WILDE LOVE

LUCY LENNOX

D1528091

Cover Art by: AngstyG at www.AngstyG.com

Cover Photo: Michael Stokes Photography https://michaelstokes.net/

Editing by: Sandra at www.OneLoveEditing.com

Beta Reading by: Leslie Copeland at www.LesCourtAuthorServices.com

To the readers who begged for Doc and Grandpa's story. Thank you.

ACKNOWLEDGEMENTS

Many, many thanks:

To my sister for her help with line-edits, concept discussion, trouble-shooting, and blurb help.

To Sloane Kennedy for inspiring me to lean in to the emotion.

To Leslie Copeland, Bishop Michael Beckett, and Chad Williams for excellent beta feedback.

To my editor Sandra for her unprecedented willingness to put up with my nonsense and deadline ~~begging~~ suggestions.

To Michael Stokes for taking gorgeous photographs.

To AngstyG for nailing the cover.

WILDE FAMILY LIST

Grandpa (Weston) and **Doc** (William "Liam") Wilde
    Their children:
    Bill, Gina, Brenda, and Jacqueline

Bill married Shelby. Their children are:
    Hudson (book #4)
    West (book #1)
    MJ
    Saint (book #5)
    Otto (book #3)
    King
    Hallie
    Winnie
    Cal
    Sassy

Gina married Carmen. Their children are:
    Quinn

Max
Jason

Brenda married Hollis. Their children are:
Kathryn-Anne (Katie)
William-Weston (Web)
Jackson-Wyatt (Jack)

Jacqueline's child:
Felix (book #2)

GLOSSARY OF TERMS

(In the order in which they appear.)

ROTC - Reserve Officers' Training Corps, a program in which a student can receive college tuition help in exchange for future time committed to the military

PFC - Private First Class

Huey/chopper/bird/helo - helicopter

Stoke's litter - a medical stretcher sometimes used on a hoist

Mess/chow - where soldiers eat/what soldiers call food

Dustoff/medevac - medical evacuation, dustoff is specifically via helicopter

Dustoff Crew - made up of four people: pilot, flight commander (another pilot in charge of navigation and communication), medic, and crew chief (mechanic)

Fuselage - the main body of an aircraft

Klicks - kilometers

LZ - landing zone

Jump seat - an extra seat that folds back when not in use

The Clap/VD - Gonorrhea/venereal disease, sexually transmitted infection

Cherry/Grunt - bottom-level personnel, newbie

Cyclic/Stick - the helicopter equivalent of a steering wheel

PX - "post exchange" or commissary on a military base where a soldier can buy sundries

Tour - a period of time a soldier is assigned to be "in country." In Vietnam each tour rarely exceeded one year

In Country - being in a country that's the focus of military activity

Viet Cong/VC/Charlie - the Vietnamese Communist/Northern Vietnamese/the "enemy"

Tet Offensive - a series of attacks by the Viet Cong beginning in early 1968

Long Binh - the largest US military base in Vietnam during the conflict

Bien Hoa - another US military installation near Long Binh

Sitrep - situation report

FNG - fucking new guy

FUBAR - Fucked/Fouled Up Beyond All Recognition/Any Repair/All Reason

Morphine syrette - a single-use hypodermic of strong pain medicine a medic carried. Once he used it on an injured soldier, the medic was supposed to mark an "M" on the patient's forehead to prevent overdose by other medical personnel

C-ration - "combat ration" or precooked, canned food for soldiers in the field

SOB - son of a bitch

R&R - rest and relaxation, leave time for soldiers to have a few days away from the war, soldier "vacation"

Hooch - sleeping quarters, often in a quonset hut

Quonset hut - semicircular steel prefabricated building that looks like a tin can cut in half vertically and placed on its side.

Malaria - a mosquito-borne disease caused by a parasite. Despite soldiers taking antimalarial medication, over 40,000 cases of the disease were reported in army troops alone between 1965 and '70 with 78 deaths (https://www.va.gov/oaa/pocketcard/vietnam.asp)

Scuttlebutt - rumor, gossip

Bunker - reinforced area made with sandbags to provide protection during mortar fire

PCS orders - "permanent change of station" orders informing a soldier of their next duty station/assignment

Short-timer - nickname for someone leaving soon

RPG - rocket-propelled grenade

SVA - South Vietnamese Army, allies to the US Armed Forces

DEROS - date estimated to return from overseas

C-130 - large cargo airplane

Andrews - Andrews Air Force Base in Washington, DC, area

Getting your "twenty" - serving a full twenty years in the military to earn retirement benefits

PT - physical training

DL - down low, discreet

CHAPTER 1

LIAM "DOC" WILDE 1968

It's true what they say about war. It's like tunnel vision. Time gets strange and the world compacts into small, intense moments of immediate need. There is no wife back home, no newborn baby, no aging father needing help keeping his northern Texas ranch afloat.

There is only the present. The time, sometimes only a matter of seconds, between saving a man's life and letting him go. Between having your act together and losing it completely in a jungle full of fear and bravado, pain and righteous indignation.

And such a moment it was when I met the man who would turn one of those compact tiny capsules of time into a full lifetime stretched long and rich over decades, who would become the very half of my heart I hadn't known I'd been living without. The man who would take a broken army medic made up of mostly selfish immaturity and familial obligation and turn him into something worthy, something decent and redeemed.

At age eighteen I found myself the star of a shotgun wedding to my high school sweetheart. It stomped on all my dreams of getting off my parents' ranch and away from my small town in Texas. Or so I'd thought at the time. And if it was even possible, Betsy was more bitter about it than I was. She'd wanted to move to the city and live a big life, and becoming a mother right out of high school put the brakes on that plan right away. We'd gone to a school dance together and fumbled our way into each other's bodies in the back seat of my mom's Pontiac Bonneville. The result was our son Billy, William Hobart Wilde. William for my dad and Hobart for Betsy's. Her family was the Hobart behind Hobie, Texas, after all.

Needless to say, our families were both horrified and overjoyed at the earlier-than-expected merging of the two historic clans, while Betsy and I were only horrified. By the time Betsy'd figured out what was causing her to lose her lunch, I'd already committed to the ROTC university program at my father's insistence that "all good men serve."

So Betsy and I moved to College Station, Texas, where I joked I worked three jobs: student, file clerk at the student infirmary, and father. Betsy used to joke right back that I was forgetting the fourth: husband, but I admitted that one got short shrift in those days since all I had energy left for at the end of the day was a kiss and snuggle with my little boy.

At the start of my senior year in college, the twins were born. Gina and Brenda were angel newborns, thank heavens, but I still prayed I'd be around enough to help Betsy with the extra work after my stint in the army started.

But in 1968, no one was that lucky. I entered the US Army as a second lieutenant and was designated a medic because of my laughable background working at the university infirmary. It didn't matter that I'd been a file clerk, I was one of the rare specimens who'd completed an actual CPR training course.

Vietnam was the kind of nightmare you can't prepare for. It was battlefield amputations and choosing who got the last vial of morphine. It was battle-hardened men turning back into babies who needed—*deserved*—their mother when they called out for her. And they did call out for her.

My sleep was full of these man-boys calling for their mothers. Rarely did they call out for their young wives. And only once did a soldier call out for another man.

He called out for me.

CHAPTER 2

WESTON "MAJOR" MARIAN

The first time I saw Doc Wilde, he was smirking around the butt end of an unlit cigarette. I'd been in the midst of chewing out the PFC who'd fucked up a simple technical adjustment to the Huey's Stokes litter for the third time. In the middle of the harangue, I froze midstep and stared at the new arrival.

"Major?" the PFC had the balls to ask.

It was then I realized my indiscretion. I'd been gawping at the kid like a fool. I turned to the grunt in front of me and glared.

"Dammit, PFC, get it right this time! That hoist's the difference between lifting a man to safety and dropping him hundreds of feet to certain death."

As he scurried off, I couldn't help but sneak another look at the golden boy standing across the muddy tarmac from me. His slender hip leaned against the fuselage of a nearby Huey, and his dirty-blond hair looked pristine, like it hadn't been mashed for days on end under a sweaty helmet. I'd seen a man in a cigar ad recently almost as handsome as this fellow. Someone had brought the magazine from home and passed it around. All the other men had paid close attention to the pages and pages of beautiful women in ads, but the cigar man had been all I'd needed.

And now here was better, live and up close. I'd heard our new medics had recently arrived, and I was betting this guy was one of them. That gave me all the excuse I needed to introduce myself. I crossed the tarmac toward him slowly, keeping my steps unhurried while my heart raced ahead of me.

Up close he was even more beautiful than I realized. His eyes a blue that made me think of summers at the lake. And his clothes were clean, still smelling of soap instead of sweat and blood and war. If anything, it made him seem more vulnerable.

At my approach he pushed off the bird, straightening. He was taller than I expected, his shoulders strong and arms corded with wiry muscle. I dropped my eyes to the name across his chest. Wilde. My eyebrows twitched, wondering just how much the moniker suited him.

"You my new medic?" I asked.

He nodded. "Sure am. Liam Wilde." He reached out a hand to me.

I took it. My first thought was how delicate this man's fingers were as my own closed around them. They were long and thin and seemed completely ill suited for the jungle. But then he squeezed and I felt the firmness of his grip — the surety of his strength. It surprised me.

Maybe there was more to this kid than I'd expected at first sight.

He cleared his throat and I realized that I hadn't yet introduced myself. I'd just been standing there, holding onto his hand like it was some sort of lifeline to another world that only existed in daydreams.

"I'm Major Weston Marian," I told him, my voice sounding gruff to my own ears.

He smiled, shifting the cigarette from one side of his mouth to the other and I found myself mesmerized by the movement. "Nice to meet you," he said. "Any tips for the new guy?"

I wrenched my eyes to meet his. I waited a beat, wondering how honest I should be. I decided to go with the truth. "Stay safe."

My answer must have surprised him because his brows rose. For a moment I saw a flash of vulnerability cross his face, as if I'd broken some sort of code. Like we weren't supposed to talk about the reality of where we were and what we were doing—that death stalked us at every turn.

"How?" He asked.

Stay next to me. I almost said the words. Almost. I shook my head at the absurdity of that thought.

"That's what we're all trying to figure out, Doc," I told him. I didn't wait for him to respond but instead turned on my heel and stalked to my tent. I felt somehow unsteady, my pulse too fast and my cheeks too hot, my uniform dirty and uncomfortable.

He's not for you, I reminded myself. None of them ever will be.

I used that reminder to push thoughts of Doc Wilde from my mind for the rest of the day. But at night… the rules were different. Getting some shut-eye was always easier with something nice to think of, and Doc Wilde was the nicest thing around. Obviously, I wouldn't act on my physical attraction to the new medic. That was a surefire way to get beaten and court-martialed at the very least. At most, it was enough cause for my men not to have my back in the shit.

But looking was free, and remembering was easy. Even though I hadn't even had a chance to really meet him, the combat medic became the leading role late at night in my hooch.

Second Lieutenant William Wilde. Almost everyone called him "Doc" or "Band-Aid" like they called all the medics, but in my comforting daydreams where I went to escape the horror of the job, he was always Liam to me.

I knew the man I fantasized about wasn't real. I didn't even know the real Doc Wilde. Not yet.

I'd nodded to him a few times across a group of men or passed something down the mess table to him when asked, but we'd never actually had a conversation other than that quick introduction the day after he'd arrived at the base.

He'd been sent to our unit with another medic to replace a couple of good men who'd gotten the dustoff after their chopper had crash landed the week before. Since then, two of the birds had been short a medic, and it was a relief to get the new men.

Liam seemed to fit in right off the bat in a way I never had. He could slide his ass into a card game at night with enlisted men or yuk it up with fellow officers with the ease of a man who'd been born charming and easy. Because I'd started off my army career as enlisted and eventually worked my way into officer ranks, I was in that odd middle zone between the two. I was no longer enlisted, but I'd never really felt like a true officer either.

But out in the field, flying above the hot wet jungle to rescue injured soldiers and civilians, we were all the same in a way, joined in a common purpose regardless of our rank. The lines were hazier in the soup. Sometimes I wondered if that made me so eager to leave the base, to put myself in harm's way, because maybe then I'd feel like I belonged somewhere.

I watched him, that new medic. Watched him walk through base like he owned the damned place. Maybe it was because he hadn't seen the shit I'd seen or even had his combat cherry popped yet and didn't realize that at any minute fire could rain down from above or blast through the sandbag walls around us. And I wanted that to be the case, to *remain* the case. I didn't want any of the horror of battle to touch this golden boy with the easy smile.

I became a stealth intelligence seeker. My ears swiveled around anytime I heard his name or even the generic moniker of "Doc."

And from this I learned he was a married man with babies back home in Texas. The news gutted me like shot pellets in a wide spray. He'd leaned across the small group of men one night to show off a tiny square photograph of "Billy, Gina, and Brenda," who were, I imagined, absolute perfect replicas of himself and whatever Texas beauty he'd left behind.

So the Liam in my dreams became even more of a fantasy man, someone absolutely unattainable in real life, but someone I held fast to nonetheless, as it was some of the only comfort to be had in those dark days and darker nights. In my head he wasn't a twenty-two-year-old married straight man, but a thirty-two-year-old single man with certain tastes like myself and eyes as blue as the South China Sea. I dreamed about sharing leave time and flying away to a private beach somewhere no one would see us. In my dreams we spent every one of our five days naked and touching each other without the fear of sudden gunfire, of falling out of a burning helicopter, of any other damned thing that would ruin our time in the sun.

But the first time I actually flew with him was the day Moline and I were assigned to Doc's Huey for a mission. In the dustoff crew of a medevac mission, there were two pilots, a medic, and a crew chief. Doc Wilde and Specialist Rusnak had already gotten a reputation as a dynamic duo, mostly because they both had outgoing personalities and talked the pilots' ears off on every flight, so when we were assigned to their Huey, Moline turned to me with a wink. "Got your earplugs, Major?"

I laughed back, but the truth of it was, Doc could talk all day long and I wouldn't mind listening. Doc Wilde was the smiliest man I'd ever seen while stationed in Vietnam, and just looking at his sunny face was enough to lighten anyone's load. He was a ray of sunshine to everyone around him—I'd already heard plenty of stories of him and his crew chief Rusnak keeping calm while under fire and managing to distract the patients from the horrors of their injuries. I'd been looking forward to working with him and glad to finally have the chance.

"Welcome aboard, Major," he said with a crooked grin as I hoisted myself up into the chopper. "I hear you know your elbow from your asshole which I've learned is a good trait in a flight commander. Just let us know what you need from us in the back."

My heart rocketed up under his direct attention. "Stay sharp," I grunted. "Don't want you hurt." I moved around him and into the fuselage to begin the final preflight checks while trying not to notice his furrowed brow.

My pilot was already on board in the starboard seat. "We ready?" I asked. Moline nodded and held out my flight helmet. "Let's get this bird in the air."

As we took off, I heard Wilde and Rusnak chattering on about what they'd had for chow that morning, a letter from home someone had gotten the day before, and other nonsense. When I updated them two klicks out from our retrieval, suddenly they were all business.

They seemed to read each other's minds and prepped the cabin for the injured men with utmost efficiency.

Once we landed in the LZ, they were out the bay door in a flash, racing to the cluster of soldiers surrounding a man on the ground. Their movements were synchronized, their communication firm and clear. Within moments, they were safely on board with one injured man on a stretcher and another riding the jump seat holding a blood-soaked bandage around his arm.

As we tipped into the air, I continued to listen to the medic and crew chief methodically treat both patients in a manner that was meant to keep the injured men calm and reassured. It was impressive considering how cherry both Wilde and Rusnak were to the dustoff unit.

When we landed back on base and handed the injured men over to the hospital staff, Moline met my eyes. "We need to find a way to keep these two. They know what the hell they're doing."

We flew three more missions during that shift, and by the time we were due to hand over the bird to the next crew, the fuselage floor was thick with blood. I stayed to help wash it out and was surprised when Specialist Rusnak clapped me on the shoulder.

"Major, that was some good flying today. You're a legend back at Fort Sam Houston. I'm Fred, by the way. It was an honor to work with you today."

That was when I realized I'd spent so much attention on finally meeting Second Lieutenant William Wilde that day, I hadn't even bothered to introduce myself to my own crew chief.

CHAPTER 3

LIAM "DOC" WILDE

I never figured out how Major Marian had made it happen, but suddenly instead of having the pilots rotate through our helo, we were assigned a steady pair.

Once Major Marian, Moline, Rusnak and I were in a permanent dustoff crew together, it was like the puzzle pieces of my time in Vietnam slid right into place. The four of us worked together like a dream, and it got to where we could damned near read each other's minds. Over the course of the next few months, where Major Weston Marian went, so went Moline, Rusnak, and I.

The base commander once referred to us as the Dustoff Beatles since Rusnak had a voice like Paul McCartney, and the nickname stuck. It became a kind of superstition. If one of the four of us was unable to pull a duty shift for some reason, the rest of us were on edge until safely landing back on base.

We were lucky as hell. Even the dicey missions we had were nothing compared to some of the stories I'd heard. The worst we saw was in the injuries we picked up. Men whose lives were irreparably changed forever and who were honestly lucky to even be alive.

That wasn't to say that everything was hunky-dory, because it certainly wasn't. In those months, we came under heavy fire multiple times, almost lost an injured soldier in a hoist retrieval, and failed to arrive before many, many men died. But the number of soldiers and civilians we did save were in the hundreds. I learned emergency medicine while the hot Vietnamese wind blew through open bay doors and Moline and Rusnak argued over whatever poker games they'd played the night before. And every moment of every rescue, Major Marian sat sentinel over all of us, making sure we did our jobs, but more importantly, making sure we got home.

Moline flew that bird like a dream, and Major Marian had a sixth sense for when we needed to abort and when we needed to stay and tough it out. There was obviously a reason the major had earned a Distinguished Flying Cross although he'd never told us what it was.

At first, Major Marian wasn't much of a talker. He was more of a grunter, a commander, a stoic authority presence like a gruff school principal or parole officer keeping watch and judging silently. But before long, Rusnak, Moline, and I were able to break him out of his shell.

It started on a mission to pick up the base commander's mistress from a nearby village. While completely against the rules, this kind of command from on high wasn't uncommon. But boy-oh-boy did it piss off a certain major.

"What's the damned point of this? So he can take the clap back to his wife? Leave fatherless babies all over the goddamned Vietnamese countryside? The man has a different woman every goddamned week," he muttered under his breath as he did the final preflight checks. "I'd rather be shot at trying to rescue a pack of cherry grunts. Christ."

Moline looked back at me and winked. "Major Pain in the Ass, why don't you tell us how you really feel?"

Major Marian glared at Moline for a split second before coughing out a laugh. "Fuck you."

"Not tonight, dear, I have a headache," Moline quipped in a high-pitched voice before turning back to grasp the cyclic. "Now get your ass in gear, Major. We're airborne."

Major glanced at me with a straight face. "Did you bring the antibiotics and sedatives?"

I pretended to nod off and then jerked awake. "Sorry, did you ask if I'd taken my sedatives? Affirmative, sir."

Major grinned and swiveled back around and spoke through the comms. "Rusnak, maybe you can loan the good general some of the rubbers your brother sent you from home. Wait. Did I say brother? I meant mother."

Rusnak's response was clipped. "Major, I told you that in confidence."

The four of us lost it, laughing and teasing each other until we were several thousand feet above the base and heading east. Rusnak and I kept watch out our respective bay doors while Moline flew the Huey and Major Marian navigated and watched out the front.

The flight was straightforward, but it marked a new kind of "us against them" mentality. Griping about the general was never smart, but that day I realized just how much the four of us trusted each other. Over the next several months through some very challenging and heartbreaking rescue attempts, we shared moments that would forever bond us together. I learned how true it was that there was just something between brothers-in-arms that was impenetrable.

And it got to a point that I truly thought there was nothing that could break the four of us apart. For as horrible as the war was and as dangerous as it was for all the men stationed on smaller firebases or in the field, the four of us were lucky. We were able to return back to the large, relatively safe base at Long Binh at the end of each shift where there was an officers' club, a PX, cold soda, hot meals, hotter showers, and clean clothes when we needed them. I began to think it was right-eous, that those of us who were tasked with helping evacuate and treat the injured would somehow be kept safe.

How naive could I have been? I'd heard plenty of stories of other Hueys going down, pilots and crews getting severely injured, but I stupidly thought that wouldn't happen to us. We were under the flight command of a fourth-tour, high-ranking pilot with almost fifteen years of army experience. The man had a Distinguished Fighting

Cross, for god's sake. If he hadn't been shot down or killed by now, surely that meant there was some kind of angel looking down on our missions.

And maybe there was. But on one particular day, it was the angel of death.

CHAPTER 4

WESTON "MAJOR" MARIAN

It had never occurred to me—and maybe it should have—that the first night Doc and I would spend alone together would be one of the worst of our lives, pressed injured and terrified into the red muddy soup of the jungle floor.

The night before, the base itself had come under heavy mortar fire since it was right around the year anniversary of Tet. The Viet Cong didn't want us to forget.

So that afternoon when we got into the Huey for our shift, Moline turned to me with an uncharacteristically grave expression. "Gonna be a crazy one today."

He was right, and it was the worst kind of crazy.

We were called out to rescue two men injured in a VC attack on a patrol unit. It was a fairly standard mission, but no dustoff mission in Vietnam was ever safe, especially near the anniversary of Tet.

After standard preflight checks, we were on our way, tipping through the skies above Long Binh on our way northwest, past Bien Hoa toward the coordinates of the injured men.

Since I was the flight commander, I was responsible for navigation and radio communications while Moline was on the stick. I could hear Doc and Rusnak banging around behind us as they prepped the hoist.

Suddenly there was the boom and flash of an air strike and everything went dark and strange. My hearing didn't work, my vision didn't work. Flickering light and shadow snapped here and there as my brain tried to put the puzzle pieces back together. I couldn't feel anything other than bright, sharp stinging on my right hip and low, dull throbbing in the back of my skull. I shook my head to clear it and realized we were going down fast. Moline was slumped over the controls, so I quickly pushed him back and tried my best to take over. My brain swam and my own equilibrium was off, but it didn't matter. It was like the cyclic was no longer connected to anything.

My training somehow kicked in, and I grabbed for the switches that I was supposed to flip in the event of a crash landing. Had you asked me then what they were at the time, I wouldn't have been able to tell you, but muscle memory from my hours of training and the many missions I'd already flown came through. The fact we were already halfway down from altitude helped because the Huey was still semi-upright when the skids hit the trees.

We tumbled through the canopy, banging side to side in seat restraints so badly I worried for the safety of Doc and the crew chief in the back. The bay doors had already been sliding back when the blast hit us, but I couldn't spare a single second to turn around and confirm we even still had Doc and Rusnak with us.

After making a mayday call on the radio, I shouted out orders from my seat about preparing to crash land. I knew if we landed in any semblance of one piece, I'd be responsible for getting Moline out, so I prayed the younger medic and crew chief remembered enough of their training to get the medical supplies and fire extinguisher respectively.

It all happened so fast, and when we finally came to a stop, we were on our left side with fires in the front and back. Moline's hands hung lifelessly toward me from his position in his seat above. I quickly unbuckled and began moving backward into the cargo area before grabbing for him and releasing his body from the restraints. The entire right side of his uniform was wet and slick with blood, and there was a large hole through the fuselage on that side of his seat.

"Doc! Rusnak! Out now! Grab your weapons." I barked. The air filled quickly with the stink of fuel and smoke as I fought to pull Moline out of the wreckage. When I finally got under the open bay doors above me, I realized how hard it would be to heft him up and out.

I felt a hand above my injured hip and turned to find Doc right beside me.

"You're hit," he said, quickly manhandling the pilot away from me. "Hop up and help lift him from above."

I didn't even have time to argue before Doc began nudging me skyward. I scrambled up before reaching back down to grab the unconscious pilot. It was hard work, and we tried not to inhale too much of the noxious air around us. The heat from flames from the cockpit warmed the side of my face, and all I could think about was needing the medic and crew chief out ASAP.

"Where's Rusnak?" I called down.

The horrified look on Doc's face was answer enough. The whites of his eyes were stark in the darkness of the cargo hold, and sweat-streaked smoke smudges already covered parts of his face.

"You sure?"

He closed his eyes and nodded. With a quick glance back inside, I could see the reason why. Rusnak's body lay crumpled in the rear corner of the cargo area behind Doc. He'd been mostly decapitated by a piece of sheared-off metal from the side of the fuselage.

I swallowed back vomit and gestured for Doc to hop up. "Grab your things, let's go."

It wasn't until we were out of the fire and away from the wreckage that I confirmed my suspicion that Moline was in bad shape. Doc laid him down to assess his injuries and quickly discovered the piece of metal in his neck.

"Shit, Major," Doc said, reaching for the rucksack of supplies he'd thrown out before climbing out. "We need a bag of fluid, and... and... *shit*. Here, hold this."

He shoved stuff at me while he worked quickly, his hands rock steady and his movements efficient. I did everything he told me while trying desperately not to think of the hours and hours of flight time I'd spent with easygoing John Moline right by my side.

While Doc raced to suture the shrapnel wound he'd found on the right side of Moline's neck, I studied the brush around us for any sign of VC soldiers. If they saw their shot had been successful, they'd be on their way here to intercept any survivors and scavenge the chopper. I wasn't about to let what remained of my crew get taken by the enemy.

He continued cursing under his breath while he worked on Moline, and eventually the words came out louder, taking on an edge of panic.

"Major, I can't... he's... it's too much damage... he's not..." As he spoke in a broken voice, his hands continued to move, trying everything in his power to save one of our brothers. "I... Weston, help me... he's gone. I—" His last words came out choked even though his hands were still working. I could tell Moline was gone, but Doc didn't want to acknowledge it.

I grabbed his hands, pulling them away from the broken body. It took a moment, but Doc finally looked up, his eyes meeting mine. I could see determination and desperation reflected in their depths. If I'd let him, he would have worked on bringing back Moline until the sun went down. But we didn't have that kind of time. "We need to move," I said softly.

"I'm so sorry," Doc breathed.

I nodded a brief acknowledgment. "Same here. Rusnak was a good man."

First Lieutenant John Moline and I had served together for two years and flown hundreds of missions together, but now wasn't the time to let his death sink in. Now was the time to assess our situation and get the hell outta Dodge. We were sitting ducks at the very obvious site of a US helicopter crash.

I drew a deep breath. "Calling in sitrep," I said to Doc in my most authoritative tone. "What's your status?"

"Unharmed, sir," he said quickly. "But you—"

I cut him off. "I'm fine. Stay alert. Any sight of the patrol unit we were looking for?" I clipped out the words while getting the emergency handheld radio out of my vest.

"Negative."

I called in our current coordinates as best I could, but informed the dispatch about our precarious situation. They said to head west in hopes of joining the patrol we'd been trying to rescue and they'd send another bird out after all of us.

As soon as the call was out, I put the handheld away and grabbed Moline's sidearm, K-Bar knife, and anything else of value I could think of that the VC would strip him of if they got to him before we could retrieve his body.

When I stood, my head swam and spots flickered in and out of my vision, but I didn't have time for any of it. I gritted my teeth and started into the jungle, urging Doc to keep up a good pace even though he was having an easier time than I was.

He kept pestering me to stop and let him treat my wounds, but I refused. The idea of Charlie getting a hold of him, or either of us, was too abhorrent to consider. I knew my wounds were superficial enough to wait until we were a little safer in a larger unit.

We made slow progress since the vegetation around us was so dense, and by the time I thought we were far enough away from the crash site to stop and rest, the sun had begun to set. My hip and head throbbed from the crash, and the pain gradually slowed me down even further. I was tempted to tell Doc to go on ahead, but I knew that wasn't protocol. It was suicide. Plus, there was no way a medic would leave an injured man alone in the jungle before at least treating him, and that would have taken more time.

I heard the sound of metal clink somewhere up ahead and wondered if by some chance it was the injured unit we'd been looking for. My ears were still ringing too much to make out any talking.

Doc's eyes met mine with a combination of surprise and relief. "I think that's them. I hear English," he said excitedly. "Let's go."

I grabbed his arm and held him back. "Wait! We can't just run in there. We have to approach carefully so they don't shoot at us."

He narrowed his eyes at me and hissed, "I'm not the FNG anymore in case you hadn't noticed, Major."

Doc was right, of course, but I still worried about him doing something that would wind up getting him hurt.

"Stay behind me," I grunted.

We approached carefully, and when we finally came within sight of them, it was a bad situation.

An already severely injured American soldier was being held with a machete at his throat by a VC soldier. A second American soldier writhed on the ground under the knee of another VC, yelling for them to let go of his brother-in-arms and getting a gunstock to the back of the head for his troubles.

I felt Doc's hand grip my left elbow hard. "What do we do?" he whispered almost silently into my ear.

I pulled out my weapon and gestured for him to do the same. My brain sorted through ideas for how I could take down the man with the machete before he could draw it across the soldier's throat.

The decision was taken out of my hands when a shout in Vietnamese came from behind us. I swiveled around and threw Doc to the ground while bringing my gun up to shoot at the VC scout. As soon as he went down, I turned back to the men in the clearing.

The first thing I saw was the VC kneeling on the soldier bring his rifle up to aim at Doc, so I shot him as quickly as I could, causing his own shot to go wide. I screamed at Doc to stay down while turning to aim at the other VC soldier, but by the time I aimed, he'd already drawn the machete across the American's throat. A second before my own shot fired, I heard Doc's pistol pop from my left. The soldier with the machete went down, falling on top of his victim.

"Noooo!" Doc's anguish propelled him toward the American who'd had his throat slit, but it was clearly too late.

A fourth VC scout stepped into the clearing from the other side and shot at me before I could take him down.

The bullet burned through the side of my calf, but I was already pulling the trigger. The shooter crumpled to the ground after my second shot.

"Major!" Doc cried a split-second too late to warn me.

"Check him," I grunted, tilting my head at the American at Doc's feet. I knew there was no chance since the man had already been severely injured and bleeding heavily before the final blow, but I also knew Doc needed to be sure.

Suddenly, Doc and I found ourselves the only two survivors in a clearing filled with both Viet Cong and Americans. The soldier who'd been smashed on the back of the skull was already dead. When Doc turned him over to try and help him, we discovered he'd already been severely injured. These men had to have been the injured ones we'd been sent to rescue.

I left it to Doc to confirm the status of the dead while I did a sweep of the clearing to make sure there weren't any more enemies hiding in the undergrowth. The minute I tried to take a step, however, I fell down onto one knee and keeled over into the mud with a splat.

The familiar smell of cordite, body odor, and blood hit me as I sucked in a painful breath. The hot, humid press of the jungle air suffocated me. This was the Vietnam I'd known for the three tours I'd already done here. But this time there was something else. A strange kind of panic to get Doc Wilde to safety at any cost.

He was by my side in an instant. "You were hit," he said, his face pale with shock as he reached for my tattered pant leg. I batted his hand away.

"We need to move," I told him, my voice more a wheeze than a command. "Someone will come looking for those VC soldiers."

Doc's hands hovered over my calf, his fingers slick with blood. He stared at them, looking suddenly lost, as though without the focused action of having to treat someone, he didn't know what to do with himself.

He sunk back in the mud, his blood-soaked hands trembling. "Oh god," he whispered, his eyes taking in the bodies littering the clearing. "It's all my fault. They're all dead because of me. Oh god. Oh *god*."

"No," I growled. "They're dead because of fucking Charlie."

He shook his head. "I should have been watching your back. I could have shot him while you shot the one with the machete. If I hadn't been so worried about the men in the clearing—"

I grabbed the front of his shirt, forcing him to look at me. "Did you slit the corporal's throat?"

"Of course not, but if I'd just—"

"Did you toss a grenade at a group of American soldiers in the first place?"

"Major," he whispered, eyes filling. "I was so stupid. Maybe we could have saved them if I'd only had your back."

My heart was breaking for him. When you made a mistake as a chef, it might result in an inconvenient case of the runs for a customer. When you made a mistake as a soldier in Vietnam, it might result in the deaths of several people. But I knew in this case we'd hardly stood a chance at saving those men. They'd been FUBAR the moment they'd run into the enemy.

"It's not your fault, Liam. Got it?"

My use of his name seemed to startle him enough that it snapped him out of his downward spiral. He blinked several times before eventually nodding. I dropped his shirt.

"We need to get out of here," I said, struggling to get my shit together. My brain scrambled to come up with a plan, but everything I thought of carried more risks than I was comfortable with.

"I need to treat you first," he said, reaching for my leg.

I started to protest, pulling out of reach, but then his hand landed on my knee, his grip firm as he said, "Please."

I looked at him. Dirt was smudged along his cheek and chin. Blood was smeared all over Doc's uniform and lingered in the crevices of his knuckles and nails. It took all my sense of self-preservation not to stare at him, or worse, crawl over the top of his body and protect him with my own.

He needed this, I realized. He was a medic. It was his job to heal. He felt like he'd failed Moline and the men in this clearing and he needed a reminder that yes, there was death in this jungle, but there could also be healing and hope. I could give that to him.

"Get it over with," I growled. In order for him to examine my calf, I had to lie on my injured hip with cause me to wince.

Doc's eyes snapped up. "Do you need morphine?"

"No. Hell no. Just bandage it up so we can move." I needed my wits if I was going to get him home.

As he worked to bandage the bullet wound to my leg, I finally called in a sitrep. The dispatcher informed me that they'd already tried to send another medevac chopper to the site but it had come under heavy fire. After ours and the second one had both experienced an air assault, they'd decided it would be better to wait until daylight to try again.

Basically, our instruction was to find a place to hunker down and stay alive until morning since we didn't have any critical wounds needing immediate treatment.

"What do they call a bullet wound to the leg if not critical?" Doc hissed after I put the radio back in my vest.

"The bullet's not in my leg anymore, and it didn't hit anything important," I said. "This is nothing. It's like a scratch compared to most dustoff missions. Gather the corporal's pack." I nodded toward the nearest rucksack belonging to the last soldier we'd examined. "It probably has food and supplies we can use."

If we were going to spend the night in the jungle, we were going to need it. All we really had was what I wore on my survival vest which wasn't much.

Doc grabbed what he could and slung the pack on his back. "Let's get out of here."

He came over and helped me up, sliding a strong arm around me under my shoulder. I tried not to lean on him too much, but with a bad hip and a worse calf, there was no way for me to cover any distance without help.

We moved in the direction dispatch had instructed, taking it slowly both because of my injuries and also because of our unwillingness to bungle into another bad situation. After a while, I began to feel faint. Maybe my adrenaline was crashing.

When spots began flickering in my vision and my body felt like it was moving through molasses, I considered warning him in case I fainted. But before I could get the words out, I went down, nearly landing on my face before Doc caught me and lowered me onto my back in the slick mud.

"Major!" Doc called from a distance. "Where... dammit, man, you're bleeding again!"

I tried to open my eyes, but all I could see was the South China Sea. I was drowning in it, but I couldn't think of a better way to go.

CHAPTER 5

LIAM "DOC" WILDE

I helped him land on his back and quickly checked his breathing before moving to his wounds. What was the problem? He'd told me he was fine.

Both the shrapnel wound on the major's hip and the bullet wound on his leg had opened up and been bleeding for what looked like a while. I cursed him for not telling me even though he was in no state to respond.

I pulled off the pack and dug out the supplies I'd taken from the slain soldier's packs. This time, instead of slapping bandages on the injuries, I dosed him with a morphine syrette before cleaning and stitching the wounds properly. After a while, I tried to wake him up enough to drink a bit of water and eat some C-ration peanut butter, hoping the sugar and protein would help him perk up.

"Wake up, Major," I snapped. "We don't have time for you to catnap."

He looked at me with a wrinkled brow of confusion, no doubt due to the blood loss, dehydration, and low blood sugar. No wonder he'd looked so pale. I'd mistakenly thought it was fear, which hadn't made any sense. Major Marian was one of the bravest SOBs of all the air ambulance pilots. This was his fourth tour of combat duty in Nam, and he was unflappable.

But I hadn't been able to save one of his best friends. Moline had bled out right in front of the major. Of course he was going to be upset and shaken.

And if I let myself think about Fred Rusnak and the young wife who'd just unknowingly become a widow, I would lose it. Instead, I concentrated on treating the major.

"Hells bells, Major," I whispered, brushing the sweaty hair back from his forehead to draw an *M* there, indicating the dose of morphine I'd given him. In case something happened to me, any rescuing medic would know not to overdose him. I continued murmuring at him. "It's just you and me out here. I'd really like it if you could perk back up and boss me around a little. Tell me what the hell to do here before I get us killed."

He mumbled something that sounded like "Liam," but I chalked it up to confusion. I reached into his vest to pull out the radio to call in a sitrep again and inform them we were making slow progress but we were still okay. I shoved down the panic that encroached, silently thanking the major for lasting long enough to give me someone else to live for. I needed to get him safely back to base before I could lose my mind with fear and self-recrimination for my inability to save anyone that day.

He was counting on me. He needed me. I wasn't going to be the reason this three-time combat veteran of this damned war didn't make it home.

"Liam. Are you safe?"

He was mumbling, and it made him sound too vulnerable. I tried to block it out, tried not to hear it.

"Wake the fuck up, Major," I hissed in his ear after his eyes slid closed. "I need you to stay with me because I don't know what I'm doing and…" My voice broke. "I'm scared."

"Doc," he said again. "Doc, 's okay."

I stared at him and wiped smudges of dirt and blood off his craggy, scruffy face. His eyes opened long enough to show me the faded denim blue of his irises. It wasn't much, but it was enough to feel less alone.

"There you are, you stubborn bastard," I said with an exhale of relief. "You were bleeding again, so I patched you up. A little bit farther to the LZ."

"Rifle," he breathed. "Grenades."

"Afraid not. Unless you have some hidden in your pants."

I watched him reach a hand down as if to check his pockets. Stifling a chuckle, I grabbed for his wrist. "Easy, buddy. I was kidding. I've already been in your pants, Major. There's no rifle in there."

"You went in my pants?"

"Stitched up your leg and hip. Good as new, if I do say so myself. So let's get going."

He tried moving and groaned, clutching his head. "Fuck."

"Yeah, um, I dosed you with the good stuff. Gonna make you dizzy. Plus I think you hit your head in the crash."

"Yeah," he mumbled.

I tried to put an arm around his back to lift him partway up. He paled and poured sweat, but clenched his teeth against whatever he was feeling.

"Let's go," he grunted. "Ready."

He was nowhere near ready. But I really wanted to get us closer to the LZ before the pain meds began to wear off.

I kept my handgun ready on my right and held on to the major on my left. After being scared of the dark Vietnamese jungle earlier, I was finally grateful for it. While we wouldn't be able to see them, they wouldn't be able to see us either.

We made slow but steady progress for a few hundred yards in the direction of where we'd been heading for the rescue before I felt the major's legs wobble. I quickly lowered him to the ground and pulled out my canteen to wipe his face off with clean water.

He met my eyes through the dark. "You're okay?" he asked softly. "You hurt?"

"I'm okay. Not hurt, just..."

"Yeah," he said before I had to finish. "Gonna be okay, Doc. I'll get you home to those babies."

The mention of my kids grabbed my heart and squeezed it until I almost choked.

"And, uh, your lady," he added, looking away. I thought of Betsy struggling to take care of three kids under three and wondered, not for the first time, how the hell she was staying sane. I thought about Rusnak's wife and said a quick prayer of thanks that at least he hadn't left behind three little kids.

"What about you? Who do you have waiting for you back home?" I checked the bandage on his calf to make sure it wasn't bleeding too much. It seemed to be holding up okay. Whenever the four of us had spoken of our families, Major hadn't been very forthcoming.

After I was done checking his bandages, I realized he hadn't answered. "Major?"

"No one. I'm a lifer." His voice was gruff and a little slurred from the drugs. "My men are my family."

I glanced at him in the dark. "Oh."

"C'mon," he said, standing up without help and gritting his teeth again. "Let's go."

Whether he liked it or not, I slid an arm around his back again to support him.

We moved slowly but covered a decent amount of ground before he stopped again.

"Close enough," he muttered, moving over a few feet and lowering himself to the ground at the base of a tree. Somehow I got the feeling he was probably right. The man most likely had a sixth sense for common landing zones after flying so many missions.

I set the pack down before sitting next to him and offering him one of the canteens of water. I took a second one and drank the tepid liquid while trying not to think of the dead man who'd originally filled the vessel. How the hell was I ever going to tell my commanding officer about this when we returned to base? Four American soldiers had died on my watch. Some medic I was.

After closing the canteen, I pulled my knees up and crossed my arms over top of them before burying my face in them and letting out a long breath. A strong hand squeezed the back of my neck, digging a thumb in the tight muscle there. It hurt, but in a way that reassured me it would feel better in the long run.

I got up the guts to ask a question that had been gnawing at me. As a pilot, he shouldn't have had that many opportunities for direct combat, but I didn't know what his previous assignments had been. "You ever killed anyone before tonight?"

He sighed. "Yes."

"What does that mean?"

Silence for a few beats. "It's not a story I tell people."

"Even when you might die in the damned jungle and never get a chance to unburden your soul?" I asked, reaching a tipping point with his mystery-man bullshit. I was stuck in enemy territory scared to death. I wanted connection. I *needed* a friend.

"We're not going to die," he said. The major's low voice sounded a little stronger than before. The morphine was finally working its way out of his system which was both good and bad. I selfishly wanted him to be more lucid, but I hated to think of him in pain.

"I wouldn't have volunteered to keep coming back if I planned to die in this place," he continued.

I closed my eyes and concentrated on the sound of his rough voice as his strong fingers continued working out the kinks in my neck and shoulders. I knew he was trying to calm down my overwhelming feelings of fear and guilt, and I wasn't too proud to accept whatever comfort he was willing to give.

"I had an older brother and a younger sister," he began after a while. I tried not to let my surprise show. "Well, I suppose I still do, but that's a story for another time." He cleared his throat and started again.

"Anyhow, when I was a senior in high school, my little sister was fourteen and had been in love with seventeen-year-old Clayton Burns for what seemed like forever." He chuckled. "She was all big-eyed and stupid whenever he came around with his mom. You see, his mom worked for our family business. My dad owned a chain of supermarkets, and after her husband died, Mrs. Burns came to work as my dad's bookkeeper."

He sighed and pulled his hand away from my neck, sinking back against the trunk of the tree and rubbing his face with his hand.

"I, uh… I was different, you see. *Am* different, I mean to say."

I didn't see, but I nodded along anyway if only to keep him talking.

"There was this man." The major clenched his jaw, highlighting the tendons along his neck. His face was rough with dirt and stubble, and smears of dried blood ran along his chin like he'd scratched it with bloody fingers at some point.

"He and I were… well, let's just say I was under his spell. I…" He stopped and looked up at the jungle canopy as if it would help him find better words.

Listening to this normally confident and commanding officer scramble for words finally clued me in to what he was trying to say.

"Like… like you were like *that?*" I asked, thinking of the two men I'd seen touching each other behind one of the buildings on base before we deployed. It had been the dead hours of the middle of the night, and I'd been late getting back from my grandmother's funeral. "Queer, like?"

Major Marian's jaw ticked again. "Yeah. Like that."

I wondered why the hell he was admitting that to me. If anyone found out he was queer, he could be kicked out of the army. Or worse.

"Go on," I said softly. I had to admit, if only to myself, seeing him vulnerable like this was a gift. And after a while, I realized that was exactly his intention. Not only was he giving me the gift of connection and companionship, he was giving me the gift of his trust.

Major Marian was entrusting me with his secrets.

"The man I liked… his name was Bobby, and he was twenty-five. I was only seventeen at the time, still in school at home, but I worked part-time for my dad too. Bobby had a job loading produce at one of my dad's warehouses."

He glanced over at me before looking back down at his hands. "Bobby said he was going with some of his friends to a place in Los Angeles where there were other… men like us." He took a breath.

"God," he said, rubbing his face again. "I wanted to go so badly. Just to see. Just for once to feel like I wasn't the abomination the church and my father seemed to think I was." He shook his head and chuckled softly again. "But it turned out I was."

My heart felt tight in my chest. I hated seeing anyone feel like dirt, especially a man who'd fought like hell to survive several tours in this shithole while flying hundreds of missions to save others.

"You're not," I said roughly, reaching for his arm to squeeze it. "You're *not*."

"My dad had already caught me once with Bobby. He could tell by the way we were standing and touching that we were more than just friends. So when he caught me sneaking out that night, he was furious. He gave me an ultimatum: stay home and change my ways or go with Bobby and never come back."

There was a trace of pain in his voice and my heart ached for him —both for the kid facing such a decision and for the man who'd lived with the consequences of what he'd chosen. I held my breath, waiting for him to continue.

"I was stupid and stubborn and left anyway, meeting up with Bobby and his friends down the street. The two friends were even older than him, and I got a bad feeling right away. We only got a few miles away when they pulled over and parked on the side of the road. They said they needed to get some money. I thought they were stopping at one of the other guys' houses or something. It wasn't until they told me to get behind the wheel and keep the engine running that I got suspicious. I asked what they were really doing, and Bobby laughed. Said my father had caught him with a man behind the warehouse and fired him on the spot. Bobby figured my dad's bookkeeper, Mrs. Burns, owed him some payroll money, and he was going to collect before we went to the city."

I put details together. "Oh god."

He nodded. "They were going to rob her. I realized it when they were halfway to the Burnses' house, so I got out of the car and went running toward them, yelling, trying to stop them. The noise I made must have woken up the Burns family because suddenly the lights were on and Clayton came racing out of the house with a hunting rifle."

His voice was rough, like it was being poured over jagged rock. I scooted closer to him so my left arm was pressed solidly along his right one from shoulder to elbow.

"What happened then?"

"Bobby shot him," he whispered. "Pulled a little six-shooter revolver like a sheriff in one of those Westerns and shot that kid right in the gut. And then... and then Mrs. Burns came up screaming, and he shot her too."

Major Marian's eyes were full, and he turned to me with a look of pleading that nearly broke my heart in two.

"Doc, it was my fault."

"No it wasn't," I snapped. "No it goddamned wasn't. Don't you say that. Don't you say that."

He shook his head. "If I hadn't yelled, or, hell, if I'd have figured the whole thing out sooner and talked them out of it, Clayton and Mrs. Burns would have been safe in their beds. Bobby and his crew could have gone in and robbed the place blind without even bothering a soul. But because of me, because of my screaming, everything was FUBAR."

I reached my arm around him and pulled him in close to my side. "You couldn't have known Bobby was carrying a weapon or that Clayton would come to the door to confront them. You didn't shoot anyone."

He looked up at me from where his head had fallen naturally to my shoulder. In the dim light of the moon, his eyes were still light denim blue. His face was still dirty and rough, but up close, I could see it was a face full of life... experience... pain. It was the kind of face I found hard to look away from. It was like the man's face wanted to tell me stories, and I wanted to sit and listen to them.

I'd always been the kind of person to get along better with older adults than other kids, and when I looked at Major Marian, I wondered if maybe that's what it was—my same old attraction to interacting with more mature people. Or maybe it was the feeling of being safer in his company than out of it. Either way, I knew I wanted to learn more about this interesting fellow. He was so much more than he appeared.

His eyes searched mine for judgment, and I hoped to god he didn't find it.

"What happened next?" I asked, clearing my throat and backing off a little.

"I ran."

CHAPTER 6

WESTON "MAJOR" MARIAN

I couldn't believe I was telling Doc Wilde my most horrifying secret. Not only did it implicate me in a crime, but it also revealed my true nature to someone who had the power to turn me in to a surefire court-martial.

If the US Army learned about my attraction to men, I was as good as dishonorably discharged, and as many times as I'd prayed to leave Vietnam way behind, I'd never really meant it. If I no longer had a home in the army, I no longer had a home. It was that simple. I didn't even know who the hell I was without the army.

Uncle Sam had saved me.

"What do you mean, you ran?" he asked softly.

"I mean Bobby and his friends shouted for us to get back to the car, and then the four of us hightailed it to Los Angeles as planned. I sat in the back of that car for two hours trying to hold back vomit. My ears rang with the echo of gunshots, and my entire body felt separate from my soul. When they pulled up outside of some kind of nightclub, I was too scared to defy them by pleading sick so I could stay in the car. I dutifully followed them into the club, but then I waited for them to get drunk and distracted before sneaking right out of there into the dark night of the city."

"Did you call your folks?"

I let out a soft chuckle. Lieutenant Wilde was a small-town boy from Texas who probably thought big daddy could save you from just about anything. He'd obviously never met mine.

"No way," I told him. "My father was a strict tyrant who would have flayed me alive. He'd told me never to come home and I believed him. Instead, I walked into an army recruitment center, lied about my age, and prayed to any god who would listen that they wouldn't arrest me on sight."

"I guess they didn't," Doc said with his crooked grin.

"They didn't. They took me right in and sent me to basic. Never been so relieved in my life. It was like a do-over."

"Whatever happened to your parents, your family... the Burnses?"

I felt that old, familiar lump in my gut. Guilt, fear, shame.

"I don't know. I haven't talked to anyone back home since that night."

"Not even your mother or sister?" he asked.

I shook my head. "My father wouldn't have allowed it, and I didn't want to put them in that position."

We sat in silence a while then, the weight of my tale hanging heavy in the thick, humid air.

Doc turned to me and looked me right in the eyes, his face so full of empathy I almost couldn't bear it.

"You told me that so I wouldn't feel so responsible for what happened back there to those soldiers."

I nodded. He was perceptive.

"Major... did you... did you make that up just to make me feel better?"

The whites of his eyes stood out in the night, and I wished with every bit of my soul I could reach out and touch his face, hold his hand, *anything* to forge a closer connection and offer him—both of us really—comfort.

"No, Doc. I wish I had, believe me. I'm sure if you went home and searched it up in the library, you'd find an awful story in the *Bakersfield Californian* about the Burnses that night."

"Did you ever look it up to see if the Burnses survived their injuries or if anyone saw you there?"

I shuddered. "Hell no. I don't think I can bear to see the story in print. Until tonight, I sort of... put it away, you know? I can't... I can't let myself think about it. It happened in another life to another person. And it doesn't much matter now anyway. What's done is done. I can never face my family again from the shame. Once they associated me with Bobby, they'd know we were birds of a feather."

"You're nothing like that criminal," Doc insisted, bristling with indignation. "You're a good man, Major. Brave, honest, strong. I've never seen you hesitate, not one moment, to do the right thing. If anyone ever associated you with a man like that, they'd be dead wrong."

His words warmed something in me, releasing a tight buckle of anxiety I'd carried for fifteen years. Finally, someone else knew the worst of me and hadn't judged me for it.

Doc was silent for another beat before speaking hesitantly. "I promise you on my life I will never reveal any of your secrets, Major."

"Nor I yours, Lieutenant," I promised. "We came upon that unit, tried to save our fellow soldiers, and failed. That is the beginning, middle, and end of the story."

"But—"

I cut him off. "Those men had already been severely injured in the grenade attack, Doc. If anything, it was the delay of our crash that killed them. Corporal Atkins was missing a leg. Private Sanchez was missing his—"

Doc grabbed my forearm with an iron grip. "No more. Please. I remember all of it in vivid detail that will never leave me as long as I live."

I nodded and patted his hand on my arm, squeezing it quickly before forcing myself to leave him be.

After a few more moments of silence, Doc spoke again. "You know all of their names."

I blew out a breath. "Their families will want to know."

"Of course. I'm an idiot. I should have—"

"No. This was your first time in combat like that, Doc. You did the best you could without shitting your pants or winding up dead."

"Who said I didn't shit my pants?" he asked with that crooked grin.

I snorted a laugh. "If you did, I don't want to hear about it."

"I would have been dead if it wasn't for you. You saved my ass. Time and again. The Huey. The clearing. Now. Keeping me from going crazy. I'll never forget this, Major."

"No, I imagine you won't."

"That's not what I meant," Doc corrected.

"I know."

After a while we spoke of normal things. The movie they'd played on base the week before. How grateful we were to be at a base with cold beer every once in a while. We talked about where some of the men took their R&R time. Doc told me about growing up on a ranch and the pressure to never leave it.

"I thought if I went into the military, I'd at least get to get out of goddamned Texas," he joked. "Fat lot of good that did me. Stupid cowboy."

"You're out of Texas," I teased gesturing at the sticky mud under us and the bug-filled jungle surrounding us. "Lucky you."

He snorted. "What was I thinking? At least I got a college degree out of the deal. Not sure it was worth it."

"Why didn't you go to medical school and defer?" I asked.

Doc laughed softly. "I never wanted to be a doctor. I had a clerk position in the infirmary at school for extra money, that's all. Apparently it was enough to flag me for combat medicine. My plan was to get in, get out, go home, and take over the ranch like I was expected to. *Am* expected to."

There was something in his voice that had me tilting my head. "Is that what you want to do?"

He seemed to think about it before responding. "I never wanted to be a rancher like my dad. Look at me. One hard stare from a bull and I tip right over."

If the man was going to give me permission to size him up, I was going to take it. My eyes started at his boots and made their way up his slender legs in filthy, wet uniform trousers to his narrow hips and trim upper body. He wasn't thick and muscular by any means. I'd been wide-shouldered and strong since puberty, but Doc Wilde had a body type better spent indoors on academic pursuits than in the field doing manual labor. Not that I minded. I thought he was the most attractive man I'd ever met in person, and his slighter form was A-OK with me.

"You're young yet," I said, my voice coming out rougher than I'd expected. "Still time to fill out."

Doc shrugged. "Maybe. I had a science teacher in high school I adored. Mr. Ackley made science interesting, never boring. Sometimes I think about having a normal job like that, you know? Use my brain more than my brawn. Drive into town, teach at school, and then drive home to Betsy and the kids at night."

The reminder of his family was bittersweet. I was both grateful he had that anchor and jealous as all hell it wasn't me.

"Why not do it?" I asked.

"The Wildes have been ranching in that part of Texas since before the Civil War. Betsy's family, the Hobarts, have been there almost as long. That's why I…" He didn't finish.

"That's why, what?" I prodded.

"Why when she got pregnant, we had to… you know." He waved a hand in the air.

Ah.

"Get married?"

He nodded. "Well, yeah. I mean, I would have anyway, of course! But, the pressure from our families was pretty intense. They were ecstatic."

"I can imagine."

"So now it's like… even worse. Because she's an only child which means she inherits her family's land and I inherit mine. Two thousand acres of cattle and six hundred of corn. What am I supposed to do? I can't just… walk away from that. It's guaranteed stability for my family. It's history and heritage and…" He sighed. "It would break my mother's heart, and it would kill my father. No. I can't do it."

"So, you'll go home and become a rancher like your father and his father before."

"Yeah." He sounded resigned.

I thought about the irony of it. My own college degree in agricultural studies and my secret wish of having my own piece of land to work. If Liam had been my father's son, he could have pursued a degree in business and taken over a chain of markets. If I'd been born on the Wilde ranch, I could have lived out my dream of minding my own damned business in peace. But as my dad had always reminded me, no one ever said life was fair.

We sat in silence for a while, startling every now and again when we heard something through the dense vegetation. The wound on my hip was throbbing, but I knew if I told Doc about it, he'd want to dose me with the pain medicine again. I didn't dare risk losing my focus in case trouble showed up. But after a while, my head was throbbing in time with my hip, and I started to feel cold, dizzy, and nauseous. I wondered if it could be a delayed reaction of shock or blood loss. I glanced down at where Doc had cut off part of my bloody uniform pants to get to the bullet wound on my calf. The bandages still looked clean.

I reached down to feel it and noticed my hand was shaking. I watched it for a little while, wondering what would cause it. No matter the cause, it meant I wouldn't be as good a shot if trouble showed up. I turned my head to tell Doc to keep his eyes open. He'd need to be ready with his own weapon in case I...

In case I...

The muddy floor came up to meet my face.

CHAPTER 7

LIAM "DOC" WILDE

Eventually, the barest hint of light began sinking through the canopy above, and I knew we'd made it through the night. Just as I turned to share the good news with Major Marian, he toppled over onto the ground.

I quickly pulled his shoulder back until he was lying against my front. One of my arms wrapped around his chest while the other felt frantically for the pulse in his neck. Alive.

After listening to his shallow breathing, I reached down to run hands over both wound sites, assuring myself he wasn't experiencing blood loss I hadn't noticed. I'd done my best to keep an eye on both areas while we'd been talking, periodically clicking on the flashlight to make sure everything still looked copacetic.

But now he was panting and sweating with no obvious cause. Infection shouldn't have set in this fast, so what else could it be?

"Steady on," I murmured to him, settling into the familiar comfort of my training. "Slow breaths, Major."

One of his hands came up and clasped mine on his chest. It was cold and clammy, dirty and rough. Large, capable hands full of healthy veins. My brain scrambled to determine what had caused the sudden decline in his condition. I checked his again, sweeping over his body, searching for something I may have overlooked but finding nothing.

"Liam," he breathed, and the name clutched at me in a death grip, like we were Liam and Weston out there in the field instead of green second lieutenant and battle-hardened major.

"What is it, dammit? I need to know what's wrong so I can fix it." My voice was shaking almost as badly as my hands were.

"*Liam*," he said again. The way my name sounded when he said it was unlike anything I'd ever heard before. It was the deep mournful groan of an old barn door and the high expectant trill of new baby birds. It was acres of golden Texas pasture land, herds of fat cattle, and three happy children sitting in the summer sun.

It was everything I'd ever thought of as home, and it centered me in an instant. I took a breath and let it out. He needed something to rally for.

"Let's go, Major," I said quietly but firmly. "I'm calling in the cavalry. Your men are counting on you back at the base, and there's no way I'm showing up back there without you. Get your lazy ass up." I knew talking to a superior officer like that was disrespectful, but I also knew he needed any energy the anger might give him.

He turned his head on my shoulder until we were almost nose to nose. "Let's go," he said, repeating my own words. "Get you home."

After finding the radio in one of his pockets, I called and insisted on the medevac now. No more waiting. By the time the crew arrived, the sun should have risen enough anyway.

It took twenty minutes to go the remaining half kilometer through the tangled vegetation with the major draped over my back. But just as the sunrise turned the gray trees to green, we heard the familiar beat of the chopper blades. Major Marian reached for my hand and squeezed. "Home."

It was strange to be on the receiving end of a medevac flight when I'd already flown a thousand of them. Granted, I hadn't seen any hand-to-hand action before the crash, but it was still odd to be a passenger rather than a member of the dustoff crew.

The medic on board had a hard time convincing the major to lie down and be seen to until I finally got in Major Marian's face and told him to stop being a horse's ass and let the man do his job.

Major's eyes went wide, but he shut his trap awfully fast nonetheless. The specialist and crew chief both dropped their jaws open in shock at the way a lowly second lieutenant had barked at a major. If only they'd known how the previous night had changed things between us.

The flight through the sunrise was shorter than the flight out had seemed, but then again, it always was. When we landed back at the base, the medic and crew chief immediately off-loaded the major to a medical crew waiting to take him to the base hospital.

It was the last I saw of the major for a little while. I'd asked around the hospital for an update, but all they would tell me was that he was still recovering and I'd done a good job suturing his wounds and caring for him in the field.

Over the next couple of days, I found myself missing the gruff man unexpectedly. His solid presence beside me that night, his quiet strength in a crisis. With ten years and three tours on me, Major had eons more life experience to draw on when facing the challenges inherent in Vietnam.

At the time, I chalked my new semi-obsession with the man up to wishing I had a kind of guardian angel. He was larger-than-life, a commanding officer who could handle a bad situation, who knew how to stay calm in a crisis, and who persevered even in extreme pain.

And he was all of those things. But after settling back at base when my head finally seemed to sink in about the events of that night, I realized it was more than that. He was someone I'd forged an unbreakable bond with in a way I never had before. He'd come to embody the ideas of protectiveness and security. In many ways, I now felt closer to Major Weston Marian than even my own wife.

And if something happened to him, after losing Moline and Rusnak, I thought I might lose the tenuous hold I had on my sanity.

Two nights later I was awoken from a deep sleep by a private I recognized from the hospital.

"Lieutenant Wilde," he whispered in the dark hooch. "You're needed in the ward."

Despite the panic that suddenly set my heart racing, I didn't ask why or what for. I'd been a soldier long enough to know better, but I wondered those things. And it wasn't until we neared the open front door of the building that the private began to explain.

The major had been diagnosed with malaria of all things. It was common enough where we were, but to come down with the symptoms on the same day as our crash was an unlucky coincidence. The nurse said it may have hit him harder because he'd been weakened by blood loss and fatigue already. I didn't know if that was true or not, but I was damned glad we got him to the hospital to be treated. Any more time in a buggy jungle would have been awful for him.

"So we got the malaria symptoms under control, but now Major Marian is fighting an infection in his calf and won't settle. He's been calling for you. Captain Samuelson said you might as well come calm him down if it'll help."

My steps slowed. "You sure he was calling for me?" I asked, surprised.

He shrugged. "Kept saying Liam. The captain says you were the only Liam he knew, and you were there when the chopper crashed."

When I entered the long room of metal-framed hospital beds, I found two nurses trying to hold Major Marian down. My gut churned with anger immediately. "Let him go," I hissed across the dimly lit space. I didn't want to wake up the other patients, but I needed them to stop manhandling the major like he was just another pesky patient.

The nurses turned in surprise which alerted the major to my presence. I expected him to look at me in confusion, to clarify, maybe, that he'd been calling out for a brother or childhood friend with the same name, but he didn't.

He let out a big breath and relaxed into the bed, his blue-gray eyes filling quickly but never looking away from mine.

"You came," he croaked softly.

My throat felt tight, so I simply nodded and stepped forward, reaching out to grasp his hand. He was a wide man with brawny shoulders and a slender waist. His muscular form looked strange in the narrow bed, and it reminded me of my son Billy's ten-pound body overflowing the newborn bassinet behind the window in the hospital nursery.

And seeing a gruff, strong major pale and feverish in a hospital bed to begin with was all wrong. It made me feel antsy, almost like I wanted to find a way to sneak him out of there.

I perched a hip next to his and leaned in to speak quietly. "How you doing, Major?"

"Ready for duty."

I reached a thumb out to wipe a tear from below his eye and smiled like it was no big deal. "Not quite yet, Major, but soon. I came by to tell you to do what these nurses and doctors tell you because I don't trust anyone else to fly my pampered ass anymore now that I know you can land a dead bird like Superman."

His troubled eyes searched mine. "I killed them so Charlie couldn't get you."

I nodded and knuckled a tear from under his other eye, swallowing hard at the horrible memory from the clearing. "You saved me. Charlie didn't get me, Major. My kids still have a daddy thanks to you."

Something shuttered in his eyes and he looked down at his hands, clasping them together and squeezing hard enough to make his knuckles white.

"Billy, Gina, and Brenda," he said softly. "And Betsy." He took a breath and looked at me with confusion. "But not Charlie."

I coughed in surprise. He was either out of it with fever or from pain medicine. "No, sir. Not Charlie."

The major nodded but then frowned. "The men?"

"What men?" I asked, thrown by the swift shift in topic.

"Moline, Rusnak, Atkins, Sanchez, Sandoval—"

I cut him off, unwilling to have a complete breakdown right there in the quonset hut ward. "Shhh," I said, reaching out to cup his cheek. I needed him to think of the good instead of the bad. It was the only thing that had kept me sane since returning from the jungle. "They're at peace."

"I killed them. Are you safe?"

The words he'd asked me before. The ones that shoved a ragged blade straight into my heart and ripped it open. Those deaths should be on my head, not his.

"Yes, sir. I'm safe. Thanks to you."

He seemed to drift off, but when I tried to release his hands, he held on tightly. "Don't go," he whispered. "Not yet."

"Okay," I murmured softly. "I'll tell you a story about a tiny town in Texas called Hobie where everyone knows everyone and all the little old biddies are in each other's business." I'd told him plenty about the ranch, but not much about my hometown.

He smiled softly, his eyes closed again. "Yes. Hobie. Sounds nice."

So I told him about the popular soda fountain at Walsney Drug and the old drive-in movie theater out past the Hobarts' place. I told him about Old Man Ritches, who ran his hardware store like a fiefdom and whose son wasn't much better.

As I spoke, the major seemed to relax into his bed and sleep easier, the stories of an idyllic all-American small town half a world away giving him respite from the awful situation around us in Vietnam. When he was finally asleep, a doctor checking the patient next to Major looked over and nodded at me.

"Sounds like they did the right thing when they made you a medic."

I thought about how wrong-footed I'd felt when they'd assigned me to the medical detachment, but then I thought of the training I'd excelled in and the rescue missions I'd already performed. Helping people gave me a high like a good drug. It was addictive.

"I guess sometimes the powers that be know better than we do," I said with a chuckle. "Who woulda thought it?"

The doctor nodded down at the major. "He was involved in the Battle of la Drang Valley in '65, did you know?"

The news shouldn't have surprised me, but it did. "No, I didn't know."

"Yes. Earned the Distinguished Flying Cross for flying in super hot like a hundred times to perform medevac. During one of the loads, he held the bird off the ground with one hand and shot out the window with his other like some kind of movie star. He personally killed like seven VC that day who were trying to take the Huey down. The man's a hero. After that, he pretty much writes his own ticket. I treated his crew chief for shrapnel wounds and got to hear all about it."

I was stunned. When I'd asked him if he'd ever killed anyone, he'd told me the story of the night he left home. I'd thought he meant he'd felt responsibility for killing Clayton and Mrs. Burns. So if he'd already killed VC during the war, was that the battle he was remembering in his fevered mumblings?

I made a point of visiting Major Marian the next day after returning from a flight. He was more lucid which made things a bit more awkward between us. It was as if the realities of our ranks were settling back over us, leaving us unable to forge the friendship I was so keen to have again.

Thankfully, within days of his return to the duty roster a couple of weeks later, things seemed to settle back to normal. We were kept together, thank god, and assigned a new crew chief and pilot.

I found myself following Major Marian around like a devoted puppy and doing everything in my power to stick by his side. Was it hero worship? Maybe. But something deep down inside of me wanted, *needed*, to be there for the man who had no one, who was on the run from a guilty past, the man who'd begged to be discharged from the hospital in favor of returning to duty, the man who didn't have anyone but me to call out for in the deep dark tangle of the jungle night.

CHAPTER 8

WESTON "MAJOR" MARIAN

I couldn't get rid of him, and I secretly thanked god for that.

When I returned to duty after finally kicking the infection, I was angry and irritable. For the first time in all my years in country, I resented the war. I hated it deep down to my very soul and wanted to rage against every damned part of it. When I'd been half-delirious with fever, I'd overheard a nurse say the life expectancy of a combat medic in a firefight was six seconds and a medic's life expectancy in Vietnam was only fourteen days. I thought of Doc Wilde's smiling face the day I'd first seen him. He deserved better than that. Hell, we all did.

So when I returned to duty, it was with a renewed vigor to protect my men and rescue as many soldiers and injured civilians as I could. I'd heard scuttlebutt at the hospital about the protests back home, and I hoped like hell our country's leaders knew what they were doing. In the meantime, all I could do was stay alert and do my job.

It took me a good five days back on duty before I realized the two of us had become inseparable. At first, I'd thought Doc was simply checking up on me to make sure I wasn't overdoing it after my injuries. But then I realized he was feeling unsure about our two new crewmates, Dial and Lynch.

One night we had to suddenly hunker down in one of the nearby bunkers because there were warnings of mortar attacks. Doc used the opportunity to ask me a million questions about my previous tours, what it was like working in the air assault division, how a Chinook differed from our Huey, why I'd chosen to become a pilot, and anything else he could think of to be actively learning something new while we were stuck between rows of sandbags.

I was used to his inquisitive nature after thousands of hours spent with him on missions and during downtime, so I told him as much as I could remember, and at one point the corporal on the other side of him gave Doc hell for it.

"Jesus, Doc. Give the major a break, will ya? You interviewing the man for a newspaper or something?"

Doc's eyes went wide with surprise, and then they flicked down with embarrassment. "Sorry, Major," he mumbled. "Just… making conversation."

I wanted to punch the corporal in the jaw. Instead, I cleared my throat in a kind of grunt.

"Passes the time as good as anything," I mumbled, but it was too late. The corporal's words had made their mark and shut up the sweet medic between us.

But several hours later when most of the men around us had dozed off, Doc spoke again. This time it was in a low voice so as not to disturb anyone around us.

"What do you think of Lynch and Dial?"

"They've been competent and efficient as far as I can see. Why?"

He remained quiet for a little while, and I wondered if he was going to tell me about a problem he had with one or both of them.

"It's just… I don't know. It's not the same."

Ahh.

"No, it's not," I agreed. "Lynch is very upright and by the book. Very different from Moline."

"Yeah. And Dial is nice and all… but…"

"He's not Rusnak," I finished for him.

Doc's eyes met mine, flush with grief. "I don't think I can—"

Someone nearby got up, presumably to visit the latrine. As he walked past us, Doc jumped back into a safer topic.

"You never told me why you got an ag degree," he said, clearing his throat. "I figured a career guy like you'd get a military science degree or something."

I went along with his need to change the subject. I explained my crazy dream of living on a quiet farm one day where I could keep myself to myself and raise chickens and goats.

Doc chuckled. "You should see the chickens my mom has. Stupidest things ever, but man oh man there are some nice-looking ones."

He went on about the peahens and the many coops he'd had to build for his mother over the years to keep her stock happy. As he chattered on, I realized how very different we were. Liam Wilde was a people person, eager and sociable, whereas I keep myself to myself for the most part. I hadn't always been that way. I remembered one time my sister had held her hand up like a stern teacher and said, "Just stop all that nonsense. Weston Marian, you exhaust me."

She'd been six at the time, and I remembered everyone laughing their fool heads off at her chastising me.

"Why're you laughing?" Doc asked with his crooked grin. "You think it's funny when a farm kid gets a walloping?"

"What? Oh, I missed what you said," I admitted.

"What made you smile like that, Major?"

I wanted to tell him to call me by my name, but after fourteen years in the army and several at this rank, my name pretty much *was* Major.

"You're a chatterbox like my little sister."

Doc's face softened. "Yeah?"

"Yep," I said with a smile. "Sassiest loudmouth you ever did meet."

His grin flashed white teeth in the surrounding darkness. "Opposite of you, then?"

"I reckon that's about right," I said with a chuckle. After a beat of indecision, I pulled out the little photo I carried in my breast pocket and showed it to him. "That's her. It was in my wallet when I left, thank god."

"What's her name?" The gentle look to his eyes told me he remembered about why I hadn't seen her in so long.

"Matilda," I said, hearing the name out loud for the first time in fifteen years. "But I called her Tilly."

The silence stretched thin between us but didn't break. I slipped the photo back into my pocket to keep it safe.

"You should write to her, Major," he said so softly I almost didn't hear it. I turned to look at him, unsure of how I felt about him using my rank when we were discussing something so close to my heart.

"Weston," I corrected just as softly. "And I don't think I'm brave enough."

Doc's beautiful eyes studied me. "You're the bravest SOB I've ever met."

"Says the corn-fed kid from small-town nowhere," I teased.

"Hey, I'll have you know our small town was featured in *Landman Monthly* magazine," he said with false indignation.

I chuckled. "Don't know what that is which oughta tell you something."

Doc grinned back. "It's a periodical for oil and mineral rights management in Texas."

We both cracked up at that until someone nearby farted, which only made us laugh some more. When we finally settled down, I told him about the class I'd taken on land use and mineral rights management. Part of me hoped it would be boring enough to help him drift off to sleep and get some shut-eye, but part of me just wanted to keep the conversation going a bit longer with the man who made me smile and forget where I was for a while.

My mention of land use set him off on another round of questions. Doc Wilde was hungry for knowledge. He'd interrogate any interesting fellow so long as the man would stand still long enough to answer him. But that night was the first time in a long time I felt the full force of someone's interest solely on me. Doc made me feel like I had something important to say, so we stayed up all night talking about everything from my background in the army to Doc's daydreams about getting an advanced science degree after the war.

Doc chuckled when the subject came back around to his father's huge Texas ranch and how Doc himself had had a special love affair with a particular brown-spotted Texas longhorn when he was a young boy.

"I named him Perry after Perry Como since I figured I'd love him till the end of time," he explained with a glint in his eye. "You know, like the song."

I couldn't help but notice how this quirky kid from Texas was the only person who'd ever made me glad to be in Vietnam. I wouldn't have given that moment up for the world right then. Seeing him grin and describe the lovesick little boy sneaking out to moon over a cow was a treat.

"What happened to him?"

Doc gave me a look that made it perfectly clear. I chuckled. "Ah, the great green pasture in the sky?"

"Smart alec," he scoffed. "I'll have you know, I didn't eat meat for a full three days in protest."

I put my hand on my heart and gasped. "Three whole days? My oh my, now that's dedication to a cause."

We laughed softly into the steamy darkness until I realized the corporal was awake again.

"What the fuck, Band-Aid? How'd you get Major Hard-ass here to crack a smile? You got some magic touch?"

Doc's eyes met mine for a split second before turning to look at the man next to him. It was only the briefest moment, but it was the kind of connection I'd been missing since twenty years before when I'd goofed off with my baby sister.

"I was treating the man's funny bone, Perkins," Doc said. "Leave the major alone or I'm sure he'll make you go fetch us some coffee."

I swallowed down my grin and remembered my rank, narrowing my eyes in a glare at the corporal before getting up to check on the security status. When I returned to my spot, I noticed the corporal had dozed off and Doc was still wide-awake.

We sat in silence for a little while until Doc turned to me. "That night... the crash... it's..." I could tell from his voice what he was trying to say.

"It's going to stay with you, Doc. And the first time's the worst," I said only loud enough for him to hear. "It never gets easy, but the first casualties that happen right in front of you in combat are like... well, they're like the ones that reset your compass to how bad it really is here. It's like a damned wake-up call of the worst kind."

I felt him turn to look at me, but I kept my focus on my clasped hands over the rifle in my lap.

"How can I keep from remembering?" Doc asked in a desperate voice. "All I can see is Rusnak in front of me one minute and..."

He didn't need to say the rest. I reached out to clasp his biceps and squeezed. "You think about those babies you got back home, Doc. That's what you do. You remember Billy and how much you want to get home to teach him how to throw a ball. You think about giving the girls away at their weddings one day. And you focus on that when the bad memories come. Now show me that picture you have."

The edge of his lip turned up in a grin as he shifted his weight to pull the little square from a pocket. "Yeah? You want to see three perfect angels?"

I snorted. "Perfect, huh? Not sure as I believe you, Lieutenant Wilde."

He passed the photo to me and then pulled out his lighter so I could see the image.

They looked like three little pill bugs all in a row. I'd never seen anything as pure and good as that little smiling boy and the two newborns he held.

"You were right," I said, trying not to feel envy snake around my heart and my gut. This golden boy had it all. The wife, the kids, the family ranch back home. Everything a good man with a kind heart deserved. And everything I would never have.

I handed it back and met his eyes. "When those bad memories hit, think of those three perfect angels, Doc. They'll guide you home."

"And what about you? What do you think about when the bad memories hit, Major?"

You, I wanted to say. *And that deep blue endless sea.*

"Peace," I said instead. Because to me, they were pretty much the same thing.

CHAPTER 9

LIAM "DOC" WILDE

At the end of three more months, we were all due for R&R. Lynch, Dial, Major, and I decided to take our leave together, and we planned our trip to Bangkok like it was the greatest thing since sliced bread. I wasn't sure why I even cared, since I certainly had no plans to be unfaithful to Betsy. All I wanted was time away from Nam, time away from the constant threat of death, the smell of blood, and the same faces everywhere I looked.

But when we finally got there, I was out of sorts. Seeing my fellow soldiers in their civvies was strange, and when Dial and Lynch started talking about renting women, I felt wrong-footed. Dial was single, but Lynch had a wife and baby back home in South Carolina. It wasn't my business, really, but perhaps I was most bothered by the major. Because I knew that he wouldn't want to rent a woman, but I also knew that no matter how close the four of us were by that point, and we weren't nearly as close as we'd been with Moline and Rusnak, Major wasn't about to pursue male companionship when any of the rest of us could see.

The first night was spent getting drunk off our asses and dancing like idiots at the closest club to our hotel. At some point both Dial and Lynch disappeared into the back with different women only to reappear later looking more relaxed. It was enough to take the edge off, I imagined, and we kept drinking until we were barely able to crawl back to our rooms.

But by the second night, it was clear everyone wanted more. Sure enough, Major Marian shined himself up and told the rest of us we were on our own that night. When he walked out of our shared hotel room, he took one last look at me. Our eyes met long enough to acknowledge what wasn't being said by either of us, and when the door closed behind him, I felt such a sickness in my gut, it surprised me.

I'd never thought of myself as particularly bothered by men who liked other men. Sure, I didn't have much experience with men who were like that, but to each his own, really. So why did it make me feel torn up inside knowing he was going out into the Thailand summer night to find a body to lose himself in?

When Lynch and Dial knocked on my door a little while later to see if I was ready, I admitted that my stomach was all out of sorts and I thought I needed to stay in. They teased me for being a chickenshit, but I told them to go to hell and remember to use a rubber when they got there.

I lay in bed and thought of home. I'd had a chance to call Betsy when we'd gotten to Danang two nights before but before we'd boarded the plane to Bangkok. Hearing her voice had been both strange and wonderful. My throat had damned near closed up with the familiar comfort of that sweet sound. I'd heard one of the girls crying in the background, and even that had been a gift. She'd told me all the news from home, including the story of Brenda taking her first steps for the sole purpose of trying to get her hands on Gina's tippy cup of milk. She'd described all of our parents doing well and finding enough seasonal hands to get the work done on the farm and ranch.

My wife was a strong woman who was single-handedly raising our three children while not knowing what would become of me over here. She had the unspoken task of making sure not only our kids were cared for while I was gone, but also our parents. And if that wasn't enough, she'd told me her doctor wanted to do some testing on a birthmark on her scalp, which would involve shaving part of her hair.

"Not going to do it, Liam," she'd said firmly. "I may not look like much these days with little sleep and half-covered in baby crud, but at least I have nice hair. I'm a Texas girl after all."

I'd laughed but then had tried to talk her into letting him do the test, but she was stubborn as hell.

"It's been there my whole life, hon. Ain't gonna kill me now. Unlike this boy here." The affection had been clear in her voice. "Billy, say hey to your daddy."

And then the little voice of my four-year-old boy had washed over me like a spring breeze through a field of Texas bluebonnets. "Hey, Daddy, we miss you."

"Hey, buddy. Daddy misses you too. So much." I'd pressed the phone so hard against my ear it hurt.

He told me about riding on Grandpa's tractor and helping Granny feed the chickens.

When it had been time to say goodbye, the thought had flashed through my head that I might never hear my family's sweet voices again. I squeezed my eyes closed and told Betsy I loved her.

"You shut the hell up, William Wilde," she'd snapped. "Don't you dare talk to me like this is goodbye. You do not have my permission to get yourself blown up over there, do you hear me?"

I barked out a laugh, getting the attention of several soldiers walking past the bank of telephones in the R&R center.

"Yes, ma'am," I'd replied with a smile. Little Brenda hadn't gotten her wildcat tendencies from me. "Ten-four and roger that."

Ending the call like that had left me in lifted spirits, which had made me appreciate her even more. But now here I was feeling sick and troubled in another country half a world away, and part of me wanted just to be home once and for all. I turned out the light and lay down on my bed in hopes of calming myself enough to at least go out for a meal.

I must have dozed off because after a while, the sound of a key in the door woke me.

It was dark in the room. The cheap brown curtains blocked out most of the light except for a sliver where they didn't quite meet in the middle.

Major came into the room quietly and slipped his shoes off before coming around to sit on the bed next to mine. My eyes were only halfway open, but they probably looked closed in the dim light.

He unbuttoned his shirt and pulled it off, laying it across the foot of the bed before reaching for his belt. I noticed how wide and strong his shoulders were, how big and capable he always seemed. His muscles flexed under his skin as he continued undressing.

I didn't realize I was staring until the metal clink caused me to startle. He didn't seem to notice because he continued as if nothing had happened, pulling the belt from the loops and setting it on top of the discarded shirt. Finally he stood to remove his trousers and socks, leaving him in plain boxers and an undershirt.

He sat and stared at me before letting out a deep sigh and stretching out on his side with his head on the pillow. The two of us were like mirror images of each other, me on my left side facing him and him on his right facing me.

A thousand questions tumbled through my head. How did one find male company in a city like this? Was it safe? Was it dangerous? Was it… satisfying? What was it like, being in bed with another man? I'd never had reason to think about it before, but if this man I looked up to so much found it satisfying, then there must be something to it. Right?

Was he attracted to big men? Small men? Did he like to… give or… receive? And why the hell was I thinking any of those things about someone I worked with?

"I couldn't do it," he said softly after a while.

"Why not?"

He continued to watch me, and my stomach flipped around as if the nap had done absolutely nothing for it.

Our eyes stayed locked on each other as the tension in the room thickened.

He finally sighed. "Go to bed, Liam." And then he turned on his other side to face the wall.

I could feel my heart thumping in my rib cage, and it felt like it was going to lift right out of my chest. My eyes examined the width and breadth of his muscular upper body in the fitted T-shirt, trying to determine what another man would see when he looked at the major like that.

As my eyes slid down his back, I noticed a stretch of skin where the shirt had ridden up, exposing his lower back above the low elastic band of his shorts.

In all the times I'd thought about my gratitude to him for what he'd done for me that night in the jungle—for getting us out of the Huey after the crash, for keeping me sane after the disaster in the clearing, for distracting me through the night—I'd always come to the conclusion that if there was ever any way of repaying him, of providing any ounce of security or comfort to him the way he'd done to me, I'd do it.

So my mind went there.

I knew I'd never act on it—of course I wouldn't. But I couldn't say I didn't consider it for the briefest of moments that night in Bangkok. I thought about giving him the gift of human touch, of physical pleasure, of male company if only to take him out of his goddamned head for a night and let him be cherished for once.

He deserved it.

But I was married. And I wasn't gay. And he was in a city with hundreds of willing participants of any size, shape, or gender, and he'd chosen not to partake.

I closed my eyes and willed myself to go back to sleep, but of course I couldn't.

And three hours later, I was glad I hadn't, if only to be able to hear the pained whimper from across the room.

"*Liam.*"

I slipped out of my bed and into his without thinking. Pulling his back against my chest, I wrapped an arm around him and held tight.

"I'm here," I murmured behind his ear. "You're okay."

"I killed them," he breathed. "Liam, are you safe?"

How many nights had he been haunted by the memory of the men he'd killed? And why was he so obsessed with making sure I was safe?

The guilt damned near broke me.

"I'm safe, Wes," I whispered. "I'm always safe with you. Sleep easy, Major. *Please.*"

He drifted back off, and after a while I decided I'd better move back to my own bed before he woke up and things got very awkward.

But getting back in my own bed felt strange after being in his. I wasn't sure if it was the lack of physical touch and comfort that we all experienced on deployment or whether there was something specific about Weston Marian that made me feel protective and possessive. I didn't want to look at it too closely because doing that brought with it the guilt of what had happened the night of the crash. I hadn't been able to save his best friend or any of the other men we'd been sent to rescue. I hadn't even watched his back the way I should have. I wasn't sure how he could have forgiven me for it, but he didn't seem to think I'd done anything wrong.

There was no denying the major and I had a connection that would last the rest of our days.

War did that to people. It took practical strangers and tied them together in knots of steel. When we returned to base, I felt closer to him than ever.

But two weeks later, Major Weston Marian got PCS orders to return stateside. To Texas of all places.

He was going home without me.

CHAPTER 10

WESTON "MAJOR" MARIAN

For as much as I prayed for an end to my time in Vietnam, I would have given it all up for the chance to send Doc home in my stead. When those duty orders came through, I felt numb. Clutching the papers in one fist, I wandered out behind the quonset hut where the colonel's office was and squatted down with my elbows on my thighs, lowering my head down so I could catch my breath and steady myself.

"There you are," Doc's familiar voice said after a few minutes. "Check it out. Taylor's wife sent a care package with…"

I finally looked up at him and stood, rolling my shoulders back.

"Who died?" he asked.

I handed him the papers and rubbed my face with both hands before clasping them behind my neck and waiting for his reaction.

"Oh."

"Yeah."

"Wow. That's…" Doc let out a huge breath and smiled at me. "That's great news, Major. Congratulations."

I'd been assigned to oversee flight training logistics at Fort Wolton with the implication time spent in the position would set me up for possible promotion to lieutenant colonel in less than two years. It was an incredible duty assignment with one very unspoken exception.

Doc wouldn't be there.

His clear blue eyes locked on mine. "Don't," he said swiftly. "Don't you fucking dare, short-timer. Get your shit together because this is not happening."

Doc's nostrils flared in anger, and I knew he was right. If we let emotions come into play, we might as well break down into jelly blobs on the ground.

I swallowed the lump in my throat. "You snag one for me?" I asked, nodding toward the candy bar he held.

His familiar crooked grin appeared. "Yeah, this one's for you. I snarfed mine down in two seconds." He handed me the bar, knowing full well I would give him half of it. He thought I wasn't much for chocolate, but the truth of the matter was, I knew he liked it more than I did.

When we joined Lynch, Dial, and several of the other dustoff crew for our nightly card game, there was a general cheer of congratulations for me but also enough regrets to make me feel part of a real family. And I was leaving them behind in hopes they'd make it home from Vietnam too.

"I'm going to send him to my daddy's ranch so he can see what a steak is supposed to taste like," Doc teased. He shot me a wink while passing me a bottle of tepid beer. "And fuck Vietnam. My dad'll put him on horseback with the bulls during breeding season and teach him what *real* danger's like, right, fellas?"

They all chanted, "*Fuck Vietnam,*" and clinked bottles.

We made the most of the time we had left. I got stupidly superstitious on the last few dustoff flights until Doc finally chewed my ass and called me out in the middle of a mission for being a chickenshit. I knew he was just feeling angry and resentful, but our emotions were so jacked up that by the time we closed up the bird and headed toward the mess, we were both screaming at each other and the men around us were backing away in anticipation of someone throwing a punch.

Doc's anger reddened his face. "I've never once known you to back down from a failed pickup and hand it off to another crew because of live fire. Never once!"

"We already had injured men on board. We needed to get them to base." My teeth were pressed together so tightly, I thought my jaw would ache.

"Bullshit. You were—"

"Can it, Lieutenant," I growled, reminding him of our respective ranks.

Dial shoved at Doc's shoulder, pushing him toward a cargo container we used for storage. "Take it behind closed doors, assholes. I for one am glad the major got us the fuck out of there before we got our asses blown off."

I followed Doc into the dim space and closed the door until there was only a sliver of light left from the opening. It was hot and stuffy, but at least it was away from the eyes of the other men.

Doc rounded on me, his index finger coming up like he was going to poke me in the chest with it. I grabbed his wrist and held it firm, meeting his eyes.

"Stop." My voice was low and firm.

His nostrils flared. "Write me up. I don't care. We should have gone back for those men."

"The other unit got them out with a gunship escort. They're all safely back, and you know it."

"Since when do you let another crew take our dustoff? Since when do you turn tail and run? Since when—"

"Since there was an RPG aimed right at your fucking face, Liam!" I roared.

Doc froze. His mouth hung open in shock.

I continued. "You question me like I'm a fucking cherry grunt who doesn't know his ass from his elbow! Do you have any idea how many men I've rescued under live fire?"

"I know, that's why I—"

"No, you don't know. But when some VC asshole with a rocket-propelled grenade launcher points his weapon at my..." I swallowed. "At my *medic*, I'm not going to hover there like an idiot and take the hit."

Suddenly, I had two arms full of lieutenant. Doc clung to me like a jungle leech and squeezed hard. I wrapped my arms around him and held on. We both smelled like dog shit, but I'd take Liam Wilde's dog shit smell any day of the week.

"I don't want you to go." His voice was muffled by my shirt.

"Yeah," I grunted back. Because if I said all the words I truly wanted to say, I'd choke on them and drown.

"You're the best friend I ever had, Wes." He pulled back and sniffed, running the back of his arm across his cheeks really quickly. "I'm going to miss you like hell."

"Yeah," I mumbled again before taking a step back to keep myself from grabbing his shirt and pulling him back against me. "Uh, same."

Doc met my eyes. "I'm sorry for..." He flapped his hand back toward the Huey.

I blew out a breath and nodded. "I know you are."

"Can we go get some chow now and maybe forget this ever happened?" The crooked grin from my dreams appeared in the dusty light. It never failed to make me smile in return.

"Not a chance. You're my servant tonight at dinner and my beer boy at poker." I turned and opened the door farther. "And I expect the beer to be cold."

Doc sighed. "I'm going to have to sleep with Private Samuelson in the mess in exchange for ice, aren't I?"

"Nah, a little blowie'll do the trick."

Doc's laughter rang out as we stepped out of the storage container. "As long as you don't speak from personal experience."

"Hell no. That kid has VD written all over him. I heard his middle name is Boom-Boom."

We joked the rest of the way to the mess where we joined our friends for a hot meal and thought for the thousandth time how lucky we were not to be cracking open C-rations in the field.

When the day finally came for me to bug out, I did my best to avoid being alone with Doc Wilde. I didn't trust myself not to tell him how much I cared about him and how, if something happened to him, I may as well lie down and die myself.

So when I gave him a quick final hug, I limited my words.

"Stay sharp. Don't want you hurt," I grunted.

His eyes widened and I drank in the cool blue for the last time.

"That's the first thing you ever said to me," he said.

"Maybe you oughta listen to me, then," I teased, ruffling his hair like he was a pesky baby brother instead of the man I loved most in this world. I kept up the stupid smiling until I was a thousand feet in the air over the base.

And then I don't think I truly smiled again until six months later when the first letter arrived.

As a senior officer in helo training operations at Fort Wolters, I spent more time at a desk in an office than I had at any of the past four duty stations. While I appreciated the ability to keep my uniform dry and clean, I felt antsy and untethered. I had too much time and energy on my hands. There were no emergencies to distract me or inside jokes with close friends to entertain me. I made friends easily enough with several of the other officers since this wasn't my first rodeo, but it wasn't the same as having men with you who'd been in the shit right beside you.

So when that first letter came several months into my time there… well, it was like holding a tiny piece of home—the only home I'd had in a long, long time.

Major,

Do I even still have to call you that if I don't serve with you anymore? Just kidding. You'll always be Major to me, even when you're a lieutenant colonel or brigadier general.

So today we almost lost Dial. FNG tried to get the man out on the skids with a rifle and shit went fubar. Dial tipped out and dropped twenty feet to the ground while Lynch was pulling up. It was bad, Major. Real bad. Multiple leg fractures, severe contusions, and they had to do surgery for internal wounds. We're lucky he's still with us, no thanks to the flight commander.

Needless to say, we miss you.

Okay, I miss you. And I probably won't send this. I'll probably trash it like all the others before. But damn, Major. Being here without you is like walking around with only one shoe on. I keep stepping wrong and it hurts.

I've never had a best friend before, and things with you were just... easy. I miss that. I miss having someone I can look at across the table and know I don't even need to say the words. Remember that time Franks told us he was going to the infirmary because he wasn't feeling well and you and I looked at each other and started hooting with laughter? He still sneaks off to visit that nurse nearly every day, and lord only knows how many times she's had to tell him she's married. Poor girl.

So, what's it like back home? Have you had a decent meal at a restaurant yet? Taken a shower and put on clean civvies? I miss my cowboy boots and jeans, but just the thought of wearing them makes me sweat even more than I am already. Oh, you'll get a kick out of this. Captain Sanchez somehow got his hands on a window air-conditioning unit for our quonset. It keeps things drier. Of course we got it just in time for the dry season, but I'm not complaining. Maybe the sound of it running will drown out Sanchez's snoring.

Dammit, Major. There's part of me that's so damned happy you're safe, but then there's the selfish SOB in me that would give just about anything to have you back in the portside pilot seat of our bird where you belong.

I miss you, asshole.

Doc

P.S. Send us a care package. Lynch wants Kool-Aid, Dial wants Mallo-Cups, and I want Junior Mints and jelly beans. And if you can find a way to send me Doritos... well, never mind. Not sure they'd taste the same in crumb form.

I READ it over and over and over again, picturing his crooked grin and twinkling sea-blue eyes as I heard his familiar voice in my head reading the words. Surely I had a goofy grin on my face because that letter from William Wilde was about the best thing that had happened to me since seeing the man in person.

The next day I spent almost an entire paycheck at the local five-and-dime, buying up handfuls of candy and snacks for the boys including Jiffy Pop. I tossed in some new socks, a few paperback mystery novels, and a stack of newspaper comics I collected. By the time I packaged everything up and sent it off, I was kicking myself for not having done it sooner. I'd spent months feeling sorry for myself when if I'd just stopped and thought about someone else for a moment, I might have realized how easy it was for me to bring a little cheer to their lives over there.

A month later, I was surprised to get a response.

Dear Major,

You really came through for us! The package arrived today and I felt like a rock star with fans following me like the Pied Piper. When I got to my quonset, everyone gathered around for their share, and after they left, I ate the jelly beans so fast, I damned near ate the earplugs by mistake. Ha, ha. If you think a pair of earplugs will stop Sanchez from keeping me awake at night, you've obviously forgotten how he also likes to keep the damned light on until all hours so he can read those devotionals his mother sends him. I keep telling him Jesus would rather him get some good sleep, but he doesn't listen.

Three days ago, I saved someone during a mission. I know what you're thinking. "Doc, you've saved plenty of people during missions." But this one was different. The PFC had been declared dead from his wounds in battle. He'd stepped on a booby trap and lost both legs, bleeding out before they could help him. We loaded his body along with a severely injured SVA soldier and a corporal who'd been hit with a bullet to the leg, similar to yours. For some reason while treating the SVA soldier, I kept looking back over at the dead PFC's body thinking there was something not quite right about it. I finally reached over just to assure myself he was truly dead, and damned if I didn't find a weak pulse!

I barked at the crew chief to keep tending to the SVA guy while I went to work on the PFC. I checked the tourniquets they'd applied when trying to save him, did CPR and pushed fluids, and kept him alive long enough to get him back to base. The surgeon took over from there. He's in bad shape, sure enough, but they think he's going to make it. They'll know more once they get him off the vent. Before I left his bedside, one of the doctors came in and clapped me on the back. Told me PFC Glaston had me to thank for his life and asked me how in the world I didn't think he was dead when he got loaded in. It had taken me a while to put my finger on what was off about the scenario, but I'd finally realized his stumps were still bleeding.

It had been one of those days in the Huey where the floor was wet and sticky with blood. You remember the kind of days I mean—the bird's engine stayed hot for twelve hours straight and we were barely awake by the last run. I thought about how I was going to have to stay after and help the crew chief rinse her out. That's when I noticed the blood dripping from the PFC's stretcher.

Amazing the things that have become ingrained in my subconscious. I mentioned it to the doctor, and he said it's similar for them in the hospital. When they hear our rotors getting louder, they know it's time to go to work.

Weston, I think I want to become a doctor.

Am I crazy?

Doc

IN THE NEXT CARE PACKAGE, the jar of jelly beans had a sleep mask and earplugs in it for everyone in his quonset. It also had a stethoscope tucked deep inside a big jar of jelly beans. The back of the bell was engraved, "2nd Lt Wm Wilde, Medic." And the note promised I'd buy him a new one when he graduated from medical school.

CHAPTER 11

LIAM "DOC" WILDE

I was such a downer after Major left that the rest of the crew teased me mercilessly.

"Aw, don't mind our medic, gents, he's still upset about President Eisenhower passing away," Dial said when we picked up a crew that had been stranded in the wrong place at the right time. Fortunately, their injuries were relatively minor, the kind I could treat in my sleep.

"That was last year," one of the soldiers said in confusion. "Wasn't it?"

"Never mind him," I muttered, cleaning the man's lacerated hand as Lynch nosed us up into the sky. "I'm fine."

But I wasn't fine. I felt like I'd gone to Nam and gotten a bullet to the gut. I'd never had a friend like Weston Marian, the kind of man you could talk about anything with and even cry in front of if you had to. He was my best friend, and now I felt like I'd never see him again.

That night I wrote him a letter like I was some kind of member of a teenage fan club. Told him how much I missed his ugly mug and bossy tendencies, how when our new flight commander had come on board, he'd insisted on a silent flight until after the rescue, but that Lynch had quickly jollied him out of it. I told him about the cluster-fuck that resulted in two friendly Hueys almost crashing right over

73

the base. And I described in great detail a prank on Staff Sergeant Timms on his birthday.

I asked him how his new job was. Where he lived on base. What it was like having good food again. Whether or not he knew anyone on base from his previous duty stations.

I asked him if he missed this. Us. Any of it.

But then I ripped the letter up and threw it in the trash. My hero worship for Major Marian had gone too far. I was obviously feeling rudderless without our senior officer around anymore.

I was a grown man for god's sake. I went back to my hooch and wrote to Betsy instead, telling her how much I missed hearing her sing to the babies and wished I could have a taste of the blackberry jam she'd put up the first year we were married. I asked her how the kids were and told her about some of the women nurses on base and how tough they were. Before I closed the letter, I even suggested maybe she could go to college if she wanted after I got home and could help with the kids.

Over the next several weeks I wrote those two letters I don't know how many times. First I'd write the real stuff to the major, and then I'd write the sanitized version to Betsy. One would get trashed and the other sent.

Until the night our chopper crashed and Mike Dial almost died in my fucking arms. When we finally made it back to base, I was still too shaky to even consider catching some shut-eye, so I sat down to write a letter to Major.

This time I sent it, and I was so glad I did. He immediately wrote back and sent us a huge box of goodies, along with regaling us with tales of drive-up hamburgers and frosty milkshakes, listening to music on the radio that wasn't two years old, and being able to wander off the base without a sidearm. It helped pass the time so much, I cursed myself for not having written him sooner.

When my DEROS approached toward the end of my first tour and I learned I'd be home in time for the twins' second birthday, I finally knew what it was like to be a short-timer. It was like walking on eggshells, trying everything in your power not to get killed or hurt.

The day finally came, and I was grateful to learn right before leaving that Lynch would be stateside within another month too. After a trip home to Hobie, I was to be stationed at Fort Sam Houston where combat medics were trained. I was under no illusion that would be the end of my time in Vietnam. As a volunteer rather than a draftee, I was committed to three years in the army, which meant the likelihood of my final year being back in country was high.

But in the meantime, I was going home to Texas, and I couldn't have been happier.

I thought of Major Marian and the fact we'd only be 250 miles away from each other. In fact, if I drove the back-roads way, Fort Wolters was on my direct route between Hobie and Fort Sam.

Would that be strange? Seeing each other under normal circumstances instead of in a Huey under fire or sitting between sandbags in a bunker? What would we do exactly? Eat a steak at a restaurant and talk about old times?

It didn't matter. The closer I got to home on my long journey back, the more I knew I needed to see him before long, if for no other reason than to assure myself he was alive and well.

But first, I was flying home to my wife and babies. The ranch. My parents and all the people in town who'd sent me off with such pride. Thankfully, the people of Hobie were patriotic and proud of men and women who served, so I'd never gotten the feeling of hate and resentment that so many of my bigger-city friends got from home.

Sure enough, when my father's Chevy truck drove us into the town square, it was awash with red, white, and blue. I'd learned from my dad on the drive from Dallas that another kid from my high school was returning the same day. Tony Trevino had apparently lost an eye over there and had gotten a medical discharge. My dad went on and on about how awful it was for poor Tony, but all I could think was how much worse he could have had it. At least he still had his legs, his sanity, his life. I didn't correct my father, however. It was the first experience I had with keeping my Vietnam stories buckled up tight.

There were picnic tables set up on the lawn of the square, and townsfolk were gathered together on a gorgeous spring day in Texas. After Dad parked the truck and led me toward the center of the square, I spotted her.

Betsy stood talking to a friend of our parents. She had a polite smile on her face, a toddler on her hip, and a beautiful yellow dress on. Her hair was done up special, and she looked like spring personified.

I took off running, catching the attention of the crowd. Little Billy grabbed for Betsy's leg and held on, unsure of what was happening. Betsy turned to me and gasped, covering her mouth with her hand before handing one of the girls off to the lady she'd been talking to.

When I got to her, I grabbed Billy up first and then hugged them both, inhaling the hairspray scent of her and trying not to bawl like a baby.

Billy started crying immediately, and I wondered if I should have left him alone, given him more time to come to grips with a daddy he hadn't seen in over a year and probably didn't remember much at all.

I pulled back and smiled at him. "Hey, buddy, it's your daddy. I missed you so much." I met Betsy's wet eyes and thought I'd never seen anything more beautiful than her familiar face.

"Hi," I whispered, leaning in for a quick kiss. Her arms tightened around my neck. "Aren't you a sight for sore eyes?"

"Welcome home. I can't believe you're here," she said with a sniff and a smile.

"Dah-dee," a little voice squeaked from nearby. I looked over to see one of the girls staring at me with her hands up in the air.

"Gina-bonina, good gracious!" I said, letting go of Betsy so I could lean over and scoop her up. "What a big girl you are! Thank goodness your mama sent me some pictures of you three or I wouldn't have recognized you."

I saw Brenda poke her head out from behind my mother's skirt and winked at her. She immediately hid again.

"Hi, Mom." My voice croaked a little when I saw her, and her face crumpled. She lurched toward me and held on tight.

She smelled like Pall Mall cigarettes and Jean Nate After Bath

Splash. It was a combination so embedded in my childhood memories, I let out a deep breath and inhaled again.

I was home. And just like that, life managed to get in the way. Betsy had elected to stay in Hobie instead of moving into base housing with me, so for the next several months, I busted my tail at the base in San Antonio during the week and raced home to help our parents on the farm on the weekends. I rarely slept, I hardly ate, and I sure as hell didn't have time to socialize or even spend much time with my wife and children.

My friendship with Major Marian had settled into a semiregular letter-writing exchange wherein we swapped information about our relative duties, hijinks around base, the trials and tribulations of a part-time farmer/rancher, and little else of consequence. We were like distant pen pals. Every letter I got from him with its superficial bullshit made me angrier and angrier and lonelier and lonelier until I couldn't stand it anymore.

One weekend almost a year after returning from Vietnam, I hit a wall.

Instead of driving straight to Hobie, I drove directly to Fort Wolters and broke down like a baby the minute I clapped eyes on him.

CHAPTER 12

WESTON "MAJOR" MARIAN

When Doc had first returned stateside, to Texas no less, I'd spent an embarrassing number of hours trying to determine how I could concoct an excuse to see him. We were best friends, after all. It would make sense to visit each other now that we were within a few hours' drive. But then I'd come to the conclusion that my crush on Liam Wilde was dangerous, if only to myself, and seeing him in person might make things much worse for me.

So when the opportunity didn't present itself and he didn't push for it, I took it as a sign. I backed off and lectured myself to keep things cordial. Friendly. Arm's length. We kept in touch with letters back and forth, but every time I started to put real thoughts and feelings down, I remembered his wife and children. I would never do anything to break apart a loving family like that, so I kept my correspondence simple.

But the need to be close to someone, be close to *him*, burned inside me every single day. So much so that when I opened the door to my apartment and saw him standing there, I truly thought my mental instability had finally created a visual hallucination, if only to give me the slightest emotional reprieve for a brief moment.

I stared at him. His dirty-blond hair had grown out from the shorn cut he'd maintained in the army. It was wavy and thick now which made him look even younger. Maybe that was what part of my subconscious clued me in to the fact it wasn't my brain playing tricks on me. Doc Wilde was really there. His cerulean eyes were careworn and filling rapidly, and I noticed in the moment before I reached for him that he'd dropped at least ten pounds he could ill afford.

I grabbed the front of his uniform blouse and hauled him in for a hug, slamming the door behind him with a kick. He clung to me so tightly I wondered if his shirt buttons would leave permanent impressions on my skin.

I hoped like hell they would.

Doc's entire body shook, and it took me a couple of minutes to realize he was crying. I cupped the back of his head so I could hold his face tucked into my neck as long as he needed to catch his breath and calm down.

"I'm sorry," he choked.

"You'd better not be," I grumbled back. "If you can't be real with me, then what's the damned point?"

His hands clutched the back of my T-shirt. I'd just gotten out of the shower after a particularly long and hot day in one of the hangars on base and had thrown on a white undershirt and the clean khaki uniform trousers I'd laid out. The plan had been to meet up with some of the guys at the officers' club. But now, clearly, my plan was to hold on to Liam Wilde as long as I could.

I finally pulled back enough to cup his face and thumb away the wet streaks on his cheeks. My brain kicked in and started spitting out worst-case scenarios.

"The kids? Betsy?"

His eyes widened in surprise. "What? Oh, no. No. That's not... Everyone's fine. I'm just..." He let out a nervous chuckle and stepped back, dashing his palms across his cheeks self-consciously. "Hell, Major, I'm just tired, that's all."

It was an understatement, but I didn't press him on it.

"Come inside. Want a beer? Soda?"

I let him into the small living space with its standard-issue bare-bones furniture. He took a seat on the small sofa and tossed his cover and car keys on the coffee table. "Yeah. Whatever you're having's fine."

In addition to the two cans of beer, I also grabbed a bag of potato chips and slapped together some simple sandwiches before returning to sit next to him. The man looked like he hadn't eaten in days.

Doc looked at the plate of sandwiches and then met my eyes with soft eyes and a curved lip. "Strawberry jelly?"

"Of course. How many times did I have to listen to you complain about the grape jelly we had on base? Sorry it's not something better. I don't keep a lot of food here."

"No, Christ. This is perfect." He grabbed a sandwich triangle and took a huge bite, groaning in satisfaction before talking with a full mouth. "I spent the first half the day being a human pincushion for the trainee medics and the second half getting my ass chewed for failing to fill out some form or another." He met my eye with a twinkle. "Goddamned arrogant majors are a pain in my ass."

I laughed along with him while he shoved food in his mouth. To give him a chance to keep eating, I told him about why I'd been stuck in the hangar all day.

"Speaking of asshole majors, apparently I scared a grunt so badly he felt he had to show up for class today despite his wife having given birth at oh-four-hundred this morning. He kept wrecking the preflight training protocol until I was about to chew his ass for failing to focus."

Doc snorted. "Poor kid. What happened? How'd you find out about the baby?"

"His father-in-law is friends with the base commander. One phone call and my commanding officer came storming into the hangar, raging at me in front of the students."

"What'd you say?"

"I said, 'Sir, with all due respect, I didn't even know the warrant officer was married, much less expecting a child. And quite frankly, if my in-flight medic in Nam can get back on a Huey the day after crashing in one, shooting Charlie, spending a dangerous night in the jungle outside Bien Hoa, and performing in-the-field medical procedures with one hand while holding a pistol at the ready in another, I expect this cherry to be able to do a simple preflight check after a night stuck pacing an air-conditioned hospital waiting room. *Sir.*'"

"No, you did not," Doc said with a surprised snort.

"Did too."

"What did he say?"

"He barked out a laugh and looked at the trainee. Asked him if he disagreed. The kid said, 'No, sir,' like he was about to wet his pants. As soon as the commanding officer left, I dismissed the kid to go enjoy his new baby."

Silence for a beat.

"How did you know I went back to work the day after the crash? You were laid up."

I narrowed my eyes at him. "Because you just told me."

We stared at each other.

I blinked. "Doc, you were terrified, and rightly so. And I know you. You had to go back up as soon as you could to get back on the horse."

"Yeah. I did. Another medic got sick, and I was too jacked up to sleep."

I shrugged and sipped my beer. "You did the right thing, as much as I would have forbidden it had I been in my right mind at the time."

Doc's eyebrows shot up. "Forbidden it?"

I loved it when he got feisty, but we were getting off topic.

"Doc, why are you here? Not that I'm not happy to see you, because I am. And you know you're welcome here anytime. But what's going on?"

CHAPTER 13

LIAM "DOC" WILDE

Did I even know the answer to Major's question?

"I don't know really. I just… I'm tired. I'm overwhelmed. I need… I need someone to talk things through with, you know?"

I held my breath in hopes he wouldn't ask the question, but he did anyway.

"What about Betsy? Can't you talk things through with her?"

I sighed and tossed the half-eaten bag of chips on the table before leaning back on the thin sofa cushion. "I have. I mean, I do. But she's so damned agreeable, I feel like I can't get a straight answer out of her."

"Answer to what?"

"Medical school."

Major's face lit up. "Great."

I held up a hand. "Now, wait. I don't know if I can swing it yet. The UT Southwestern is expanding their medical school, and there's a new program where they're trying to encourage people to finish medical school in three years instead of four."

"That's great. Plus you won't be so far from the ranch."

I ran my hands through my hair. "Yeah, that's the thing though. I'm trying to convince Betsy to come with me. She's always wanted to live in the city."

"Doesn't she want to go?"

"I think she does, but she's afraid of leaving our parents with no help."

Major leaned forward and put his elbows on his knees. "Doc, you know I'm only an hour away from Hobie. For the time I'm still here, if something comes up, you know all you have to do is call."

I hadn't realized how much an offer like that would mean until I heard it. "Thanks. That's... thanks, Major."

"I think maybe you should think about what Betsy would want," he said, reaching for his beer again.

"How do you mean?"

"Well, what's she into? What does she like? Is there anything she's always wanted to do or study or become?"

"In high school she talked about becoming a nurse, but I think that was just because it was something her parents would support," I said, trying to think.

"Does she have any passions. Besides the kids, I mean?"

I smiled. "She loves to plant roses. Always has. She was in 4-H like most of us were, and she learned how to hybridize two of her favorite kinds together. I call her my Texas Rose."

"Maybe you should encourage her to take horticulture classes at the university while you're there. I mean, if she can swing it with the kids. Or even biology classes if you think she might want to get a degree. I remember you said she didn't go to college because of Billy."

I nodded and smiled, remembering something she'd told me a few weeks before. "Yeah. She actually joked recently that Billy saved her from having to do any more homework. So I'm not sure she wants the degree, but I think she'd really like the horticulture classes. Or, hell, even joining a garden club would probably be enough to give her something all to herself."

Major snapped his fingers. He told me about a man he'd served with whose wife ran an in-home daycare in Dallas. We talked through some more ideas for how I could juggle med school and my family's ranch, including how the hell I would break the news to my parents without giving them a heart attack. When it was finally time for me to ask about him, he dropped a bombshell.

"I'm going back."

I didn't understand what he meant. "To Bakersfield? To your family?"

He shook his head, his thick dark hair sticking up where he'd run fingers through it. "Nam."

The word sat there like a grenade with the pin pulled.

"No you're not," I said between clenched teeth. "No you're goddamned not."

Major sighed. "I wasn't going to tell you until I was already there."

My heart plummeted into my stomach. He was going to die over there. I knew it as well as I knew my own name. And what if he'd gone over there and died before I'd even had a chance to talk him out of it?

"No. You're not." This time my voice was unsteady. I wanted to punch the stubborn son of a bitch. "You asshole! No you're not. Tell them you've gone through enough over there. A *fifth* tour? Are they crazy? Tell them they can't have you. No. No way. Tell them—"

I didn't really realize I'd started yelling and banging my fist on his chest with every sentence until he grabbed my wrist and turned me around, hauling my back to his front and pinning my arms to my chest. I felt the scrape of his beard stubble on the side of my face.

He was so much stronger than I was, there was no fighting him. I'd learned that one day when I'd tried to jump out of the chopper to rescue a VC soldier who'd lost a leg right alongside our own guys. Major had forcibly held me back while Lynch had pulled us out of there just before the VC soldier pulled a grenade out of his pocket and launched it at us. Had Major not held me down long enough for Lynch to pull up or had, god forbid, I loaded the guy onto the chopper, we would have all died.

There in Major's apartment, I went limp almost immediately like a damned kitten in its mother's mouth.

"Stop," he said in his low voice, the one I'd always joked sent out shock waves of power across the land. Moline had sworn that one word in Major's "command voice" could make a grunt shit his pants.

But I was no grunt.

"No," I said like a petulant child. "No I will not stop. You're an idiot! Why? Why, Weston? Christ, do you have a death wish?" I was getting worked up again and thought for a split second I was going to have a true panic attack. I closed my eyes and tried to concentrate on breathing. I could smell Ivory soap on his skin and commercial starch on his uniform pants. Warm puffs of his breath brushed across my cheek. Something about the way he held me so tightly calmed me. It reminded me of the way the nurses in the hospital had wrapped the babies so tightly in their blankets to give them a sense of security.

Maybe there was something to it.

"*Lieutenant Colonel* Marian," he said, emphasizing the promotion, "will be on special assignment to Cam Ranh, and they said they anticipate the assignment only lasting six months."

"The air base?" That was something, at least. Cam Ranh was safer than Long Binh. And as lieutenant colonel, he sure as hell wouldn't be flying helicopters every day. It was more likely he'd be working in an office, safely staying on base most of the time.

He puffed out half a chuckle. "Yes, Liam. The air base." Something strange always happened to my stomach when he said my first name. I never could tell if it was because he usually only said it when he wasn't aware of it, or because when he said it, it just sounded so tender and incongruous coming out of his gruff self. It was like watching a bloody war hero hold a daisy.

I blew out a long breath and wriggled out from his hold so I could turn and look at him.

"Congratulations on the promotion. I mean it. You deserve it."

Major's eyes studied me. "Thanks."

"I'm not going to call you Lieutenant Colonel though. You know that, right?" I teased.

He ran thick fingers through his hair again, a reluctant smile creasing his face. "Yeah. I know."

"When do you leave?"

"Sixty days."

I thought about spending time with him before he went. If something did happen to him over there, I'd regret every single moment I'd never had with him.

"How do you feel about joining me on the ranch this weekend? I could use your help fixing some fence line and moving some equipment to a new barn." I gave him my best puppy face, which made him bark out a laugh.

"That shit doesn't work on me."

"Then what does?" I asked before standing up and stretching. I knew he was going to say yes, and I was eager to get on the road so we could make it home in time for some of my mom's pie.

He watched me stretch. "The promise of a home-cooked meal or three and the chance to meet your Texas Rose."

I laughed. "Major, if there's one thing I can promise you, it's home-cooked meals. Pack a bag and let's get going."

CHAPTER 14

WESTON "MAJOR" MARIAN

The drive to Hobie wasn't long, but by the time we arrived on the ranch, my nerves were shot anyway. What the hell did I think I was doing agreeing to meet his wife and kids? But I knew the answer to that. I was being his friend. I needed my friendship with Doc Wilde like I needed the army. It had become part of me etched deep like the letters on my dog tags.

When I met Elizabeth Hobart Wilde, she was as pretty as a picture. She was sitting on the wide front steps of the farmhouse snapping pole beans with dogs and kids running around her in the yard. When she spotted us driving up, she lifted her head midlaugh, and I knew right away I was going to like her.

I expected to be jealous and possessive, but she was just too nice and smart and funny. Betsy was perfect for Doc.

She stood up and walked forward, wearing oversized blue jean overalls like a true farmer, but they were clearly not hers. The bottoms were rolled up several times, and the floral cotton blouse she wore underneath was fresh and modern.

"My, my, who did you bring home, Liam? And does he know he's going to be put to work like a common day laborer?" Her smile was lovely. She'd already set down the white mixing bowl of beans and reached out a slender hand to me. "I'm Betsy, it's nice to meet you."

"Ma'am, I'm—"

"Oh, I know who you are, Major. Liam has described you often enough. It's a real pleasure to finally meet you. If it weren't for you, I'd be a widow right now. Thanks really isn't enough, now, is it?"

She used our handshake to pull me into a hug, her slender arms wrapping around me and her feminine scent wafting in my face. It was overlaid with sunshine and the outdoors, and I thought for a brief moment how lucky their kids were to have a mother who liked to be outside on a clear summer day.

"I didn't save his life," I corrected. "He saved mine."

"Bullshit," Doc coughed into his hand. Betsy smacked him lightly on the shoulder and laughingly chastised him for cursing in front of the kids.

Betsy turned to pick the bowl back up. "You're in time for dinner. We had a huge lunch earlier, so it's later than normal. Y'all hungry?"

I turned to Doc and must have had a wolfish grin on my face because he said, "One of us sure is, and I could eat too. Poor Major hasn't had a home-cooked meal in decades, isn't that right?"

"Feels like it anyway. Can I help?" I offered.

She led me through the old farmhouse toward the kitchen. I noticed sheer curtains lifting in the slight breeze through the open windows in a front living room as we passed through an airy center hallway. Wide wooden floorboards creaked underfoot, and I idly wondered how long the place had been there. When we entered the large kitchen, an older woman turned from the stove and widened her eyes in surprise. I recognized the bright blue eyes immediately.

"Mom, this is Major Weston Marian," Doc said. "I stopped off at Fort Wolters and kidnapped him."

Mrs. Wilde wiped her hands on the cotton apron she wore and approached me for a hug, her eyes filling quickly. "It's an honor to meet you, Major. We've heard so much about you." After a quick squeeze, she pulled back but held on to my upper arms. "Thank you for keeping an eye on my boy over there."

What the hell had Doc told these people?

"He's an outstanding medic, Ma'am. I couldn't have asked for a better lieutenant on my chopper."

"Enough of that, Mom," Doc pleaded. "Don't embarrass the major. He doesn't know how to take compliments anyway. They're dangerous to his health."

It was true. One of the colonels on base had once praised me in front of an entire squadron of pilots for a particularly dicey rescue Moline and I had worked. I'd snuck around back of the hangar afterward just so I could punch something. Unfortunately, the stack of boxes I'd chosen as my target had been full of sharp helicopter parts. I'd sliced my hand and had to ask Doc to stitch it up without telling anyone.

I held up the back of my hand so he could see his handiwork. "Not even a scar. Your stitches are as precise as any plastic surgeon's. Or the quilt ladies in the church guild," I teased.

Betsy and his mom laughed and began asking me a million questions, hungry for more stories of Doc in Vietnam. I felt right at home in the farmhouse kitchen. The smells of ham baking, the sounds of the kids playing with wooden blocks in a carpeted corner of the room by a stone fireplace, and the sight of two friendly, maternal faces smiling at me, welcoming me to their home... it was like everything I'd always dreamed about.

Even back in Bakersfield, I'd never had it. My mother was a quiet mouse of a woman who ascribed to the seen and not heard mentality my father seemed to think was commanded by God for all women and children. Our house growing up had been stifling with rules and silence. When my father had been at work, at least Walt, Tilly, and I could cut up and be silly, even if our mother never joined us in our childish exuberance. But when our father was home, no sir. I'd always wondered if that was why I'd felt so at home in the military. I'd been raised to accept authority without question, to follow orders and follow rules, and to keep a stiff upper lip even in adversity.

In short, I'd been raised to be a man. And I'd failed spectacularly in so many ways.

"Wes?" Doc asked softly. His use of my name startled me out of my daze. I caught myself staring at the town Billy and his sisters had made out of wooden blocks.

"Mm?"

"My dad wanted to show you to the bunks so you can wash up for dinner. Is that all right?"

I rubbed the stupid off my face with both hands and looked past Doc to a taller, broader version of him standing in the doorway.

After standing immediately, I strode forward with my hand out. "Sorry. Of course. It's nice to meet you, Mr. Wilde. I'm Weston Marian."

His friendly smile was identical to Doc's and put me at ease right away. The handshake was warm and firm, and I felt the same appreciative welcome I'd gotten from the rest of the family. "We're so happy to have you here, Major. Sorry I don't have a decent bedroom in the house to offer you. With Liam and Betsy in one, and the kids in two others, I'm afraid—"

"A bunk is fine, sir. I'm used to much worse, I promise."

As he led me back through the house and across a stretch of dry lawn toward one of the large barns, Mr. Wilde pointed out some different areas of the ranch we could see from the yard. When we reached the wide open barn doors, he gestured me inside.

"The bunks are in the back of the main barn. Right now I have three hands living here full-time. I hire on two more come spring to help with calving season, and Jerry—Hobart, that is, Betsy's father— hires extra for the harvest and baling in the fall. I put up any overflow since his hands live in a trailer that's seen better days."

I was surprised to hear about the extra men since I'd gotten the feeling Doc felt like he had to put in a full week's worth of work on the ranch every weekend to help keep the place afloat.

"How's business?" I asked. "If you don't mind me asking."

"Going strong right now. Been a good few years. Liam mentioned you were interested in agriculture. He said you got an ag science degree up in Kansas while you were enlisted. You ever want to get your hands dirty, let me know. I'm sure we'd love to have you."

"Thank you, sir."

"Major Marian, how about you call me Stan instead of sir?" His grin was the same crooked one I'd been goofy over for going on two years now.

"Yes, sir," I said stupidly before catching myself. "Stan. Call me Weston."

"Sure thing. Major," he said with an easy smile and wink.

We chuckled companionably together in a moment I looked back on for years to come as the beginning of something special. Stan Wilde was something special—a good man, hard worker, fair boss, and a loving father. But that night, he was still a stranger to me, a man I'd assumed before now was a tough rancher with strong opinions and a strict demeanor.

So it shocked me when he stopped me in the narrow doorway to a tiny closet-like room with a bunk bed in it and said, "I need you to do something for my boy, Major."

I met his eyes and tried hard not to see Doc's heart in them. "Yes, sir?"

"Encourage him to go to medical school. It's his dream. It took me a while to see it, but... if that's what he wants, then I want him to have it. We'll do fine here while he's gone, and he deserves to choose his own future regardless of mine. Will you tell him that?"

"Already done, sir," I said. Doc was lucky to have a father like Stan Wilde.

And when the comparisons to my own father snuck into my thoughts like poisonous gas, I did my best to breathe in a different direction.

CHAPTER 15

LIAM "DOC" WILDE

My years in med school flew by faster than I ever expected. When I wasn't studying or doing clinical rotations at the hospital, I was teaching the girls to swim at the community pool in our neighborhood or racing to catch one of Billy's Little League games at the park.

Betsy had joined a garden club and met some wonderful women who'd made a big difference to our time in Dallas. She was happy which made me both happy and relieved. Things were good. More than that, they were great. Everything was falling into place, and I felt like I had everything I could ever want.

Even when we'd discovered Betsy was pregnant again just a few weeks after we moved to Dallas, it had seemed like it was meant to be. She said it'd helped her make the decision to embrace her role as mother and stop feeling like she needed to find a career to somehow prove herself.

When little Jackie was born, the girls were over the moon. They got the real-life baby doll of their dreams. Billy wasn't as impressed, but by then he'd started school and made plenty of friends outside of the family. I pictured us staying in Dallas long-term and always being within a few hours' drive of Hobie.

But when it came time for residency assignments, all hell broke loose.

I was offered a residency spot at Johns Hopkins in Baltimore, Maryland—one of the most coveted spots in the country. Betsy was beside herself with pride and bragged to everyone who would listen that her husband was going to Johns Hopkins to become the best damned doctor the world had ever seen.

I wasn't so sure moving across the country was the best decision for our family. Would Betsy and the kids adjust to a new place knowing we may only be there a few years? Would I be working too much to spend any time with them?

Not for the first time, I wished Major had been there to talk things through with me. He'd thankfully survived his fifth tour in Nam, but then he'd been sent to Germany for a year. Now he was posted somewhere he wasn't allowed to say. Our letter writing had slowed to a trickle, but we both made a point of touching base by telephone on Christmas Day at the very least. He'd gotten along so well with Betsy and my family during the weekend visits before deploying to Vietnam, that they'd encouraged him to consider the ranch his home base for visits home.

At least three times so far, Major had come home to the Wilde ranch between assignments to help my father and give my mother someone to fuss over. Betsy and I took the kids to Hobie for the weekend whenever "Uncle Major" was at the ranch because the kids adored the gentle giant and loved having someone to "teach ranch things" to. Billy in particular had stars in his eyes for Major. It didn't hurt that the man looked like he was born to ride a horse and wear a Stetson. He reminded me of the Marlboro man or at the very least Clint Eastwood with his stern face and in-charge demeanor.

But now that I had a big, important decision to make, he was unreachable.

"You know what he'd say," Betsy said from the sofa where she was knitting something while *The Brady Bunch* played softly on the television in the background.

"Who?" I asked stupidly.

She rolled her eyes. "Weston. He'd tell you to go. He'd tell you not to be an idiot."

"I don't need his say-so." Did I sound as stubborn and petulant as I felt?

"No, honey, but you'd like his input all the same. He's like a mentor to you, and we both respect his opinion. I think he'd tell you to follow your dreams. And your dream is in Baltimore."

"But the ranch... right now we can get there in a few hours easily. What happens when we're a plane flight away?"

She put down the yarn and stood up before walking over and putting her arms around my neck. I slid my hands over her hips to her lower back and up along the soft cotton of her nightshirt.

"Liam, my parents are there. Your parents are there. All the hands are there, and every danged person we've ever known in our lives is there. If something happens, they're covered and you know it."

I leaned in for a quick kiss. I loved the way she looked after she'd washed all the makeup away at the end of the day. The little freckles that peppered her nose were starting to appear on Gina's face too. "You're pretty amazing, Elizabeth Wilde. Don't know if I tell you that enough. I couldn't have done any of this without you."

"Yes, you could have. But I am amazing too." She stepped back and twirled before taking a dramatic curtsey. "And I'm going to parade around town the wife of a doctor before long, and Patty Ritches can stuff it."

I laughed along with her. Patty Brown had been Betsy's nemesis *before* she'd married into the Ritches family. Now it was ten times worse.

"I guess that means we're going to Baltimore," I said. She squealed and jumped up and down, hugging me again.

"Just think! We can show the kids all the history in Washington and maybe even take the train to New York City."

But we'd only been living in our little rental house in Baltimore for eighteen months when Marsha Hobart was diagnosed with uterine cancer. By the time she realized her symptoms weren't just a terrible side effect of menopause, it had already spread to other organs.

Thankfully, I had gotten to know a specialist at the university hospital in Dallas, who hooked Marsha up with an aggressive treatment plan.

Betsy and the kids raced home to Hobie to help take care of her. My mom watched the kids while Betsy ferried Marsha to Dallas for treatments and I stayed in Baltimore to finish my residency. I felt torn, but the medical team in charge of her care assured me she was in good hands, and Betsy promised to tell me if she needed me to come.

I wrote to Major about all of it, pouring my worries and fears out to him the way I would a personal diary. He wrote back only to say it was all under control.

I didn't know what that meant until I came home for Billy's eleventh birthday a few months later and found Major, George Hobart, and my dad all sitting around the big farmhouse table in the kitchen crunching numbers at eleven o'clock at night.

"What's going on?" I asked, tossing my overnight bag down and shucking off my coat.

My dad's frown turned into a grin right away as he got up to give me a hug. "What're you doing here? We thought you weren't getting in till tomorrow. I was going to drive down and get you."

I squeezed him tight for a second before pulling away. "I ran into a friend of mine, who said I could hop on a C-130 at Andrews and hitch a ride." I looked over at Major. "Did you know Lynch is flying the big boys now?"

He nodded. "That's Captain Lynch to you, Lieutenant," he said with a wink.

"Never," I hooted, reaching out to clap hands for a firm shake. "You're a sight for sore eyes, Major. What crazy wind blew you in here?"

Surprisingly, it was George, Betsy's dad, who answered. "He's coming on board, so we had to go over some things."

I stared at the three of them like the village idiot. "What do you mean, he's coming on board?"

"Sit down, son. You want a beer?" my dad said kindly.

"Yeah, I guess. I'll grab it though."

When I walked over to the fridge, I felt Major get up and follow me. His large hand landed warm and strong on my shoulder. The man never failed to calm my ass down just by being nearby. I took a deep breath.

"Everything's fine," he said softly. "No need to worry."

I pulled out a few cans of beer, handing him a couple to offer the other men. When we returned to the table, I could see how tired and worn down George appeared. Marsha's illness was taking its toll.

My dad started. "I was already talking to Weston about taking over as foreman when he retired from the army."

I didn't let him finish. My eyes flashed to Major with accusation. "You're retiring? Since when? And how come I didn't know about this?"

His face remained passive and calm like it always did when I got belligerent. "We'll talk about it later, Liam."

I stared at him while something in my belly twisted oddly. It was another one of those situations in which he seemed *so* in control, it was like I had permission to not have to take charge. It was oddly freeing, but I wasn't about to give him the satisfaction of telling him that.

George cleared his throat. "I need to be able to spend more time with Marsha right now."

"Understandable," I agreed. "But I'm happy to—"

"No," Major said, cutting me off. "It's all worked out. You're staying at Johns Hopkins."

I felt my jaw click shut and my nostrils flare. I was the man in this family, dammit. Not him. "You don't get to—"

Betsy's voice came from over my shoulder. "He's right, Liam. If you'll just stop and listen to the man..."

I turned to find her leaning in the doorjamb. She wore her hair up in a messy bun and had on one of my flannel work shirts over baggy trousers. I got up and approached her, pulling her in for a hug and kiss. "Hey," I murmured. "The kids asleep?" I knew the answer since it was so late, but it popped out of my mouth out of habit.

"They'd better be," she said with a soft snort. "Or someone's getting a spanking."

I brushed the hair off her face and kissed her forehead before pulling away. She was the least likely person to ever spank a child, so I laughed and popped her lightly on the ass. "Maybe you for not reading them enough stories?"

When I turned back toward the table, I noticed Major's head was turned away and his ears were red. Had my flirting with my wife embarrassed him?

I took my seat again at the table. "Okay, I'm listening. What's the plan?"

CHAPTER 16

WESTON "MAJOR" MARIAN

That right there—that easy affection between Liam and his wife—was the reason I never should have said yes. I wasn't sure I could stay there if it meant watching Doc and Betsy be sweet to each other. But that was why I had to insist he stay in Baltimore. I couldn't... I couldn't have him here every day like that. I couldn't watch him kiss and love on his wife and live the life I so desperately wanted but could never have.

I'd only agreed to this cockamamie plan when Stan had played his trump cards.

"George has high blood pressure, and I have arthritis in my spine. If Liam finds out, our gooses are cooked. You and I both know the only way he'll stay and finish out his residency is if he trusts the ranch and farm are in good hands."

I'd been at Fort Bragg in North Carolina at the time, and had clamped my jaw shut while my brain whirred through options. The call from Stan hadn't been much of a surprise. I'd called to check on him about once a month anyway.

"Major," Stan had said quietly, "you're the only person besides my son I trust to take over. And if you weren't up for retirement from the army, I wouldn't even ask. But it's still got to be your decision, son. You know I'll respect you either way and you'll always be family to us, no matter what."

That sweet son of a bitch, I'd thought. "I'll be there in two weeks. Tell Marsha I'll clean out the chicken coop for her for a week if she'll make the chocolate chess pie," I'd grumbled.

Stan had laughed. "You'd do that anyway."

"Yes, sir, but at least I'd like some pie out of the deal."

"Roger that, Major," he'd teased.

After I'd hung up the phone, I'd thought about how warm it made my heart to hear him call me Major. I'd been lieutenant colonel in the army already for several years. Now when the Wildes called me Major, it felt like a term of endearment instead of my rank, and it made me feel loved, almost as much as the olive-green scarf Betsy had knit me for my birthday with silver maple leaves on it. In my thank-you note to her, I told her she'd have to teach me how to knit one day, but her response had been to point out that I never sat still long enough. Whenever I was on the ranch, I was outside working.

But tonight, as I watched Doc slowly accept that things were changing, I realized I'd finally be at the ranch long enough to have downtime. Betsy had been over the moon at my decision to accept the job, and it hadn't been easy convincing her not to tell the kids until we told Doc.

I could tell by watching him that Doc's annoyance was because he'd been the last to know and hadn't had any say in the matter. But George, Stan, Betsy, and I had all agreed that if we didn't have our plan in place by the time we brought Doc in, he'd abandon his residency and move home out of a sense of obligation.

The man was loyal and stubborn.

We explained to him that I was retiring and moving into the foreman's house on the Wilde ranch. Jay Mason, the current ranch foreman, was getting married, and his wife had convinced him to move back to Wichita Falls to set up house. His plan had been to commute until Stan could find his replacement.

They'd made him a deal to keep coming three days a week to help train me through calving season when he could earn a bonus that would help him with his new house. Win-win. Meanwhile, with me and Jay both at the ranch, Stan could help George at the farm. Between the four of us and all the hands, I expected we'd be able to keep things running just fine. And when I was fully up to speed, maybe I could help remove some more of the load from George and Stan's shoulders.

It wasn't until much later that night, after everyone had retired to their beds, that Doc came and found me to ask the tougher questions. I was expecting him—had, in fact, bumped up the heat a little bit on the oil heater in my tiny bunk room. But when he came in with only his thin cotton pajamas on, I cursed and reached for the extra wool blanket on the shelf to wrap around him.

"Get in the bed," I snapped. "You crazy? It's below freezing out there. Where are your socks?"

He shivered and jumped under the covers where I'd already warmed up the narrow bed with my own body heat.

"You sound like my mom," he said with his adorable crooked grin.

"I'll take that as a compliment," I griped. "Your mother is a good woman."

Doc paused and studied me for a few beats. "I'm glad you're here. Full-time, I mean. I'm... it's good. Good for everyone. Thank you, Major."

I turned around to find another sweatshirt to pull on, grunting some kind of wordless acknowledgment to his gratitude.

"Don't feel like you have to do this," he began. I turned and glared at him.

"Since when do I do things I don't want to do?" I asked.

He held up his hands in surrender. "Don't bite my head off. I just... you never said you were getting out when you got your twenty."

I pushed his legs back and sat on the edge of the bunk. "I didn't think I was. Honestly, if your dad hadn't offered, I'd probably stay in. But, Doc, when am I ever going to get an opportunity like this? It's exactly what I've always wanted to do. And if I can help George out on the farm, I can stay out of your hair over here on the—"

"Don't finish that sentence," he growled. "Dammit, Major, you know I'd be overjoyed knowing you were here on the ranch. I'd love nothing more than to know you were here watching over my family and this land. Don't think for one single minute I don't want you here."

His words were a relief. "Good. Okay…. good."

I leaned back across his covered legs until my back was against the rough wooden wall. "Marsha's not doing too good."

"Yeah. Betsy told me." Doc sat up and held out one of the bedcovers. "Here, you're going to get cold."

I pulled it over me, trying not to notice the Old Spice scent of him on my blanket. "How's work?" I asked.

"Crazy busy. But good. I'm learning a ton. It's better now that I have my feet under me a little. The internist I'm working under is brilliant. The man knows it too, but I don't mind. He's a good teacher."

I met his eyes. "You thought about specializing?" For as many times as I'd wondered, I kind of didn't want to know. It would mean more time in residency—more time away.

He shrugged and looked down, away. "I love emergency medicine, but I need some more time in family medicine if I'm going to open a practice in Hobie."

"Is that what you want to do?"

"It makes the most sense."

I reached out and put my hand on the top of his head to spin his face around until he was looking at me. His dirty-blond hair was silky to the touch. "Doc, is that what you *want* to do?"

He swallowed and looked at me with those clear eyes I loved so much. "I want to watch my kids grow up. I want to be here for my parents. I don't want my entire life to be about the job."

His words socked me in the gut like a punch. My entire life had been about the job.

"Good," I grunted, letting go of his hair before I was stupid enough to start caressing it. "Smart."

Doc reached out and grabbed my wrist, holding it until I met his eyes again. "What about you? Is this what you want to do?"

I looked at sleepy Liam Wilde, hair messed up and vulnerable in my bed.

"Yes," I said gruffly. "More than anything."

CHAPTER 17

LIAM "DOC" WILDE

Late the following summer, we laid Marsha Hobart to rest in Betsy's family plot in the town cemetery. I was two years into my three-year residency and could barely think straight, but as I was standing in the steaming August rainstorm holding Betsy's hand under the funeral tent while they shoveled wet dirt onto the coffin, I suddenly remembered something I'd seen the week before at the hospital.

I leaned over to whisper in her ear. "When was your last OBGYN exam?"

That was the wrong damned question to ask a woman at her mother's funeral, especially when Marsha had died from GYN cancer.

Shit.

I squeezed my eyes closed and felt my dad's hand rub the back of my shoulder in sympathy.

After putting my arm around Betsy and pulling her close, I whispered again. "I'm so sorry. I just… I…"

She turned her tear-streaked face to mine. "You don't want to end up like my daddy. I know."

I looked over at devastated George Hobart and saw the major holding him firmly by the elbow. Wes stood there in his full dress uniform, and it was so covered in ribbons and medals, I wondered how he held himself upright.

Honestly, until that day I'd never realized just how decorated the major—*Lieutenant Colonel*—was. I was in awe of his service as I had been many times before. Weston Marian was truly one of the best men I'd ever known.

On that day when we buried my mother-in-law and I mourned more for Betsy's loss than my own, I realized my life overflowed with riches. It wasn't fair. Out of the corners of my eyes I saw George and Major, Betsy and the kids, and my mother and father. Not to mention the entire town of Hobie had shown up to mourn Marsha. Her church guild and tennis ladies, her fellow women's club volunteers and the kids she'd mentored on 4-H projects. All around us was the reason I never should have left Hobie in the first place.

When we got back to the Hobarts' place afterward, the place was filled to the rafters with townspeople and casseroles. I noticed Major standing in the kitchen with three-year-old Jackie propped on one hip and eight-year-old Brenda hiding behind him with one of her hands in his uniform coat pocket where we all knew he kept a collection of interesting things for busy hands. The selection varied depending on the day. Sometimes "Uncle Major's" jacket pockets held a duck feather, a Buffalo nickel, a nut-and-bolt combo, and a porcupine quill. Or sometimes it was a marble, a seashell, a tangle of rubber bands, and a four-leaf clover. No matter what it was, there were always at least four items of interest in his pockets—one for each of the kids.

He was busy talking to Nancy Young, whose eyelashes batted so fast when Major was around I was surprised they hadn't caused her face to take flight yet.

"He single?" a voice behind me asked. I turned to see Mrs. McReedy from the library point her chin at the major.

I wanted to snap in her face that he wasn't single. He was *ours*.

But I knew that was ridiculous. My best friend deserved to find a partner, someone to have like I had Betsy. Someone to give him comfort at the end of a hard day.

"Yes, um. Yes, ma'am. But—" I wasn't about to tell her he was gay, of course not, but I wanted to say *something* to lead her off his trail. Otherwise he was going to be on the receiving end of a dozen or more date match-ups before the end of the week.

"He's a loner, Mrs. McReedy," Betsy said from over my shoulder. "He had someone once, but… well, you know how hard it is to get over a broken heart…"

My wife was a smooth liar.

I looked at her in surprise, and she gave me a knowing look in return. "Isn't that right, Liam?"

I glanced at Major, whose eyes were locked on me. "Yes. He… he keeps himself to himself now mostly. The private type."

"Oh, so sad!" The librarian clucked in Major's direction, which caused his brows to furrow in confusion. "I should have known. I know just the thing. Never you mind."

She wandered off muttering to herself while I turned to Betsy with a raised brow.

"I think he would rather date Max than Maxine if you catch my drift," Betsy said in a soft whisper. "And I don't want those busybodies foisting every Hobie debutante on the poor man."

"What makes you say that about him?" I asked just as quietly. I'd never told a living soul about Major preferring men, so I was curious how Betsy of all people had caught on. It wasn't like she'd had a chance to see him around a man he was interested in. Had she?

She reached out to straighten my tie. "Liam, honey, that man is in love with you. I've practically lived with him for six months now and can tell just by the way his face lights up when he hears your name."

There wasn't a jealous tone at all. It was more… pity, maybe. Almost like she felt bad she'd called dibs on me first.

"We're best friends, Betsy," I corrected. "That's all. He lights up because I'm his family. I'm his *brother.* He doesn't have anyone else."

Her face softened. "That's not true anymore, is it? He has me. And the kids. And your parents and my dad. That man has been a rock for my father these last few months. If he stepped in horse patties, I'd wash his feet," she teased, referring to the time I'd accidentally stepped in horse shit barefoot and begged her to help me hose my feet off. She'd refused.

"Wow. That is love. Are you going to throw me over for Major Marian? Do I need to watch my back?" I slid my arms around her waist and felt the scratchy surface of the black dress suit she wore.

She hummed. "I wish we knew of a man for him. For a while I thought maybe Roger…"

"Roger who works for your dad?" I thought of the short, stocky man who never said much but worked harder on the farm than almost anyone else and always went out of his way to help Marsha with her vegetable garden. "What makes you think—"

Movement across the room caught my eye, and I turned to see Patty Ritches giggle and squeeze Major's arm right next to where the man's service ribbons lay in tidy, colorful rows. She'd pulled her friend Carol Claire over with her, and I almost laughed when Major subtly shifted little Jackie until she was on his front like body armor: a baby koala bear, her skinny arms wrapped around his neck and her head laying on his right shoulder. Her blonde curls escaped the barrettes my mother had put in that morning, but Major didn't seem to mind. He simply reached up and smoothed the wildness down and out of his face.

"The man has no idea that holding that baby makes him more attractive to them, does he?" Betsy said through a laugh. "For as smart as he is, he's stupid as a box of rocks sometimes. He might as well have sprayed himself with steak juice and gone for a stroll among the wolves."

I felt the return of that strange euphoria I'd felt at the cemetery, that I was one of the luckiest SOBs on earth. I mourned the loss of my kind mother-in-law, but I was thankful my own parents were still healthy, my wife was happy and settled, and my best friend was there to watch over all of them for me. I was lucky—couldn't ask for anything more.

But that's the way of things right before the storm hits. You get a moment of perfect stillness, a chance to breathe, before the rain comes and the lightning strikes down everything you thought would last forever.

CHAPTER 18

WESTON "MAJOR" MARIAN

Doc had only been back in Baltimore for six weeks when he finally convinced Betsy to go to the doctor for a checkup. They said even though Doc was right in suggesting there was new data about women's cancers being genetic, they were sure she was fine since she had no symptoms.

But they did tell her once again that she should have the birthmark on her scalp biopsied since it seemed to be getting bigger. She came home from the appointment in the middle of a hissy fit.

"Doc Browning thinks it's no big deal for me to go have half my head shaved for that stupid test. I'd like to see how he would feel if Cora had her head shaved for goodness' sake! Does he have any idea how long it's taken me to grow this hair out from that stupid bob I got when Billy was a baby? No. He doesn't. And he doesn't care either."

I kept my mouth shut and continued to weed the front flower beds by the steps leading up to the front door of the farmhouse. It had been a hot day, but an afternoon thunder shower had cooled things off and loosened the soil for me. Made it much easier to tidy up these beds in preparation for planting fall flowers.

"What are you doing?" she asked after she calmed down long enough to notice I wasn't doing my normal chores.

I sat back on my heels and put down the spade. "Fixing your dad's tractor," I said deadpan.

She barked out a laugh. Score one for me.

"You always know how to do that," she said with a smile. Her eyes warmed in my direction. "Make me laugh when I'm upset. You're a good egg, Major."

"No so bad yourself, Mrs. Doctor Wilde." I'd called her that once as a joke and she'd blushed so red, I couldn't help but tease her with it from then on. Plus, I felt pretty strongly that she deserved some of the prestige that came with all she'd sacrificed to support Doc's time in medical school and residency. I know it killed her to be away from him so long.

"Less than a year left now," she said wistfully, referring to his remaining time at Johns Hopkins.

Seven months, one week, and two days...

"I suppose so. You know what would be a good present to celebrate?"

"I'm already getting him a medical bag with his initials on it."

I met her eyes. "A clean bill of health for his wife."

She rolled her eyes and huffed at me. "Fine, but you're coming with me to hold my hand. And then we're going wig shopping in the city. Scratch that. Wig shopping first, then the biopsy."

So three weeks later, that's what we did. I drove her down to Dallas in my new Chevy truck. Stan had finally convinced me no self-respecting ranch hand drove a Datsun even if it had been practically free in a repo auction. With Betsy looking dressed up and lovely, I was glad I'd taken Stan's advice about the truck. At least the air-conditioning worked in this one so Betsy didn't melt in the late-autumn heatwave we were having.

Doc had insisted the biopsy be done at the university hospital since he knew so many people there. At Betsy's request, I'd spent half an hour on the phone talking him down from flying home for the biopsy. It made him crazy that he couldn't leave again so soon after his visit home for Marsha's funeral.

"It's just a biopsy," Betsy had told him again after I'd handed the kitchen phone off to her. "If you make a big deal about it, I'm going to start worrying about it." She winked at me and grinned. She and I were both pretty good at pushing the right buttons with Doc.

"Besides," she'd said, "Weston promised me a trip to Sonny Bryan's for barbecue and you hate that place."

But when she came out of the procedure, she definitely wasn't up for barbecue, because the surgeon had ended up taking way more than just a simple biopsy. He'd cut out the entire birthmark and left her with a much deeper wound than anyone had expected. As soon as she realized it, she'd burst into tears.

"It's bad news, Major, isn't it?" she asked. I moved over to sit next to her on the bed, carefully sliding my arm around her shoulders and pulling her against my side. I said a silent prayer of thanks that Doc wasn't here because he was terrible at poker. One look at his face and Betsy would know how bad it was.

"No, sweetheart. It's good news. It means you'll get a chance to wear *both* wigs we got."

She laughed through her tears and wrapped her arms around me. "The second one was supposed to be for you."

"I was never meant to be a redhead. Besides, your dad wouldn't let me live it down. I still hear stories about him finding Roger in a dress that one time. I'm not so sure George Hobart can handle any of his hands expressing their feminine side." I squeezed her in a hug. "But if you end up having to get your whole head shaved, I'll do the same so we can be twins. How about it? I think the girls would laugh until their sides split, don't you?"

I shouldn't have mentioned the girls. It set off another round of tears. When she finally slowed down enough to catch her breath, she tilted her head up at me and ran her slender fingers through my hair.

"Don't shave it. I love it now that it's grown out some. Goes well with the beard." She sighed and laid her head back on my chest. "I don't want to tell him."

"There's nothing to tell right now."

"It's cancer. Why else would the doctor have taken so much out?"

I knew she was probably right, but maybe they'd gotten it all. Maybe she was cancer-free now and we didn't have to worry.

"The doctor said they'd have the results back in about a week," I said. "Let's not worry about it until we have something to worry about."

"My father won't survive this," she said in a small voice. "Major…"

"Shhh. Betsy, we're not going to worry until there's something to worry about. Okay? Promise me."

She lay on my chest for a while longer before looking back up at me again. "We're not telling either of them anything right now. You got me?"

She was asking me to keep something important from both my boss and my best friend, but I would do it in a heartbeat for one reason. Both of those men wanted Betsy to be happy more than anything. And if me keeping her confidence made her happy, I would do it without fail.

"I got you," I said firmly. "I promise."

"Good egg," she murmured sleepily. "Told you."

I kissed the top of her head as gently as I could and let her doze for a while on my chest. Despite growing up in the church, I'd never been a religious man. God and I had issues, to put it mildly, but I wasn't afraid to admit I was a colossal hypocrite. I prayed that afternoon like I was a newly baptized devotee. I prayed for this strong, sweet woman who made so many of us happy every day. I prayed for her father, who truly would collapse and wither away if something happened to her. I prayed for the four children at home whom I loved like my own. The idea of them watching their mother battle a serious illness made me feel hollow inside.

And of course I prayed for my best friend, the man who was on the verge of finally having the perfect life he'd worked so hard for. Who deserved the smart, beautiful wife he adored. I offered up every single thing I could think of if God would just keep this woman alive and well.

But God was a son of a bitch. And life wasn't fair.

She was diagnosed with cancer, but the doctors felt confident she'd get past it if she accepted an aggressive treatment plan. That was the only reason I'd agreed with her pleas to hold off telling Doc until his residency was complete.

We lied to everyone about her disease. When chemotherapy began, I had to take her to Dallas every three weeks. She told the family we were visiting a friend of hers from when Doc was in med school there. She really did have a friend named Kathryn who'd lost her husband in the war and was left with two small children. But because we used that as our excuse, I insisted on stopping by Kat's house while Betsy was getting her infusion so I could fix anything that Kat needed fixing. That way it wasn't a complete lie.

Or so I thought. Until Doc found out about it.

CHAPTER 19

LIAM "DOC" WILDE

I don't recall much from that summer. By the time I got home from my residency, riding high on the knowledge I was finally going to have everything I ever wanted, Betsy was already weak from the chemo and horribly immune-suppressed.

And I seethed with anger. My anger was a living, breathing thing. Since there was no way in hell I was going to direct my anger at my beautiful, sick wife, I thrust it all at Major Snake-In-The-Grass. He'd kept her secret from me instead of telling me she was sick. And because of that, he'd cost me five extra months with her. Five months of caring for her and making sure she was getting the best medical attention.

I'd never hated anyone as much as I hated that man the summer of 1976. If I could have fired his ass without putting more work on poor George Hobart, I would have done it ten times over. Weston Marian was a selfish son of a bitch, and no amount of sweet-talking from Betsy was going to change my mind about it.

I made sure not to notice his generosity in taking my children to do fun things off the ranch like grab a milkshake in town or visit a neighbor's new litter of puppies. I ignored all the extra work he put in around the Hobart place when it became clear that George was losing his own will to live watching Betsy suffer. And the rare times Major Asshole accepted an invitation to Sunday dinner in my parents' kitchen, I pretended like he was part of the furniture.

And throughout all of it, he accepted my abuse like it was his due, like it was part of the price he paid for accepting Betsy's confidence. He stayed in the shadows during those months. When he wasn't working his ass off taking care of the ranch or the farm, he was caring for George's personal residence and making sure my kids still got to all their extracurricular activities. It didn't matter to me. Nothing made up for his lies of omission.

The well of my anger was deep and dark, building and frothing until the dam finally broke late one afternoon in early September. I'd gotten called out on a case in the middle of the night and had come back home around dawn. After catching several hours of sleep, I woke up to find Betsy sitting by the open window in our bedroom crying quietly. It was unusual that she wasn't sitting in a rocker on the porch by her rose garden. When I'd arrived home from Baltimore, I'd realized she'd replaced the scraggly old boxwood bushes in front of the porch with gorgeous full specimens of all different hybrid versions of her roses. The fall-blooming ones were a sight to behold right now, so she usually took advantage of every spare moment out there. She'd sit and knit by the roses, although now that I thought about it, I realized I hadn't seen her with her needles in a while.

"Why are you crying?" I asked groggily. I got up and went over to her.

She tilted her head toward the window. "Listen."

That's when I noticed Major Secretkeeper kneeling alongside the flower beds with all four of our children lined up alongside him. Each of them had gardening gloves on and were listening with rapt attention. Brenda clutched the handle of a watering can, and Billy had the hose nearby. Gina held a weeding fork.

Major was talking quietly to them. "We're only helping your mama with her roses until she feels better, okay? Now, this is one of her favorites. She calls it the Bologna rose. See the pink speckles? That's called variegated, when it's speckled like that. Well, it doesn't want to get its arms and legs wet. It's kind of prissy, you know? So we only water its feet." He turned to Brenda and showed her how to water the base of the rosebush.

Betsy's voice was soft and scratchy over my shoulder. She'd been fighting a bad cough that was leftover from a head cold. "He started planting those roses the day I was diagnosed, and he's been out there every single day since feeding and watering them to make sure they bloomed like a Rose Bowl Parade for me."

I stared down at the riot of colors. The perfume from the blooms was strong enough to reach our bedroom when the breeze blew in.

"I thought that was your garden," I said. "That you planted it and took care of it."

She turned her head to give me a look disbelief. "Liam, I've barely been able to hold my own hairbrush for three months and you think I've been kneeling in the flower beds gardening while you've been at work?"

God. Now that she said it, I realized how stupid my assumption had been. I stared down at the major, my feelings of betrayal and gratitude making a murky soup in my gut.

"He's one of the best men I've ever met, hon. You bringing him here was a gift to all of us." Betsy's voice was gentle but firm. She was making sure I knew how juvenile my resentment had been toward him.

"Mpfh. He's not the most experienced foreman, you know. We could probably find someone better." We both knew I didn't mean it.

"I want him to stay here. To be here for our children when... *if* something happens to me. They adore him." She reached out and grabbed my jaw with her cold hand. "Do not let our kids lose someone else important to them. Promise me."

"They're not losing you, so just stop." I refused to consider it. It couldn't happen. Plus, the cancer was responding well to treatment. Things were looking up.

"He asked me to teach him how to knit," she said, turning back to the window where Major was now half-sodden with water from the hose. He still had his usual calm demeanor even though Billy's face was guilty as hell.

"Knitting? The major?" I couldn't picture it.

"Yeah, I don't know, but when I realized I wouldn't be able to finish the Christmas stockings I wanted to make for everyone, he offered to take over and be my fingers. I could still pick out the patterns and the yarn, but he'd be the one to knit them." She chuckled. "He's really terrible at it."

And that's when the dam broke. I realized the reason I hadn't seen her with knitting in a while. She couldn't knit because of the neuropathy in her fingers, and Major Fucking Steadfast had noticed and offered to take over to relieve her burdens. Who the hell did the man think he was? While I was working hard at the clinic, he was here playing perfect husband and father with my family?

I lit out of there like my ass was on fire. Once I flew down the front porch steps, I barked in his direction. "Barn, now." I didn't stop long enough to notice his reaction, just kept moving until I was in the wide open aisle inside the barn where the kids wouldn't be able to see us.

As soon as he walked in, I took a swing at him and clocked him in the jaw. His eyes widened in shock, but he just stood there ready for another. So I gave him one, this time a punch to the ribs. The wind whooshed out of him, but I didn't care and he still didn't do anything to block me.

"Defend yourself, dammit!" I hollered at him. My voice was broken and half-screechy. I sounded like a lunatic. "Why are you letting me do this to you?" This time I shoved his shoulder. Hard.

"I've been waiting six months for this. Gotta be honest, glad it's finally here," he said in his low, steady voice. He was breathing heavier now and blood trickled from his lip, but of course he kept his calm. The jackass.

"You should have told me!" It came out as more of a sob than a yell. "I hate you! I hate you for keeping that from me. You should have told me!" I beat on his chest with my fists until I wailed his name and he grabbed me tight around my arms and we both sank to the ground.

My breathing came in frantic gasps. "Wes... *Wes*... she's sick. And I can't watch."

"I know, baby, I'm sorry. I'm so sorry. But she's a fighter. She's going to kick this."

I didn't catch the endearment at first. It just sounded so natural and went along with accepting comfort from my best friend. It was the kind of thing I'd heard him say to my children when they'd scraped their knees or fallen off their ponies. Affection, praise, comfort. And I needed it from him like Betsy's roses needed water in the hot Texas sun.

I clung to him and sobbed, but then his words sank in. *She's going to kick this.*

If there was one thing I knew about Lieutenant Colonel Weston Marian of the United States Army it was that the man was rarely wrong about anything.

I blew out a shaky breath. "Yeah. Yeah, she's a fighter. She's going to kick this."

Two weeks later she was hospitalized for pneumonia, and before the sun came up the following morning, she was gone.

I went back to hating Weston Marian for being wrong. If he'd been right about so many other things, why did he have to be wrong about this? He was an easy target for my anger, and I was barely able to hold an adult conversation with anyone anyway, so it didn't matter.

It wasn't until George Hobart died of a broken heart and Billy went missing on Thanksgiving Day that I was forced to shake off my grief and ask the major for help.

CHAPTER 20

WESTON "MAJOR" MARIAN

I'd politely declined to join the Wildes for the Thanksgiving meal, claiming I'd already accepted an invite from an old army buddy down at Fort Wolters. It was clear to everyone that Doc didn't want me around, and I didn't blame him.

I was an easy scapegoat. Plus, whenever I was nearby, I couldn't help but try and cheer him up or make him forget, and he damned well didn't want to be cheerful or forget.

Again, I didn't blame him.

But I didn't go to Fort Wolters either.

George Hobart had fallen asleep one night in October only a week after his daughter's funeral, and simply hadn't woken up. He'd left me in charge of farm operations even though ownership had been legally left in trust for Doc and Betsy's kids. Since Doc was in no shape to focus on much more than the kids and his job at the clinic, that left me to make sure the farm was running smoothly which meant I wasn't leaving town for the foreseeable future, even if only to spend a few hours eating turkey and pie with friends.

While George's passing hadn't surprised any of us adults, it had left the kids reeling. In the span of less than a year, they'd lost Grandma, Grandpa, and Mama. My heart was broken for them, and knowing that the only cure for grief was time, I tried hard to distract them in order to help time pass.

Distracting the kids was easy enough. I roped Billy into some tougher chores on the ranch now that he could handle his mount as well as any other hand. The twins took charge of their granny's vegetable garden, cleaning and prepping it for winter, and Jackie was given the task of taking care of George's two old coon hounds. When their spirits seemed to flag, I reminded them how proud their mama would be looking down on them and how proud their daddy and I were of how grown up they'd become in such a short amount of time.

After the first two weeks of Jackie taking it hardest, she seemed to almost forget about Betsy. She was only four, so Lois Wilde's grandmothering seemed to fill whatever maternal needs she had just fine. The twins seemed to draw strength from each other. Bossy Brenda was unusually gentle with the more sensitive Gina.

That left Billy, who seemed to have gone practically radio silent since the day we'd laid Betsy to rest.

So I shouldn't have been surprised to come back to my house late the night of Thanksgiving to find Billy asleep on my sofa. I'd been over at the farm, making sure the chickens were put up for the night. Instead of driving over in my truck like I usually did, I'd saddled my horse and gone for a ride to clear my head and say my own thanks in my own way to celebrate the day.

By the time I returned Thunder to the barn and made my way back to my little house across the far pasture from the Wilde's farmhouse, it was past eleven. I'd left a single bulb light on at the front door, but the rest of the house was dark as usual. Since my house was so deep on the ranch, I'd never even considered using door locks.

I opened the door and reached to flick on the light when I noticed the small lump on the nearby sofa. The recognizable towhead poking out from the blanket clued me in right away. I walked over and looked down at him, baby-faced and serene in the protective bubble of sleep.

After kicking off my boots and sitting down on the edge of the cushion near his hip, I reached out and brushed the overgrown cowlicks from his forehead. He looked like a mini version of Doc, and

I wondered if that's what my friend had looked like when he was that age. I'd seen pictures, of course, in Lois's albums, but it was different seeing Billy here in the flesh and in full color.

After a few moments of listening to his steady breathing, I stood up to cross to the kitchen to use the phone. If Doc or the senior Wildes knew Billy was missing, they'd be frantic.

But when I reached for the handset, I thought about a midnight call tearing through the sleepy silence of the farmhouse and terrifying everyone who'd already had more than their fair share of stress lately. I decided to leave Billy asleep and walk over to tell Doc where he was instead.

I slipped my boots back on and stepped quietly out of the house. The late-November night air was frigid but clear, and I wondered where things would be when the weather turned warm again. Would the family be any better? Would Betsy's memory have softened by then into a fond recollection more than a jagged sharp edge tearing at all of our hearts? I missed her dearly. By the time she'd died, she'd been one of my closest friends, and she'd loved me fiercely. She'd never once shown an ounce of jealousy when any of the kids had flocked to me in a crowded room over her.

I loved her for loving me and for giving me the best home I'd ever had. She'd accepted me with open arms and made me feel welcome. They all had. Lois and Stan had done their best to make me feel like a part of their family. But I wasn't part of their family. And that had become clear when I hadn't felt welcome at the Thanksgiving meal that day.

Before I got to the porch steps, Doc came flying out of the front door.

"I need your help," he cried frantically, turning toward the stable. "Saddle Thunder up. Billy's missing. I need you to help me search. Please. He's gone, Wes, I—"

I reached out and snagged his elbow, pulling him around and meeting his terrified eyes. I held on to both his upper arms. "I have him. He's safe. He's asleep at my house."

He stared at me in confusion before somehow deciding Billy's disappearance was my fault. "What did you do?" he snarled, pulling out of my hold. "And why aren't you down at Fort Wolters?"

It surprised me that he even knew where I was supposed to be since he seemed so completely uninterested in acknowledging my presence lately. Anger welled up at being blamed for something I'd had nothing to do with, but I did my best to remain calm.

"I stayed to look after the farm. I was putting the chickens to bed when he must have snuck in and fallen asleep. I wasn't even there, Doc."

His eyes were still narrow and angry. He was bound and determined to blame me for something, and I was sick and tired of it. I'd been silently taking hit after hit from him for two months now—longer than that really, since he'd returned home to our deceit six months before.

"Why did he sneak out to come to your place?" he asked. "Why didn't he come to me? I'm his father, dammit. And you're just... just..."

I felt my nostrils flare wide and my teeth grind together. My hands fisted at my side. "Go ahead, Lieutenant. Say it," I growled. "I fucking dare you."

He stared at me wide-eyed, as if maybe he'd surprised more than just me with his unkind implication. I scoffed and turned my back on him, walking away before I said something we'd both regret.

"Don't walk away from me, Major," he shouted after me. "We're not done talking."

It took all my self-control not to turn around and deck him. Instead, I called out over my shoulder. "Your dad will have my resignation in the morning."

Nothing but silence followed me to my little house where Billy was just as sweetly sleeping as before. I got him a pillow from the closet and an extra blanket to tuck around him before making my way to my small bathroom to shower off the day's filth. When I got back to my bedroom with a towel around my waist, Doc was sitting on my bed with his face in his hands.

"I'm sorry," he said without looking up. "I don't deserve you as a friend."

He sounded miserable. Despite still being pissed as hell at him, I walked over and tilted his chin up so I could see his face.

"No, you don't. Not right now you don't."

Doc's eyes widened in surprise. He was so used to me giving him whatever he needed and taking one on the chin for him, he'd obviously been expecting me to roll right over and accept his apology— take whatever scraps he was willing to give me.

Which... normally I would have. But while witnessing his frantic emotional stew out there in front of Betsy's dormant rosebushes, I'd had a revelation. I could not fix this for him. And I was done trying. He was going to have to mourn his wife his own way without me tiptoeing around him like a scared cat and continuing to take the blame for every damned thing. If he wanted my friendship, he'd always have it, but I was done being his punching bag.

"I said I was sorry," he said petulantly. "And I am. I was just scared. I went in to check on Billy and found an empty bed. You have no idea what it's like to be a parent and—"

"Stop right there," I said, seething with renewed anger. "You're right I have no idea what it's like to be a parent, and thank you so much, your highness, for reminding me that I'll never have that joy as long as I live. But if you think for one minute that I wouldn't have felt the same bone-deep terror finding Billy Wilde missing, you haven't been paying attention." My voice had started to crack and step up in pitch, but I couldn't help it. I was on the verge of either sobbing or taking a swing at the man. "I love that boy like my own, and you know it. I'd do anything for those kids. If I could have sacrificed myself to save Betsy, I would have in a heartbeat. If I could spare any one of you, of *us*, the pain of losing her, I would. I would *die* for this family."

I turned my back to him and pulled out my dresser drawer so hard the entire thing flew out and landed on the floor. I swiped up a pair of pajama pants and pulled them up under my towel. As soon as I pulled the towel away and tossed it on the dresser, I noticed Doc's face in the mirror. He stood directly behind me with such a look of pity and sorrow, it was overwhelming. Suddenly, I was exhausted.

I placed my hands on the top of the dresser and dropped my head, squeezing my eyes closed and hoping nothing dripped out.

Doc's arms slid around my front and he plastered himself along my back, resting his warm face against the back of my neck. He had no idea what that kind of intimate touch did to me. At least I hoped he didn't.

I was sticking around here hoping to make this family mine in some way, but tonight had made it clear as day that Doc wasn't willing to share. And why should he? He was right. I was just... just... what? The hired hand? The bachelor uncle?

"I think it's time for me to go," I said softly.

"No."

"You don't need me anymore," I said, pulling his arms away from my front before things got awkward in my thin pajama pants. I stepped away and moved over to the little wooden chair in the corner to sit down. It had been a long, lonely day.

Doc followed me and knelt on the ground in front of me, shocking the hell out of me—maybe out of both of us. He laid his face on my thigh and put his arms around my waist again. When he spoke, his voice was full of anguish.

"I will always need you! You can't leave me. Please, Wes, *please*. Please don't leave me. I can't lose you too." His sobs were wretched, and they damned near broke my heart all over again. I slid to the floor and held him tight, holding the back of his head with one hand and rubbing his back through his shirt with the other. I smelled the faded Doc scent of Old Spice and something I finally recognized as apple pie.

"You cost me a slice of your mother's pie," I murmured into his messy blond hair.

"I'm sorry," he whispered. I felt the warm puff of his breath on my chest and tried to think of mucking stalls. "It was miserable without you there. My father was fit to be tied. Talked about you the whole damned time. 'Major this, Major that, do you think Major is having a fine time with his friends?' My mother finally admitted that you hadn't gone after all."

Doc began fiddling with the long drawstring on the front of my pants, bending it in different shapes between his thumb and forefinger. I took a slow breath and tried not to notice. "How did she know I stayed here?"

"She said you give her an emergency phone number every time you go anywhere, even into Hobie for feed. And that if you didn't leave a number, it probably meant you didn't go." He paused for a minute. "I thought maybe you went to Dallas to... uh, a club or something. Like, uh, someplace you didn't want to give her a phone number for."

He kept his head down like he didn't want to make eye contact when referring to my sex life, but I noticed he didn't move away from me either. I still held him against my bare chest.

"I don't go to Dallas for sex, Doc," I said quietly enough Billy wouldn't hear us if he woke up to use the bathroom.

Doc lifted his head and finally looked at me. "You don't? Then... how... I mean... when...?"

I moved him off me as gently as I could, unable to talk about this with his body pressed against mine. He moved over until both of us had our backs against the wall side by side.

"There are a couple of men here in—"

"*Here?*" he asked. "In Hobie?"

CHAPTER 21

LIAM "DOC" WILDE

Why was I so shocked to find out there were other gay men in our small town? Well, because it was Texas for god's sake. This wasn't the most open-minded place on earth.

"Who?" I asked.

"Doc…"

"You know I won't tell anyone. I want to know who." Why was I so bothered by this? "Who?"

Major rubbed his hands over his face before looking at me through his fingers. "Jonny Rittenhouse for one."

"Jonny?" I spluttered, picturing the big muscular ranch hand who'd been working for my dad longer than I could remember. "*Our* Jonny?"

Major lifted an eyebrow.

I tried to picture the two of them together. Naked. For some reason it made me ridiculously angry. "He's a big dumb idiot." *I did not just say that.*

Major's eyes flew open wide in shock. "He's a hard worker and a good man. What the hell is wrong with you?"

"Oh, so this is like… is he… is… I mean are you two like…"

He rolled his eyes at me. "Don't hurt yourself, Liam. Are you asking if he's my boyfriend?"

"That word sounds weird when the two people involved are over forty," I muttered.

"The answer is no. We have sex, we do not date."

"Sex?" I squeaked.

Major's eyes twinkled, and I got the feeling he was enjoying seeing me squirm. "It's a little different with guys like us. We can appreciate helping each other out from time to time without expectations of a phone call the next morning."

Which one of them pitched and which one caught? And how did they decide? Was it just understood, or did there have to be a negotiation process?

I laughed, suddenly remembering something Betsy had said a while back. "Betsy thought maybe Roger was..."

"Roger who works for me on the farm? No. I'm his boss. Besides, he's having an affair with Patty Ritches."

"Is not!" I gasped like a little old lady. "Man, I wish Betsy was around to tell that to."

Major's smile softened. "She knew. I told her. We spent plenty of time swapping intel on all the busybodies in town. She used to send me on fact-finding missions."

"How do you mean?" I asked, thinking that sounded just like something she'd do.

"If I had to go into town for feed or for something at the hardware store, she'd coach me about what to ask and who to talk to so I could bring back the best gossip." He chuckled. "She hated Patty. I had to hold her back from telling Patty's husband about the affair."

"He's sleeping with Patty's best friend, so it's karma all around."

Major nodded and grinned. "I told her that too."

I studied him with my finger to my chin. "You sure know a lot for a quiet guy."

"I'm not always quiet."

"No." I remembered he'd said there were multiple men he slept with in town. "Who else?"

He narrowed his eyes. "Why do you want to know so badly?"

"I'm your best friend." It sounded even lamer out loud than it did in my head. "I don't know."

Major's faded denim eyes assessed me. "Assistant Pastor White."

My jaw dropped to the floor. I had to admit the man was good-looking, but he was a Southern Baptist preacher for god's sake. "I don't believe you," I said defiantly.

"Yes you do."

"But... but..." I spluttered. "How? *Why?*"

"Remember that time I tried to use the winch on my truck to get his sedan out of the ditch after that ice storm and it didn't budge?"

I nodded.

Major's eyes twinkled. "He was mighty thankful after I gave him a lift home. And after Easter services, and after the Hobie Hootenanny, and—"

"Stop," I said, holding my hand up and trying not to laugh. "Gross. It's all I'll be able to think about when I see him in town now."

"I might convert. The man has nice lips. I could watch him in the pulpit maybe, but I'd have to confess after, that's for sure."

I sighed. "He's a goddamned hypocrite," I muttered. "Must make you crazy."

He shrugged. "I'm used to it. But I take more than I give in that situation. Now, with Jonny—"

This time I clapped my hand over his mouth. "Christ, Major. Please. The man sat at my mother's dining table today and cut up Jackie's turkey."

"Jonny's a good man, Doc," he repeated. Even though I agreed with him, I liked it even less when he said it the second time.

"Then why don't you want to have a relationship with him? Sure would be easy, what with him living on the farm and all." I didn't mean it. The very idea of him in a relationship with someone made me stupidly jealous. I was possessive of his time and confidence, I guessed.

Major's eyes bore into mine, but he didn't say a thing. The tension thickened between us, and I gulped.

"It's... uh, well, it's not like it's any of my business," I stammered awkwardly. "And besides, I'm not a good example of the joys and benefits of putting your heart on the line."

"Bullshit." The word didn't carry any heat when he said it.

I shrugged. "I loved her. Still do, obviously. And I don't regret loving her. But Christ, it hurts like a motherfucker, Major."

"Yeah, I imagine it does."

Comfortable silence settled between us. I wondered idly if I should offer to take Billy home or let him sleep the night on Major's sofa.

"I don't want the children growing up in a family with a shroud over it," I said after a while. "I want to remember Betsy alive and happy. Maybe if I focus on that, the kids will forget this past year of her sickness and remember her bright and shining, you know?"

"Miss Hootenanny four years running," Major quipped with a wink. He'd heard the stories a million times already. I barked out a laugh before he continued. "The woman was born to reign over a parade."

"Oh god, she was so smug that first year. Patty'd thought she had it in the bag. Someone's dad loaned me his 1962 Ford Galaxie Sunliner convertible to drive her. I'll never forget the feeling of sweat trickling down my back when I almost crashed it into the float in front of me."

Silence again, and then I turned to him and clasped his forearm. "Wes, I'm going to give myself until the New Year to wallow in it, and then I need you to help me put it away, okay? I need you to help me raise these kids to be happy and healthy and good, and I can't do that if I'm walking around with black cloth over my heart."

His large, capable hand settled on mine and held tight.

"New year, new start," he said in his calm but determined way.

"And you stay," I said, trying like hell not to let it sound like a question.

His denim blues looked like spring rain to me then, the kind that washed away the harsh winter and forced open the flowers of spring.

"And I stay."

CHAPTER 22

WESTON "MAJOR" MARIAN

After the New Year, we followed the plan. Lois and Stan were on board, and the four of us adults sat the kids down to explain that while Mommy was gone, we were going to treat her memory like one of her beloved rosebushes. We would tend it with care and watch it grow. We would only feed it good things, and when we started feeling low, we'd remember that her number one wish was for the people she loved to be happy.

It wasn't easy, and there were crying jags the like of which I'd never seen before. My own sister had been emotional, but she'd never been much of a crier. But Brenda Wilde? Crier. She was stubborn as hell and a defiant wildcat when she didn't get her way. She quickly discovered that she could play the motherless child card and get whatever she wanted. Doc was the worst. One chin quiver or dropped tear from Brenda would melt him like a chocolate Easter egg in the late-spring sun.

I finally had to sit him down one night and lay it out for him—explain why he wasn't doing her any favors by letting her manipulate everyone that way. We sat at the farmhouse kitchen table while Lois put the kids to bed and Stan took the dogs out for a stroll. The evening meal had been a nightmare. The Brenda show was becoming a nightly rerun.

"She's begging for boundaries, Doc," I said.

He threw his arms up and admitted defeat. "Then you're going to have to do it. From now on, can you just be the disciplinarian? I obviously can't do it. She has my number. Besides, you're a hard-ass anyway. Ask any of the hands."

I stared him down.

"See?" Doc spluttered. "You're just looking at me and I want to polish your damned boots. You're scary as hell."

"Well, from now on she's giving me physical labor outside every time she pulls that crap."

"Major, she's only a little girl."

I lifted a brow. "How old do the twins turn this year?"

He sighed. "You know how old they are, jackass. Ten."

"When Billy was ten, he could herd cattle with me for five straight hours and come back to muck stalls afterward. You've seen Brenda on Starlight. You know that girl can hold her own. Besides, I'm going to start her in the rose garden pruning Betsy's flowers first."

Doc met my eye across the table. "I never thanked you for that."

I blinked at him. "For what?"

"For planting those roses." He swallowed. "For loving her."

She's not the only one I loved.

I grunted. "It's my job."

Doc's face turned stony. "Like hell it was your job. You tore out those boxwoods and planted her flowers to give her something to enjoy while she was laid up. She died with a pitcher full of her favorite yellow roses on her bedside because you cared enough to bring her joy until the moment she died." Doc's voice was fierce and rough. "I will never forget that, Weston Marian. *Never.*"

I stood up, shoving my chair back and taking my coffee mug to the sink to rinse out. "Gotta go. Morning comes early during calving season. Send the girl to me when she smarts off tomorrow." I cleared my throat and set the mug on the drainboard before heading to the front door.

The sound of Doc's soft chuckle followed me out. Pretty sure he called me a stoic bastard under his breath.

Sure enough, the following day little Brenda Wilde turned up in the barn after school with her arms folded across her chest.

"Daddy said I had to come see you."

"Why's that?" I asked, hanging up an extension cord I'd been using.

"How'm I supposed to know?"

I squatted down in front of her, my suede work gloves resting on my knees and my hat tipped up so I could see her defiant glare. It didn't take long for me to wait her out.

"I told him I was too sad to do my homework and that Mrs. Trayver doesn't even care. He said I had to do it anyway."

"Then what happened?"

Her chin wobbled. "I got sad again and told him he couldn't make me do my homework when I was upset like that."

I nodded. "Well, I'd be sad if I had to do homework too," I allowed.

Her face was triumphant. "See? I told him so. It's not fair. You need to tell Daddy that—"

I interrupted her with a raised finger. "Here's the thing, Baby-Bee," I said calmly but firmly, using the nickname we'd all called her since she realized she and her mom shared a first initial. "Sometimes life isn't fair. And even when we're sad as all heck, we have to do our work."

Her little forehead crinkled, and I pulled her in for a hug. Her arms automatically wrapped around my neck, and I noticed she smelled like apple juice and cookies. She held on tight.

"I miss my mommy," she said in a soft whine.

"I know, baby girl. I do too. Your daddy does too. So much. But you know what he does every day even though he's sad?"

She pulled back and looked at me, keeping her little hands around my neck. "Goes to work?"

I nodded. "Yep. And so do I. And so does Grandpa, and so does Granny. Otherwise, it wouldn't be fair for the little boy who breaks his arm at baseball practice and doesn't have your daddy there to fix it. And it wouldn't be fair for the cattle if I wasn't around to deliver the hay. And you and I would starve every night if Granny was too sad to make her meatloaf, wouldn't we?"

"It's not the same."

"It *is* the same." I brushed her bangs back from her face. Her sister Gina had taught me how to braid hair several weeks before when Lois had gone to Dallas for a craft show, but I was terrible at it. One side was twice as thick a braid as the other. Lord only knew why she'd kept mine in from the day before instead of letting her grandmother redo them.

Brenda buried her face in my shirt again for a minute.

"Uncle Major?"

"Yes, sweetie."

"Daddy said you were going to make me do work and maybe I was going to have to prune mama's rosebushes."

"Yep," I said, pulling back. "Go find the clippers in the tool room and be sure and grab your work gloves too."

She squeezed me around the neck before letting go and turning toward the tool room.

"Brenda," I called to her before she got there.

"Yes, sir?" She turned back, knowing she wasn't getting off that easy with me.

"You owe your daddy an apology too, don't you?"

Her eyes flicked to the open barn door behind me, and I realized Doc had been probably standing there the whole time watching.

"I'm sorry, Daddy," she said in a small voice. "But I really was sad, you know."

Doc's jaw ticked. I'd known him for almost ten years by then, and I knew he was doing his best to keep steady.

"I know you were, baby. And it's always okay to be sad. I accept your apology. Now get to work like Uncle Major said."

She nodded and turned back to fetch her things. I met Doc's eyes across the dimly lit barn aisle.

There had been a million times by then that Doc and I had communicated without words. It had started back in Vietnam when I was the flight commander and he was the medic. One look from the other and we knew exactly what needed to be done. When I'd come to the ranch, there had been times we'd ridden the herd together and been able to communicate with quick glances and no words. But that day in the barn was the first time I caught a glimpse of what it must have been like to have a spouse, to silently celebrate a milestone together that you both recognized the importance of.

It was such an odd feeling because all at once my heart was so very full.

And emptier than it had ever been.

He wasn't actually my spouse. With William Wilde I had half a life, everything I ever wanted without the physical intimacy. Over and over again I made the decision that it was enough, that I was willing to accept the lack of a physical relationship with him because it was the only thing missing in a life otherwise damned near perfect.

I could have my physical needs met elsewhere. It was fine. I'd already resigned myself to it many times, but I wouldn't have said I was happy about it.

So when Doc Wilde interrupted me in the barn early that summer with one of Stan's new seasonal hands, I was already holding on to my patience with the barest scrap of frayed yarn.

It was the only reason I let it happen. If he was going to take even my private sexual moments from me, he was damned well going to get an eyeful.

CHAPTER 23

LIAM "DOC" WILDE

After Betsy had been gone over eight months, I'd started to finally feel the return of my libido. I woke up hard and aching most mornings and had gotten into the habit of taking myself in hand as quickly and roughly as I could just to get release. I tried not to think of anything—any*one*. If I thought of Betsy, the sliver of grief would send my mind tumbling in decidedly unproductive directions.

But then one day that all changed on a dime.

It had been late one night when I'd glanced out the bedroom window and noticed Major's truck was still parked outside the barn. He'd been working his ass off helping my dad in the evenings on the ranch after a full day spent working the Hobart land.

I knew he felt responsible for making sure my dad didn't over-work himself, but still going at it after eleven at night? That was too much.

I didn't bother putting my clothes back on, thinking it would be fine to wander out there in my boxers and undershirt to say my piece to my best friend before returning to bed. But I sure as hell never expected he wouldn't be alone.

After George had passed, we'd turned their ranch house into a quasi-bunkhouse for all the hands for both the farm and ranch. It served several purposes. Mainly, it gave the hands a much nicer place to live. They had their own full kitchen and a place to relax and watch television after hours. But it also got all the men out of the bunk rooms in the barn by the main farmhouse, which gave my family back some privacy.

Which is why I was shocked to find one of the hands in the barn with Major that late at night.

But after a split second, it became clear they weren't still hard at work. At least Major wasn't. Young Russ sure was.

He knelt at Major's feet in the dusty hay while my best friend stood wide-legged and shirtless against the rough wooden wall of a horse stall. His jeans were open and pushed partway down his thighs while his arms stretched high above him to a wooden peg sticking out of the wall.

Major's eyes were closed in pleasure, and a deep rumble of satisfaction came from his throat. The kid working on his knees made obscene slurping noises as he bobbed his head up and down in front of Major's body.

I stood there transfixed. I'd never in my life seen a man perform a sex act on another man. The one time in the army I'd stumbled across two men going at it, they'd been fully clothed and simply groping and kissing. This was different. This was half-naked and debauched.

And I could not look away.

Within seconds, my dick was hard and tenting my boxers. I squeezed it and sucked in a breath. What the fuck was wrong with me? I wasn't homosexual. Other than being… well, *curious* I guess you could say, I'd never imagined being with a man like that.

A devilish whisper in the back of my mind brought back memories of the times I'd lain in bed at the base in Long Binh and thought about Major having sex with other men after I'd found out about his sexual preference. I'd imagined how he'd most likely be the dominant one and pin a smaller man down beneath him. I'd pictured Major's muscular body stretched long and strong across the back of another man thrusting inside of him, but that had been more like… like me just trying to understand him.

Right?

"Take it all," Major grunted in his deep voice. One of his large hands came down and grabbed a handful of the kid's curly red hair. "That's it. Like that."

Oh god.

My dick was wet, and my throat was thick. Why was this turning me on?

Russ's hand came up and splayed across Major's stomach, drawing my attention to the dark hair there and the defined muscles he carried from working such a physical job. His shoulders were wide and defined, even more so than they'd been in the army. I'd noticed many times the way his muscular shoulders stretched his shirts when he hauled hay bales or roped a calf.

Did I notice the physicality of any of my other male friends the way I noticed his? I'd always known he was a very attractive man, but from the very beginning of our acquaintance, I'd been with Betsy. I'd never needed to think of anyone—male or female—as a potential sexual partner. But now that I no longer had someone, was I just that bad off that any sex act made me this riled up?

Or was it something more? Something I'd never really had time to think much about since I'd been with Betsy since high school?

A choking sound snapped me back into the moment. Russ groaned but kept sucking Major's dick. I wished he'd had to catch his breath or something—pull back just long enough for me to see what he'd been working on. I'd seen Major's dick plenty over the years, but never... never really looked at it, of course.

But god did I want to see it right now.

"Look at me," he growled. My eyes snapped up to his, expecting to see him staring down at Russ, but he was staring right at me instead.

I froze like a startled doe caught by a hunter.

My heart hammered in my chest and roared in my ears.

"Like that," he commanded, eyes drilling into me from across the dimly lit space. "Just like that."

I couldn't breathe.

"Touch yourself."

Oh god, no. This can't be happening.

My hand was already on the front of my boxers, pressing my cock to give it some relief. His words were spoken in his infamous command voice, and I was Pavlov's dog, conditioned to respond to it.

I slipped my hand into my shorts.

Absently, I noticed the kid on the ground grappling with his own blue jeans, assuming—as he should have—that Major was talking to him.

"Taste it."

Suddenly, I was so light-headed I almost swooned to the ground like some kind of Victorian lady. Instead, I took a shaky swipe at the tip of my hard-on with my finger and brought it up to taste the wetness there. I'd never in my life done such a thing.

It was salty and strange, but licking it off my finger while Major stared at me was one of the single most sexually stimulating moments of my entire life.

"I want to see you," he said roughly. "Take your dick out and show it to me."

I did.

"Stroke yourself off," he grunted, squeezing his eyes closed for the briefest moment before returning his stare to me.

The man on the ground stroked himself frantically while still sucking Major's dick and moaning dramatically.

I tugged at myself silently, swallowing back gasps as I got closer and closer to coming.

"Come for me, sweetheart," he said softly.

The orgasm was so powerful, I bit my tongue until it bled. Tears streamed down my face, but I couldn't look away from Weston's gaze. He saw me. He *saw* me.

And my life would never be the same.

I did what any self-respecting man would do when faced with something raw and powerful like that.

I turned around and ran.

CHAPTER 24

WESTON "MAJOR" MARIAN

Watching Doc's emotional and physical release triggered my own, and I poured myself down poor Russ's throat. In decades of sexual trans-actions, I'd never felt like I'd taken advantage of someone until that night. Having sex with him while thinking of and engaging with someone else wasn't fair to him even if he hadn't known another man was in the room, so as soon as Doc left, I pulled Russ up and took care of him, kissing and cooing and cleaning up his spend until he wandered goofily off toward the Hobart farm.

Then the reality of how I'd taken advantage of *Doc* finally hit.

No. Scratch that. I hadn't taken advantage of Doc. He'd wandered into a private moment between two consenting adults and *stayed*. Moreover, he'd voluntarily participated.

That was on him.

He was a grown man who could make his own decisions, and if he regretted anything he'd done tonight, well, that was on him too.

I leaned down to pick up my shirt from where Russ had flung it. It was covered in bits of straw and who knew what else, so I tucked it into my back pocket instead of putting it on. It was still plenty warm outside anyway, and now my blood was boiling.

Really, I was angry at myself for doing something so unprofessional in Stan's barn. While I didn't work directly for the ranch, I still considered myself one of the managers of the entire enterprise encompassing the Wilde ranch and Hobart farm. If I was going to dally with one of the hands, I could have at least had the decency to do it in my own home. At the same time, it wasn't like I'd planned it.

Russ had been flirting with me for weeks, and he'd deliberately stayed late tonight in order to put the moves on me. Now that Jonny was seeing a man on the regular over in Valley Cross, I hadn't had sex with anyone in several months. So I let the kid go down on me.

And Doc had walked in.

I ran my hands through my hair and blew out a breath. Jesus fuck that had been hot. Hottest thing I'd ever experienced, and I'd been to bath houses all over the world. It was different when there were feelings involved, and *that* was something I wasn't used to.

As I trudged out to my truck, I noticed the bright orange flare of a cigarette tip in the darkness near the corner of the barn. I squinted to be sure of what I was seeing.

"Since when do you smoke, Dr. Wilde?" I tried not to let on how fast my heart rate had ramped up when I saw who it was.

Doc looked at me for a moment before taking another long drag. "Since I got all the way to the kitchen and spotted my mother's Pall Malls," he muttered on the exhale. "I figured coming back outside for a smoke was better than breaking my hand by taking a swing at something."

"You that disgusted by what you saw?" I asked defiantly. "Or what you *did*?"

Instead of answering right away, Doc took a few more puffs on the cigarette. He finally blew out the smoke and dropped the butt under his boot. I'd noticed his bare legs in cowboy boots before, in the doorway to the barn, but now I took my fill of them again.

"I wanted to take a swing at Russ," he said.

His words surprised me. "For what? For preferring men?"

Doc stepped in front of me and got close enough to almost touch chests.

"No," he growled. "For preferring *mine*."

We stared at each other, practically nose to nose. My heart thundered and hope damned near took all the oxygen from my lungs.

"You're grieving," I whispered. "You're confused."

"Grief doesn't get my dick hard, Major. Confusion doesn't make me want to kill some idiot cowhand for moving in on something that's supposed to belong to me."

"Since when do I belong to you?" I breathed.

Doc's hands shook when they tentatively reached up to land lightly on my upper chest. They were warm and dry as he smoothed them up to cup the sides of my neck. Every single hair on my body was standing up straight like I'd put my finger in a socket.

"I don't know, Wes. You just do. Part of me feels like somehow you always have. But..." His voice caught. "I loved her too. So much, Major. So fucking much."

I held his hips before running my hands around to his back to pull him in closer. "I know you did. And I know you still do. It's enough for me just to know I mean something to you. I don't ever want to take Betsy away from you. I hope you know that. I loved her too, and I'd do anything to bring her back for you. For all of us."

There was enough ambient light from the safety light in the barn to show me his eyes were full to overflowing.

"I know. And I... I don't think I'm ready for... for..."

I cut him off. "Shh, it's okay. I will never push you. And if you're never ready for more, that's all right too." I pulled him in for a hug and held him tight, truly exhaling for the first time in my forty years. "Just please let me keep on loving you, Doc. I don't know how to stop."

He turned so his face was buried in my neck and his lips brushed right next to my Adam's apple. I tried to keep my hardening cock from pressing into him and scaring him off.

"I don't want you to stop," he whispered into my skin. "Ever."

I pulled his face away from my neck and cupped his cheeks. "Get some sleep, Doc. It's late." I pressed a kiss to his forehead and relished seeing his eyes flutter closed.

When I stepped out of his embrace, he swayed a bit but then gazed at me steadily. "You, uh… you gonna be here for breakfast in the morning?"

He was so damned beautiful when he was unsure.

"I promised a certain rose gardener I'd give her double braids before school," I said with a grin. "So I'll be there with bells on."

It seemed like he wanted to say something important, but he held back.

"All right, well… I'll, ah, see you in the morning, then."

I couldn't help it. I reached out and pulled him in again with a hand around the back of his neck. This time I pressed the kiss to his cheek about a millimeter away from the side of his mouth. "Sleep tight, sweetheart."

He melted against me for just a brief moment before he nodded and pulled away. When he got to the top of the porch stairs, he turned back around to find me watching him. He smiled at me and went into the house.

I'd never wanted to follow someone into bed as much as I did in that moment.

Doc was right.

I was his and he was mine. But I wondered if and when anyone but us would know it.

After blowing out another breath, I turned to hop in my truck. The drive back to my house had never been quieter, nor my bed emptier.

CHAPTER 25

LIAM "DOC" WILDE

I didn't sleep a wink that night. The interlude in the barn replayed in my mind like a film on a loop. The thick veins on the back of his hand as he held Russ's head to his dick. The way his eyes never left mine, the hoarse roar of his release as soon as I turned my back on him. The way my insides turned to jelly both times he'd called me sweetheart.

I couldn't make my heart slow down, much less my brain. What the hell did all this mean? Did I want him... like *that*?

I barked out a laugh. Of course I did. There was no denying my body's reaction regardless of how surprising it was to me. By the time I got to the privacy of my bedroom, I was hard for him again just remembering. I masturbated three more times until I was sore and my balls ached. I wanted him desperately. After imagining him naked against the barn wall, I pictured myself being the one to kneel at his feet. I wanted it to be my hands that explored the trail of dark hair up his belly to his defined pecs, my mouth that teased his red-brown nipples to tight buds, and my name on his lips as he came in a rush, hot on my skin.

Once I started thinking about it, I couldn't stop.

I obsessed over what it would be like to lie naked in bed with Weston Marian. And I wanted it.

While the next morning at breakfast was incredibly awkward, things were the way they'd always been between us. On the outside anyway. Major proceeded to do his work around the farm and join the family for meals the way he always had. On Friday as usual he took a break from work long enough to take Billy to baseball practice where I met him from the clinic to take over. Only this time, I asked him to stay.

"Do you… do you have to get back? I mean, I know things are busy right now at the farm." I sounded like a kid with a crush. "Never mind. I'm being ridiculous. I just thought, if you didn't have to race back, you might want to stay and watch the scrimmage with me, but you're probably busy with things on the farm and things are probably busy… on…" My eyes widened in shock at my runaway mouth.

Major's eyes widened too, and the most amazing grin lit up his entire face. "On the farm?" he teased.

"Christ," I muttered with a self-conscious laugh. "I'm sorry, I—"

"I'd love to stay."

Once we took a seat on the bleachers, I relaxed and told him about the phone call I'd had from Billy's middle school science teacher asking if I wanted to help chaperone a field trip to Dallas for his class.

"I can do it if work is too busy," Major said before cheering for one of Billy's friends who'd made it to second base. A group of moms leaned over and waved to Major.

"Yoo-hoo, hi, Lieutenant," a woman named Letty called out with a wave. "I keep meaning to ask if you're free for Sunday dinner sometime soon. My two younger sisters just back moved to town from nursing school, and I'd love for you to meet them."

Major shifted his weight until the length of his thigh pressed up against mine. A rush of warmth filled my chest while my face lit damned near completely on fire.

"Unfortunately, the Wildes are riding me pretty hard these days, ma'am. Rain check?"

Had I been drinking something, I would have spewed it out all over the back of poor Lally James, who'd obviously just gotten her hair out of curlers to come to the game.

Major turned to me with a sly grin. "Isn't that right, Doc?"

"I don't... it's... I mean... we're not... that is to say..." I clamped my teeth shut with an audible click. "Mm-hm."

His laugh was wild and free. It boomed over the field and made the ladies swoon. I wasn't sure I'd ever seen Weston Marian let go like that. His entire face was unlined and full of joy. A deep dimple appeared to the right of his lips, and his eyes sparkled in the late-afternoon sun.

It was goddamned glorious.

And when he met my eyes while his were still full of mirth, I fell a little bit in love with him right then and there. He was my center. My steady rock. The man who made sure our lives had kept spinning without scratching the record.

I must have looked at him like I'd just escaped an insane asylum.

"Doc? You okay?" he asked softly. "There's a water fountain over by—"

"I..." I swallowed and looked around. There were too many people sitting close by. "I..." Since when had I become this snidely, stuttering person? I swallowed again and spoke as softly as I could. "Can, um, can I come over tonight?"

His fingers twitched where his hand lay on his thigh. "Of course you can."

I nodded. "Okay... Okay, good. Yeah."

Now that it was out there, I tried to focus on my son. The scrimmage lasted approximately six thousand hours and fifty-nine minutes. When they were finished, Billy asked if he could ride home with "Uncle Major." I ruffled his hair and took his baseball gear from him. "Sure can, bud. Remember not to track mud into Granny's kitchen if you get there before I do, all right?"

Billy tilted his head at me. "Dad, Uncle Major would make me do fifty push-ups if I did that. No, thanks."

I bit my tongue to keep from laughing when I met Major's eyes. "You giving my kids PT on the DL, Major?"

He pulled Billy in with a side hug and gave him a knuckle to the head. "That was supposed to be just for us tough guys, Billy. So we could win in a fight against your super-strong dad if ever we were down to just one piece of Granny's pie."

Billy pulled out of Major's hold, but he was smiling. "Don't be silly. Granny always saves the last piece for Grandpa. It's kinda gross."

Major met my eye over Billy's head. "It's kinda wonderful."

I was glad Billy didn't look at me since I probably would have won the World's Goofiest Grin Award right then. "See you two at home."

On my solo drive home, thoughts of Betsy snuck into my dreamy reverie. I'd always assumed Betsy would be my last-piece-of-pie person. I thought about what she'd say if she knew how I was feeling about my best friend.

Her voice was so clear in my head, I realized she'd said the words over and over while she was alive to make sure I'd know exactly how she felt.

He's one of the best men I've ever met. You bringing him here was a gift to all of us... I want him to stay here. To be here for our children when... if something happens to me. They adore him.

She'd even known he had feelings for me, yet she'd never once pushed him away or said a single negative thing about him. Instead, she'd recognized how much he'd needed us and had given him the gift of love right back in spades.

Was it possible for lightning to strike twice? For me to be loved by two incredible people in my lifetime?

I got home on a bed of clouds and floated into my parents' house with the same goofy grin. My father looked up from the newspaper he was reading and saw my expression. "The boy must have scored a home run."

"Nah, but he played great. He's with Major. I think they stopped off to pick up some ice cream at the store."

I pulled off my tie and unbuttoned the top button of my shirt. "Mom, you need any help before I run upstairs to change?"

I thought about my plans to go over to Major's house after the kids were in bed. Maybe I needed to shower before I changed my clothes.

"We're just making hamburgers tonight," my mom said. "Nothing fancy. Go on ahead and change."

I turned to head up the stairs when I overheard my father mutter about Anita Bryant and the Save Our Children Coalition. Something about his tone stopped me.

"Pastor Dickerson mentioned this at Bible study last week," he continued. "The coalition is trying to raise money here in case the gays come to Texas to do what they did in Florida and California. They're organizing a fund-raiser. Sounds like he's jumping the gun a bit. We don't have gays here like they do in those other places."

My stomach plummeted. I'd never thought of my father as particularly bigoted. In fact, he was downright open-minded compared to most of our neighbors. But the man had been born in 1906. He and my mother had tried for years to have children, and by the time they'd finally had me, he was forty. Which meant he was already in his seventies and stuck in his small-town ways. He was ignorant about things he didn't know much about. Well, I guess that was the very definition of ignorance anyway.

"Dad, there are plenty of gay people in Texas," I said carefully.

"Maybe in Dallas or San Antonio," he muttered. "But I don't see why our small-town church needs to participate when it doesn't affect us at all."

I pulled out a kitchen chair and sat in it, facing him. Confidentiality reasons and fear for the man's livelihood insisted I not mention a word about Assistant Pastor White and hypocrisy, but it was a near thing.

"First of all, there are plenty gay people in small towns. Second of all, there's no threat from gay people. Why would we need to raise money to fight anything?"

Dad lowered the paper to the table and seemed to think it over. "That coalition says they prey on little children, Liam. They're immoral. And that's in the Bible."

My stomach churned with mixed feelings because he wasn't wrong. According to our church, it *was* in the Bible. But so were many other things that didn't make sense and were contradictory.

"Patty and Hal Ritches are both having extramarital affairs," I said. "Are we going to ask the church to raise money to fight them?"

"Liam!" my mother gasped from across the room. "What in the world?"

"Sorry, Mama, but it's true. I'm pointing out some basic Christian hypocrisy right now. If the Ritches' affairs aren't hurting anyone else —which by the way I would argue they damned sure are or will hurt those children—then what business is it of ours if two men or two women want to be together?"

"Two of God's children temporarily losing their way isn't the same thing as the deviant behavior of homosexuals," my father said. "Obviously, I personally would be more concerned about the Ritches because that's actually happening in our community."

"Dad, homosexuals aren't deviant. And I assure you, there are plenty of gay men in our community. Nice men. Good men you wouldn't ever expect or consider deviant in any way."

My parents both stared at me. "Who?" my mom asked.

I felt light-headed. This wasn't the way this conversation was supposed to happen. And no amount of questioning would make me reveal anyone's sexuality like that. I loved my mother dearly, but I also knew full well she would mention it "in confidence" to a close friend who'd mention it "in confidence" to another until the entire town was in an uproar over it.

The front door opened and Billy's voice could be heard chattering to Major about going to a Texas Rangers game that weekend. The low rumble of Major's short responses made me feel strangely emotional. When his familiar face appeared in the kitchen, his eyes found mine immediately.

"Hey," I said. It came out as more of a squeak. His eyebrows furrowed and he flicked his gaze to my parents before looking back at me. "Everything okay?"

What would my parents do if they found out their beloved second son was a gay man? What would they do if they learned that their very own flesh and blood wanted to lie naked with him that very night?

"I, uh—" My breathing came fast and shallow. "—was just going upstairs to change."

Major ran his hands through his hair, undoing some of the damage his cowboy had done. "Can I come up there and get that Creedence Clearwater album you said I could borrow?"

I had no idea what he was talking about.

"Yeah, right. Of course. Come on up."

He said a quick greeting to my mom and dad before following me up the stairs to my bedroom. I closed the door behind us and turned to find him with his hip propped on my dresser and his hands clasped loosely in front of him. He didn't say anything, just looked at me with the same patience he'd always had.

The man could read me better than anyone, even Betsy. After a few beats, he held his arms out in invitation and I stumbled over to fall into them. While my seeking physical comfort from him was fairly new, it was as natural as breathing. I thought back to the night in Bangkok when I'd snuck into bed with him and held him tightly. Who exactly had I been trying to comfort that night, him or me?

Major's warm hands rubbed up and down my back.

"You're shaking," he murmured into my hair. "What happened?"

I shook my head. "Nothing. Just… I needed this right here."

"Liar," he said with a smile in his voice. "You know you're the worst liar ever, don't you?"

"Shut up." God, he felt good. And smelled good too. Like outdoor work and sweat. Hay and horses. The scent of my childhood.

"You still coming over later? You know it's okay if you've changed your mind. I won't pressure you, Liam."

When he said my real name, it made me shudder. I remembered all the times he'd murmured it in his sleep over the years. Every single time he said it was like him hand feeding me a morsel of gourmet chocolate.

"I don't feel any pressure. I'm coming over because I can't get you out of my damned mind, and I can't stop wanting to take your clothes off." I pulled back and met his eyes. "And because I'm desperate to know what it feels like to kiss you on the lips, but I'll be damned if I'm going to do it for the first time with my parents downstairs." I grinned at him, trying to wash away the conversation with my father and tuck it into a box to keep it safely away from the man in my arms.

I never wanted him to feel prejudice or pain, and I'd fight like hell to ensure he especially didn't hear it in this house.

Major stepped away from me before casually adjusting himself with a large hand on the front of his blue jeans. My stomach flip-flopped wildly with nerves.

"I'm, uh… I'll be a little while. I'm going to take a quick shower," I stammered.

His grin was slow and knowing.

"Wash yourself real well. Don't forget the cracks and crevices, Lieutenant."

Christ on the cross.

If what my dad had said was true, I was going to hell for sure. But I wasn't so sure I minded all that much.

CHAPTER 26

WESTON "MAJOR" MARIAN

Liam Wilde flustered and blushing was a sight to behold. If I'd thought he was attractive before, that was nothing compared to how he looked now that I knew he might want me. I grabbed the first record in the stack of albums by his turntable and returned back downstairs, stashing the album by my boots so I wouldn't forget to take it home. When I put it down, I noticed it was Loretta Lynn. I snorted. Betsy and her country music crooners.

When I returned to the kitchen, I asked Lois where the girls were.

"They took all their dolls outside to play. They're probably under that big oak with all the shade. Will you go bring them in for dinner, please, Major? It's time to wash up."

"Yes, ma'am."

I made my way back outside and found them not under the oak but by one of the far pasture fences. It looked from here like Brenda and Gina were encouraging little Jackie to climb through the slats into the pasture where a handful of Stan's greenest horses grazed. They knew better than to go into a pasture without permission.

"Girls," I barked, taking off at a swift jog toward them. The twins scrambled to hide Jackie but were clearly still trying to force her into

150

the pasture. Suddenly, I noticed Jackie's little pink overalls on the other side of the fence. "Get her out of there!"

The horses heard my voice and looked up, assuming if I was there that meant they were getting feed of some kind. *Dammit.*

"Brenda, Gina, grab your sister and pull her back," I yelled again. Jackie was only five years old and no match at all for the nervous horses who were now wandering over expecting dinner.

I heard Doc's voice behind me. "Wes, what the hell is going on?"

I reached the fence at a dead sprint and vaulted over it, grabbing Jackie up and holding her to me right as the first horse reached us. She burst into tears against my neck.

"Git," I snapped at the closest horse, motioning with one arm for it to move off. He hopped to the side a bit and blew air out through his nostrils. I turned to hand Jackie over to Gina so I could climb back over the fence, but Jackie wouldn't let go of my neck.

Brenda grabbed Gina's arm and said, "We're in so much trouble. Run!"

Even though Gina looked unsure, she followed her stronger-willed sister as usual and the two of them took off for the barn.

"Running makes for more work, and you know it," I called after them. "Might as well get started while you're in there by mucking stalls. And you can explain to your granny why you missed dinner."

Doc watched them race past him and then looked up at me, holding his arms out for Jackie. "What just happened?"

Jackie still wouldn't let go, so I began climbing carefully with one arm wrapped tightly around her little body. When I landed on the other side next to Doc, he reached out a hand to rub Jackie's back.

"You all right, sweetie?"

"Day said to wide Pink Pony," she said with a sniff and a hiccup, peeking out at me with one blue eye. "Sowwy, Unca Mage."

Pink Pony was the name the girls had given one of Stan's new horses who'd been delivered by a man with a pink logo on the side of his horse trailer. Despite the sweet name, the stallion was a royal pain in the ass and nowhere near safe enough for the kids to approach.

Doc brushed her blonde curls out of her face. "You know better than to go into one of the pastures where any animals are, baby."

More tears appeared, and she ducked back into the crook of my neck. Doc smiled up at me. "C'mon, let's go eat. Mom was hoping I'd man the grill for her. Jackie, I think I saw some cut-up strawberries on the table. You know anyone who'd want to eat those?"

They were her favorite, and I felt her little body let out a shuddering breath. "Uh-huh."

"You want me to get the twins?" I asked, following him and trying not to stare at his ass in his Wranglers.

"Nah. I think you're right. Let them eat it cold and explain to Granny why they missed it."

As I followed him into the house and helped Jackie out of her little cowgirl boots to leave them on the boot trays by the door, I thought about how grateful I was that he allowed me to co-parent the kids as much as he did. Not only did it prove his trust in me, but it also allowed me to be even closer to the family I loved so much. Billy choosing to ride with me home from baseball and Jackie staying in my arms instead of automatically reaching for Doc were signs of love and acceptance I'd never gotten anywhere other than the army. And I would never have described the army as particularly loving in the first place.

When we got to the kitchen, Billy was begging Doc for tickets to the baseball game in Dallas he'd been talking about earlier. When Doc explained he had to work and I had to stay close to the ranch to help Stan with the herd, I was surprised to hear Stan pipe up and offer to take him. Since we were going to be elbow-deep in castrating the calves, it was highly unusual for Stan to take off to Dallas and leave it to the rest of us.

Stan met my eye when I walked in the room. "That okay with you, Major? Can you handle things without me?"

"Sure. Of course." I still hadn't spilled his secret to Doc about the spinal arthritis, so Doc was shocked at Stan's change of plans. He looked from Stan to me.

"Good for you for taking some time off, Dad. You know I think you should consider retiring. You and Mom deserve some years with less stress."

Stan was in his seventies, and the life of a rancher wasn't kind. He definitely deserved retirement. But the man had never replaced his lost ranch foreman back when I'd come on. He'd acted as his own foreman sort of using me as his unofficial second-in-command even though my main job was managing the Hobart farm. If he retired, something would have to change. He'd either need to hire a foreman or he'd need to replace me on the farm. As it was, I was already working around the clock most days, especially in spring and fall.

Stan glanced at me for the briefest second before looking at Doc. Something about his look didn't sit right with me.

"I've been thinking about selling."

Oh hell.

"What?" Doc asked. His eyes jumped to me, and I shrugged. Obviously this was the first I was hearing about it, but I wasn't any happier about it than he seemed to be. "Why?"

Lois handed Billy a tray of burger patties. "Honey, why don't you put these on the grill for Granny? It's already hot."

Once Billy was outside and I'd sent Jackie to the bathroom to wash her hands, Doc asked his dad again.

"Why? I get you wanting to retire, but I never thought you'd sell the ranch."

Stan's eyes slid over to me again and back to Doc. I felt like I should have offered to leave the room along with the kids. I moved to stand, but Doc put a hand on my arm.

"Stay."

Stan cleared his throat. "Son, you're a doctor, not a rancher. Billy's too young to take over anytime soon and that's if he even wanted to. There's no future for the ranch in this family."

Doc looked at me again, and I knew exactly what he was thinking. He'd always assumed I'd take charge of the ranch one day, and to be honest, so had I. I'd never expected to inherit it, of course not. But I'd expected to be its caretaker at the very least to keep it profitable for the sake of Doc and the kids.

I stayed quiet and kept my eyes down on my clasped hands on the place mat in front of me. The silence in the room was deafening. I finally couldn't take it any longer.

"I'd better help Billy with the burgers," I mumbled, standing and heading for the rarely used rear door.

When we returned with a plate full of cooked burgers, the conversation had clearly ended to no one's satisfaction. We ate quietly until the girls came crashing in covered in bits of straw and stinking like horse shit.

"Straight to the bath," I called out, pointing to the stairs, before they could step foot in Lois's clean kitchen. "Don't even think about coming in here like that, girls."

Doc, Stan, and Lois all stared at me while I took another bite of my burger. Billy just snickered under his breath.

Lois looked over at Doc with a smirk on her face. "You think Betsy's haunting Major?"

Stan cracked a smile. "Possessing, more like," he added.

Doc seemed to relax a little for the first time all evening. His crooked grin was my favorite. "You should have heard him one time when one of our rescues in Nam got sick all over the back of Major's seat in the chopper. He made me and the crew chief clean it with a toothbrush." He stopped for a second, remembering, and then blushed deep red to the roots of his hair. I quirked my head at him in question. He cleared his throat. "He, ah... well, let's just say I'll never forget him barking at us that day."

Suddenly I remembered what I'd said to him when I'd instructed him to clean out the mess.

Don't forget the cracks and crevices, Lieutenant.

CHAPTER 27

LIAM "DOC" WILDE

After Major left and the girls were in bed, I gave Billy permission to stay up a little later so he could read his book out on the screened porch off the side of the house where it was nice and cool.

My parents sat me down in the kitchen and brought up the subject of selling the ranch again.

"Why wouldn't you let Major take over the ranch?" I asked.

My parents exchanged a look. "He's not family, honey," my mom said. "I mean, we love him like a son, but..."

After everything that man had done for this family, it hurt like hell to hear her say that.

I spread my hands out flat on the kitchen table. "I don't mean passing ownership of the property to him. I only mean having him take over as foreman and caretaker. We can have him oversee both properties and hire accordingly," I suggested.

"Liam," my dad began. "You know Weston is forty now and still unmarried."

The nerves frothed up in my stomach. They were already plenty high for what I was planning with him later, but after our conversation before dinner, I thought I knew where my parents might be going with this.

"He's an excellent foreman," I said angrily. "A good man. And one of the hardest workers we've ever had here."

My mom's soft hand landed on mine on the table. "We know that, honey. We're just concerned that he doesn't have enough roots to stay here. We love him like a son and think that maybe he should go somewhere he can meet a nice girl and start his own family."

"He has a family! Our family. He loves those kids like they're his own. He loves you like you're his parents. He loves me like..." I tripped over the word for the first time but said it anyway. "Like a *brother.*"

My mom's face softened, and my dad looked at me with affection. "Of course," my mom said. "That's why we want him to be as happy as he can be."

"Maybe staying here will make him happy," I said, hoping I didn't sound as belligerent as I felt. But deep down I wondered if they were right. Was he only staying here for me? And by staying here in Hobie, was he giving up all chance at a happier life, a fulfilling relationship?

He could have moved to San Francisco or New York and been able to be more himself instead of hiding such a big part of himself.

"Maybe so," Dad said. "But now that we're discussing it, I see maybe I should have asked him rather than making the decision for him."

"Well... I was going to go over and watch *Logan's Run* and *Quincy* with him if that's all right with you two. Maybe I could talk to him about it then."

Dad squeezed my shoulder as he stood up. "Sounds good. You boys have fun. One of these days maybe you two should go down to the city for the weekend and have some fun now that you're both single at the same time. I saw an advertisement for a disco club in Dallas. It sounds like American Bandstand or something. I don't know, maybe you could meet some ladies at a—"

"Stan," my mother interrupted with a laugh. "I don't think poor Liam needs dating advice from his father."

I tried to picture meeting and dating women I'd never met before, and nothing about the idea appealed to me. "I think I'll stick with hanging out with Major for now. Not sure I'm ready for much else, you know?"

Mom frowned. "Of course, dear. We didn't mean to push. I think your father just wanted you to know that it's all right for you to have a life outside of work and the ranch. And the kids. We're happy to help out so you and the major can get out and meet some people when you're ready. That's all."

"Thanks, Mom. I appreciate it. Major mentioned there may be a card game later with the hands, so if I'm not back in the morning, I just bunked over there, all right?"

They sent me off with smiles and a six-pack of beer from the fridge. My mom even handed me half a sheet cake she had leftover. When I turned up at Major's house with my hands full of alcohol and sweets, he laughed.

"If you're trying to seduce me, Lieutenant, it's working."

"Shut up. I'm so embarrassed. I lied to my parents like I was sixteen years old again. By the way, we're going to have to watch TV in case they want to talk about *Quincy* tomorrow."

"It's reruns tonight," Major said with a shit-eating grin.

"Hot damn."

I followed him into the small kitchen and helped put things away. When we were done, he handed me a beer and gestured toward the sofa.

My hands were shaking so hard, I put the beer on the coffee table and forgot to sit. Instead, I stood with my back against the wall and didn't know where to put my hands. This was going to be awkward. We were going to sit here making excruciating small talk and pretend to watch TV until one of us finally got the nerve to make a move. I started to babble. "Oh, this coffee table looks familiar, because it is, because it used to be in our—"

Major walked right up and grabbed my face with both hands before crashing his mouth onto mine. He was hard and hot and tasted like beer already even though he smelled like clean Ivory soap. The stubble by his lips scratched at my skin, his tongue demanded entry, and someone, somewhere was mewling. All of my senses were overloaded and overflowing. Every nerve suddenly zinged with need and want.

I noticed absently that my wrists had been pinned above my head against the wall by one of his strong hands. His other hand was clasped gently around the front of my throat so he could use his thumb and forefinger to angle my face exactly where he wanted it. I was breathless and panting within seconds, following his lips and tongue wherever they went.

Oh god oh god oh god.

His erection pressed hard into my belly, and one of his muscular thighs pressed between my legs until I was practically humping it. Noises I'd never made before were coming out of me—groans and whimpers, gasps and pleas for more.

Major's mouth owned me. It took complete control over me, and I dropped my head back against the wall to take whatever he wanted to give.

But instead of taking my mouth again, he drew in a deep breath and settled his face in the crook of my neck. His skin felt hot against mine and I swore I could feel him trembling, He'd moved his hands to claps my upper arms. His flexing fingers spoke of something unleashed within him. Something I couldn't wait to discover.

"Liam," he breathed against my neck. His voice shook and a sudden, inescapable fear took over me that he'd changed his mind about this... that I wasn't who he wanted after all. But then he repeated my name and it came out as a plea this time.

"Baby, what is it? What's wrong?" I croaked. I settled my hand over the back of his neck and stroked him as gently as I could.

Major lifted his head so his cheek was pressed against mine. He was breathing harshly. I clasped his cheeks. I swore that his eyes looked wet, but in the lighting, I couldn't be sure. "Wes, you're scaring me," I admitted, my own voice sounding shaky.

He shook his head. "No, no," was all he managed to get out before he kissed me softly. Reverently. I returned the kiss. It was so soft and sweet that it stole more of my breath than the first one had. I'd never felt more cherished in my entire life.

Major sighed. "Don't be scared, Liam. I just... I've been waiting so long for this. So fucking long," He kissed me again. His tongue traced the seam of my lips and when I opened, he dipped inside. The more he consumed my mouth, the more I understood what he was feeling because I was feeling it now too. I'd always feared losing him and that had been bad enough, but to lose him now, after this... after discovering this new part of who we were together...

Fuck.

"We're not," I began, but had to stop when Major's tongue chose that moment to tangle with mine. I was breathless by the time he released me and moved his lips along my cheek to my hairline.

"We're not going to lose this," I managed to get out. The words sounded more like a question, but Major's response was unequivocal as he lifted his eyes to meet mine.

"No, we're not," he growled. "You're mine now, Liam, do you hear me?"

He didn't give me a chance to agree because his mouth crashed down on mine again. I clung to him as we battled for control. Major took the decision away from me when his lips slid down my neck and he gentled his touch so that he was dropping a row of small, nibbling kisses down the side of my face to my neck.

"Oh god," I breathed. "Oh god."

"You're so beautiful. You have no idea how beautiful you are to me, Liam."

"Oh *god*." I felt like I was going to explode. Or implode, or simply just faint and slide down the wall in a puddle at his feet.

I brought my shaky hands up to thread through his thick dark hair, something I'd always wanted to do but thought was kind of strange. He immediately moved his hands down around to my lower back and pulled me in closer.

"That's it, touch me please. Anywhere," he murmured between kisses inside my collar.

I didn't know where to begin. Did I just... put my hands wherever I wanted? And where would that be, exactly?

You've had sex before, idiot.

I blew out a nervous laugh. Major pulled back and looked at me. His eyes were dark and intense, pupils inky and bottomless. It made my stomach swoop low and straight back up again.

I tried to explain my weirdness. "No, I just... I was so nervous, and I just realized that I can stop acting like a virgin. It's not like I've never made out with anyone before."

Major's mouth twisted up on one side. "Made out?"

"Dammit, I really am a virgin, aren't I?" I asked with a smirk.

"Thank you for coming over, Liam," he said, pressing his forehead to mine. "Stop me if you need to. I'm having a hard time keeping my hands off you. This is... this is already more than I ever dreamed of."

"I, uh, I like it when you take charge, Major," I admitted softly. "Then I don't have to decide or... or worry. I trust you."

Major's eyes drifted closed, and he blew out a slow breath. "Christ what you do to me. The things you say."

I slid a hand down from his hair to feel his cheek. "Will you take me to your bed, Weston? I want to know what it's like."

He opened his eyes to study me. "To be with a man?"

I shook my head and pressed my lips to his simply to feel the contradictory softness of his lips and roughness of the surrounding stubble. I let my lips trail over his slowly. It was the first time I'd been the one to make the move.

"To be with you. To be with *my* man."

Wes reached for my hand and led me across the small living room down the hall to his bedroom door. For as much time as I'd spent hanging out with him in the old foreman's house, I'd never been in the bedroom. The space wasn't large, but it was very tidy and sparse, the way I'd imagine Major would keep any personal space of his. A large bed took up most of the room, and a simple chest of drawers held a plastic tray on which lay a few personal items I was surprised to recognize. A wooden hairbrush with a chip out of one corner. A set of dog tags on their chain. A tiny picture frame with the photo of his sister that he'd shown me that night in the jungle. Besides those three things, there was very little of importance in his living quarters, and it made me feel an odd combination of sad and angry. I wanted more for him.

My parents had been right. He deserved a bigger life.

Major's hands landed on my shoulder and his lips on the back of my neck. "What are you thinking?"

"I want you to have everything you've ever wanted," I said softly.

He turned me around and lifted my chin with the back of his index finger. There wasn't a single line of stress on his face, and he looked more at ease than I'd ever seen him. Major huffed out a low laugh. "You have no idea, do you?"

The dimple that rarely appeared was distracting, and his denim-blue eyes were truly beautiful. "Hm?"

"*You* are everything I've ever wanted. You. And now you're here in my bedroom. Even if you let me hold you fully clothed above the bedspread, I would consider myself the luckiest man on earth tonight."

"You deserve more than a half-broken widower who doesn't know what the hell he's doing," I muttered, reaching out to straighten the collar of his shirt. It was only then I realized he'd dressed up for me. He wore a rust and cream checked button-down shirt tucked into pressed chino trousers. "God, you look nice. I'm sorry, I should have said that earlier. Only I don't normally notice what you're wearing, you know? I should though. You're... you're really nice-looking. I've always thought that. Is that weird? Do other men say things like that to each other?"

I looked up at him in an embarrassed panic.

Major's callused thumb brushed lightly along my jaw. His lips widened into an affectionate smile. "Doc, you can say anything you want to me. You already know that. And right now you need to stop worrying so much. I have an idea if you're willing to humor me."

"Okay. Yes. Tell me what to do." I stepped closer and laid my fore-head on his chest, wrapping my arms loosely around his waist. "I feel so stupid."

He dropped a kiss on the top of my head and stepped back out of my embrace. "Go into the kitchen and make us a couple of screwdrivers. You know where everything is. Before you bring them back in here, I want you to take a shot of vodka, okay?"

I couldn't help but grin at him. "Screwdrivers are my favorite."

Major's eyes twinkled. "Yes, I know. Now git." He smacked my ass and moved toward the bed. I tried not to think about what he was doing or planning. Instead, I followed the orders like a good little soldier, taking the shot first thing and gasping as the sharpness hit my throat and nose. By the time I had the ice cubes cracked and out of the tray to add to the tall drinks, I was already feeling a little looser. Major Marian was a smart man.

I returned to the bedroom to find him stretched out on the bed still fully clothed with the exception of his bare feet. His hands were clasped behind his head, and his gaze sent a shiver through me.

I handed him one of the drinks. "Does it bother you that I still call you Major instead of Lieutenant Colonel?" I asked.

He took a big swig of the cold drink before answering. "Doc, you're my best friend, not my subordinate. When you call me Major, I don't hear rank. I hear respect and affection. Just like when I call you Doc, I'm not thinking of your medical abilities."

I took a gulp of my own drink before setting it down on the bedside table. The room was lit by the two lamps on either side of the bed. The warm glow was doing pretty nice things to Major's handsome face. "What would you prefer I call you?" I asked, sitting down next to him and fiddling with the cuff of his shirt. Apparently, I enjoyed touching him.

"Unbutton it please," he said softly. I unbuttoned it without a second thought. He continued. "Doc, I'm fine with you calling me whatever you want. Sometimes I like it when you call me Major because it reminds me of when we first met and it makes me feel a little bit in charge of you which is a turn-on to me. But sometimes you call me by my name and it's like a shot of adrenaline straight to my heart because I'm not used to it and it feels very intimate. So I don't really have an answer for you." He held out his other hand, and I immediately moved to unbutton that cuff. When I was done, I took another sip of the drink.

Major's eyes tracked every movement. When I set the glass back down, he took my hand and moved it up to his chest. "Unbutton my shirt please."

My fingers went to work before my brain kicked in. "Why?" I kept doing as he said, but my nerves had returned too.

"I want you to undress me while you stay fully clothed. That way you can examine me or touch me or just get used to seeing another man naked without feeling too vulnerable."

With every open button, more of his chest hair was revealed. I couldn't keep my eyes off it. There were one or two silver hairs mixed in with the dark ones, and I found myself reaching for them with a fingertip.

"Old man," I teased. "Are you robbing the cradle right now?" Movement under the fly of his pants caught my attention out of the corner of my eye. I gulped and reached for another quick sip of my drink without realizing it. When I returned my hand to his chest, he hissed.

"*Cold.*"

"Sorry." I chuckled. The vodka was doing its job. I moved his open shirt wider, revealing the twin bird tattoos on his chest that matched mine. Lynch, Dial, Major, and I had gotten them in Bangkok after discovering they symbolized safe homecoming.

I skimmed my hand across one. "God, I should have never gotten the same tattoos as you," I said with a laugh. "On you they look all masculine and tough. On me they look ridiculous. Birds on a bird chest."

Major's eyes went dark and hot again. "I'd ask you to show me, but I'm trying not to push, remember?"

I kept my eyes on his as I moved to take off my own shirt. My hands were shaking, but it wasn't like he'd never seen my bare chest before. He had. Plenty of times.

Major's hand came up to rest on one of my own bird tattoos, his thumb brushing lightly along my sternum. My nipples hardened and my dick wasn't far behind. I swallowed before getting up the nerve to straddle his thighs. "This okay?" It came out as more of a squeak, and I closed my eyes in embarrassment.

Major's warm hands landed on my thighs and rubbed up and down them in an effort to reassure me.

"Unbuckle my belt, Liam." His voice rumbled so deeply, I almost lost my breath. What the hell was it about him that suddenly lit all my fires and made me feel inexperienced and desperate to please?

My trembling hands moved to the buckle.

CHAPTER 28

WESTON "MAJOR" MARIAN

Of all the ribbons and medals I'd earned in the service, none were as hard to achieve as keeping myself from flipping Doc onto his back and ripping his clothes off so I could shove myself deep into his body once and for all. The number of times I'd imagined it, had gotten off to it, was staggering. But now that he was here in my bed in the flesh, I was terrified of doing something to scare him off.

His dark pink nipples pearled up, making my mouth water. The bulge in the front of his pants was promising if I could only be patient.

Doc's hands moved to my belt, and the tip of his lip caught between his teeth in concentration. The rasp of the leather through the buckle seemed loud in the quiet bedroom. Doc's chest heaved with a fortifying breath before he spoke.

"It feels weird to be…" His voice faded and his neck and chest turned blotchy red. He took another breath. "It's just… I guess I thought… I mean…" He shook his head with a self-deprecating huff and smirk before meeting my eyes. I held my tongue to give him a chance to get it out. "I thought *you* would be the one undressing *me*."

My cock filled and my balls tightened. "Is that what you want?"

His gorgeous eyes looked unsure and vulnerable, but they didn't look afraid. He nodded. "Yes," he whispered. "I want you to take off my clothes and touch me. Show me what to do to make you feel good. Show me what to do in bed with another man. You're... you're being so careful not to scare me, Wes, but I want this. Want *you.*"

The words were too good to be true. Hearing him say it, believing he felt it, was just... simply unbelievable. It was everything I'd ever wanted with him, and I was terrified it would get yanked away from me at any moment.

I was torn between feeling the need to distrust it and wanting to ignore all my doubts and sink into him—lose myself in him.

I reached down and squeezed myself, trying to stave off an embarrassing situation. My knuckles brushed his crotch, and he let out a groan that damned near pushed me over the edge.

His hands suddenly landed on my chest, and he leaned in to kiss me. I brought my arms around his back and moved one hand up into his hair to hold him close so I could devour his mouth. This time he tasted of orange juice and vodka, so damned sweet.

I flipped him beneath me and ground my hip against his hard cock, making him groan and curse again. After pulling off my shirt and tossing it over the side of the bed, I knelt up and finished unbuckling my belt. All bets were off now, and I couldn't wait to get him naked underneath me.

Doc's eyes were kiss-drunk, and his face was flushed. I leaned in and took one of his nipples into my mouth, sucking gently at first and then harder.

"Wes, fuck." His hand in my hair encouraged me, so I continued tonguing and kissing his nipples and collarbone and neck while my hands fumbled open my fly. Once I got it open, I moved down his body, kissing everywhere and running my fingers along his smooth, pale skin.

Doc's hand stayed in my hair, but his hold gentled until his fingers were caressing my head and cheek. I looked up at him and saw such naked affection in his gaze I almost blurted out how much I loved him and how grateful I was he was sharing himself with me in this way.

His hips arched, pressing his dick into my chest for friction. "Oh god, sorry," he muttered, putting a hand over his face. "Sorry, Wes."

I moved back up to kiss him on the lips. "No sorries. None. I love that you're turned on. I love knowing you can't help it. Sex between two men is different, Doc. You don't have to be afraid of upsetting or offending me. Your desire isn't shameful or too aggressive for me."

He nodded and breathed out. "My dick is so hard right now I need it out of my pants." His shy smile was adorable. "I've never used the word dick during sex before."

I grinned at him. "You've probably never put your mouth on one either. But it's a new day, Dr. Wilde."

He put both hands over his face and laughed. His ears were beet red as I unfastened his fly and pulled his pants off. When I climbed back up the bed, I studied every slender inch of his muscular calves and thighs before peeking up the leg of his boxer shorts and catching sight of dusky pink skin in the shadows.

I dropped a kiss on the blond hair of his inner thigh. God, he smelled amazing. Clean, musky, warm.

As I moved up toward his balls with small openmouthed kisses, he began to squirm and breathe out my name. I nudged up the leg of his boxers with my nose so I could continue kissing a path closer and closer to his sac. When it was clear I couldn't go any farther without removing the boxers, he was the one who spoke.

"You can take them off," he said softly. "Please. Please take them off."

Instead of taking them off right away, I moved off the bed and took off my own pants and boxers. My cock slapped against my lower belly from being so damned hard for him. Doc's eyes landed on it and didn't move. I tried not to think of all the men he'd examined over the course of his medical career, all the dicks he'd undoubtedly seen and cataloged subconsciously in his brain.

"C'mere," he said roughly, reaching out for me.

I climbed back over him and pulled his shorts off, revealing dark blond curls at the base of his dick. I leaned in to bury my nose in them.

Doc bent his knees up on either side of me and put his hands in my hair again. "Christ, Major, are you... *please*."

I put my tongue at the base of his shaft and licked upward before meeting his eyes just in time to see them roll back. He continued murmuring pleas for me to suck him and lick him. His fingers twitched in my hair but never gripped too tightly.

After taking his entire length into my mouth, I began to bob up and down, always watching his face for his reaction. Within seconds, I could feel his balls draw up tight as he got ready to climax. I cupped them gently with one hand.

"Major, Wes, Wes, Major," he babbled. "Gonna—*hnngghhhh!*" His entire body arched as he emptied into my throat, hands clenching in my hair and toes stretching and then curling again.

As I lapped at his spent cock, I held my breath, waiting for the inevitable letdown in which he'd realized he'd just come in another man's mouth and panic.

He looked at me with dazed eyes, almost confused. "I need to, ah..." Doc looked around. "I should..."

"You're not going anywhere," I said, trying to hold back both my hurt feelings and anger.

His eyes widened in surprise. "Even to go clean myself up in the bathroom? Or, um, hand you your drink to, ah, wash your mouth out?"

"There's nothing to clean up. And I don't need to wash your taste from my mouth."

I sat back on my heels with my hands on my thighs trying desperately to ignore my still-hard dick. Suddenly Doc scrambled up and threw his arms around my neck, tackling me onto my back on the mattress and kissing me like a man possessed.

When we had to separate long enough to breathe, I asked, "What the hell? Not that I'm complaining. I just thought you were getting ready to bolt."

Affection was clear on his face. "You thought I was regretting it."

"Well, yes. I was afraid of that, anyway."

Doc's crooked grin squeezed my heart. "Not leaving, not regretting. In fact, I didn't tell you this yet, but I'm staying over."

"All night?" I asked in a higher pitch than I'd intended.

"Yep. Whether you like it or not. I told my parents the hands might have a late-night poker game and I'd probably bunk with them."

I wrapped my legs around the back of his and noticed the scratchy texture of his happy trail on the thin skin of my erection. I pressed up into him and groaned. It would probably only take a few pathetic humps to get off.

The edge of his hairline was damp, and I reached up to brush the hair back from his forehead. "You're even more handsome when you let go."

"You're the handsome one. Ask anyone in Hobie. I can't tell you how many times people ask me to set you up with them." He looked down at my lips and licked his own without realizing it. "Even before, um, Betsy passed… it used to bother me." Doc's eyes flicked back up to see my reaction to that.

"Bothered you that they wanted to date me?"

"Well, I mean… at the time I just thought I was jealous because I didn't want to share your time. If you'd met someone and fallen in love with them, they'd have become your best friend instead of me, plus you'd have moved off the ranch."

I continued running fingers through his silky blond hair. "But I wouldn't have because I'm gay. You already knew that. Plus, my wife would move into this place with me."

His narrowed eyes almost made me laugh. "I didn't say my jealousy was rational, Major. And just hearing you say 'my wife' makes me want to punch something."

I couldn't believe my ears. I sat up and moved him until he straddled my lap with his legs around my back and my arms holding him close. His ass teased my dick, but I tried not to lose focus.

"Tell me more about how you want to keep me all to yourself," I demanded with a euphoric grin.

Doc cupped my cheeks and kissed me softly, slowly, before reaching down and tentatively grasping my hard shaft.

I sucked in a breath. "Ohh fuck, Liam. Yes, just like that."

He moved his lips to my neck and nipped at the thin skin over my pulse while he continued to move his hand up and down my length, squeezing and twisting as if he was jacking himself off.

I grasped the globes of his ass and squeezed, imagining what it would be like to slide between them one day and watch his face as I introduced him to his gland.

"Fuck, god, oh god," I breathed. "Don't stop."

While I looked down, mesmerized at the sight of his pale hand gripping my ruddy cock, he surprised me by taking a swipe over the top with the thumb of his free hand and sneaking it into his mouth for a taste. That was all I needed. I came with a shout all over his fist and stomach.

I laid my head on his chest and panted, feeling the thundering of my heart in my rib cage and the tingly aftershocks of my climax in my legs and groin. After catching my breath, I leaned up and kissed him before gently moving him off my lap so we could clean up.

Doc followed me to the little hallway bathroom and washed his hands in the sink while I turned on the shower. Out of the corner of my eye, I saw him watching me in the mirror. I kept quiet, assuming he needed time to think and process, so I was surprised when he turned and ran his hands along my back to my shoulders and down my arms. He leaned in and pressed his cheek to the top of my spine.

"I think about all the times I've seen you shirtless or completely naked, you know?" he began. "And I've always looked and thought how muscular you were or how strong and manly or how fit. I've admired your body in a way that I always assumed was... like... not really *envy* I don't think. I mean, sure, maybe part of it was wishing I had a body like yours, but it also had this different feel to it than the way I felt looking at other men."

While he tried to put his thoughts into words, I stepped into the tub and pulled him in after me, nudging him under the spray and closing the curtain.

He rinsed off before changing places with me and continuing. "I looked at your body and thought how strong and capable my best friend was. How you could protect me with a body like that or fight next to me if I ever needed it. It was like... I looked at your body and thought of how much I liked it in a way that *involved me*. Does that make sense? Like, I could look at another man showering on base and think, 'Yeah, he's good-looking and fit,' but it wasn't the same as when I looked at you. It wasn't as *personal*. I wonder now if I was sexually attracted to you all along and just didn't see it."

"It must be confusing for you. Had you ever been sexually attracted to a man before?" I reached for the shampoo and poured some into my hands. Doc's fingers gripped my hips, his thumbs moving up my sides without conscious thought.

"You know, it's funny. There was a night in Bangkok, do you remember it? Where you went out to get laid and came back frustrated?"

After shampooing both of us, I reached for the bar of soap. I pictured him in that Bangkok hotel bed only two feet from me. "Yeah, I remember. It was the only time in our lives we slept in the same room. Of course I remember it, Doc."

"I thought about letting you fuck me."

The bar of soap shot out of my fist and hit the tiled wall before banging to the floor and ricocheting around the ceramic tub walls until it landed on the drain.

My dick filled and stood at attention within seconds, enough to make me say a little cheer for forty-year-old men still having it.

"Jesus Christ, Doc. What the... *what?*"

CHAPTER 29

LIAM "DOC" WILDE

Between the soap rocket and the expression on his face, I couldn't hold back laughter. I howled with it. "Oh my gosh," I cried. "Where is a camera when you need one?"

His hands gripped my shoulders, and he leaned down to meet my eyes. "Story. Now."

I loved it when my Major got bossy. It had always gotten my attention in an odd way, but now with the added sexual attraction between us, it did things to me that were new and exciting.

"Can we get in bed first? I want some more of my drink." I was mostly stalling for time. When the subject of anal sex came up between us for the first time, I wasn't sure if it would make him want to try it. And I wasn't quite ready for that. It wasn't like I thought he'd pressure me, but I still didn't want to disappoint him.

Major turned off the water and reached across me to grab two towels from a nearby hook. We dried quickly and returned to the bedroom where it felt at once strange and also natural to climb into bed next to Major's naked body.

We sat side by side, propped up against the headboard enough to enjoy our drinks, and like before, my hands naturally sought out a physical connection with him. I reached for his free hand with mine, and our fingers automatically threaded together.

After setting my drink aside, I turned to face him and scooted down a bit until my head was propped on the pillows. "You looked so sad that night, and I felt like it was all my fault. I hated thinking of you being in need." I drew fingertips along the dark hair scattered on his forearm. "So I thought about what it would be like if I offered myself up to you like that." I turned onto my back and looked at the ceiling. "I was watching your wide shoulders and muscular back through your undershirt. And, um, your shirt had ridden up. So there was this... hey, turn over onto your stomach."

It took him a second to process what I'd said, but then he moved over and flipped. I ran a fingertip across his lower back, right above the crack of his ass.

"Here," I whispered. "I could see it and... and it just made you look... god, I don't know. But I thought about what it would be like. And I wondered what you liked in a man and what you..." I swallowed thickly. "What you did with a man in bed. What you liked to do or to have done to you."

Goose bumps had prickled along his skin where I touched. Major's head was turned in my direction, and his eyes bored into me. "It wasn't your fault that I wanted you more than any of the men in the city that night, Doc. It's funny because I got out there to a club I'd heard about, and my plan was to find someone to get my mind off of you for at least a little while. But the whole time I was there I realized I'd rather be lying in that crappy hotel room listening to you snore than thrusting into some stranger's body for a quick release."

"I don't snore," I lied, trying not to picture him thrusting into a stranger's body.

Major's grin was adorable. "You're such a bad liar, it's comical. When your dad finds out you weren't at the hands' poker game, I'm going to tell him I had to distract you all night with other things to keep you from betting away the ranch. Before you know it, I'll have him thanking me for keeping you in my house overnight."

At the mention of my dad, something must have changed on my face.

"Doc, you know I don't expect you to tell them, right?" he asked softly. "They don't need to know your private business."

"They think gay is a perversion."

He sighed and looked sad, but it was a sadness for me more than himself. "Of course they do. That's what they've been taught at church, same as you."

"I guess I just don't see what the big deal is if it's private and no one else's business. It wasn't anyone's business what I did with Betsy in the bedroom, so why would it be anyone's business what I do with you here?"

"If it's any consolation, I think things are changing a little bit. But yeah, it's tough. Especially here in Hobie. Maybe it would be different in California or something," Major said with a shrug. "But I really like farming and ranching, Doc. And I love this land. And the kids love their safe, small town. I don't think we should have to leave the things we love in order to live more openly."

His use of the word "we" startled me at first. Again, he could read me like an open book.

"Doc, I'm not expecting anything," he began carefully. "I don't want you to—"

I swallowed and met his eye. "What if... Wes, what if *I* do? What if I want more than just trying it on?"

He turned on his side and pulled me in close, our legs tangling together under the sheets and blankets. "Then we will figure it out together, and we will find a way to make it work. You know I'd do anything to make you happy, right?"

I did. More than anything. He'd always shown me how important I was to him. The reminder filled me up with such warmth and hope, longing and rightness. This man was home to me, and even if our physical relationship was brand-spanking-new, I was 100 percent convinced my future was tightly woven together with his from here on out.

"I, um." I did an internal check for the millionth time to be sure of what I meant before I put the thought into words. I never wanted to hurt him or give him false promises. Major's usual stoic calmness prevailed. He waited while I gathered my courage.

"I love you, Wes. So much." I choked on the last word, the enormity of what was happening between us slamming into me and taking my breath away.

In the blink of an eye, his lips were on mine, a mixture of savage and possessing, tender and sweet. He absolutely owned my mouth and my body, and part of me sat by, idly wondering how it had all happened so quickly and fully. But another part of me knew it didn't matter.

This was simply how it was between us now.

I was his and he was mine. It was that easy.

Except, of course, it wasn't.

CHAPTER 30

WESTON "MAJOR" MARIAN

Not only did Doc sleep over that night, safe and secure and sexy as hell in my arms, but he managed to stay over two more nights over the course of the next few weeks. I tried like hell to take things slow between us since I knew the minute any inkling of our new relationship got out, there would be big trouble not only with his family but with the entire town. I may have been a well-respected retired lieutenant colonel from the army and foreman to the large Hobart farm, but in many Hobians' eyes, I was a simple cowhand. And luring the vaunted Dr. William Wilde over to the dark side would make me persona non grata in a skinny minute.

So during the day, especially around his parents and the kids, we were best friends as usual. Well, probably less so than usual because I was so worried about my feelings for him showing like neon lights on my face.

But those few times he was able to sneak away to my house and we could be ourselves together made up for it. We'd gotten ourselves off with quick mutual masturbation sessions, and then I'd teased him for over an hour with my mouth everywhere on his body before sucking him down while sliding a finger inside him and introducing him to his prostate. He'd been so thankful, he'd even offered to reciprocate by trying his hand at a blowjob. But his blissed-out face and half-lidded eyes were too sweet to ignore. "Sleep, sweetheart," I'd murmured to him. And then I'd watched him fall into slumber with a goofy grin on his face.

Summer was a busy time for me on the farm. Thankfully we had extra help including Billy, who'd begged me for a more official job now that he was twelve. We'd sat and had a mock interview in which I asked his interests, strengths, and weaknesses. Both of us were surprised to discover he got most excited when we talked about finances and accounting rather than the physical work outside we'd both assumed he'd prefer.

So I took him to talk to Stan, and we came up with a plan. In the morning he'd do his usual work outside whether it be on the farm or ranch, and in the afternoons when the heat got too much, he'd spend some time checking our invoices against the ledger and bank book. It would be a good way for him to start learning the money side of how an agriculture business worked while also giving our books a good double-check.

He was so excited and proud that when Doc arrived home from work that afternoon, Billy almost burst with it. We'd been sitting on the front porch, and Billy jumped up to race to his dad's side. "Guess what? Uncle Major hired me to be his accountant!"

Doc's eyes flashed over to me with his usual crooked grin. He swooped Jackie up into his arms and gave her a loud kiss on the cheek. "Did he? Smart man. What say we celebrate your promotion with dinner out at Dairy Queen? I know Jackie here doesn't much like ice cream, but the rest of us—"

"Daddyyyyyy!" Jackie cried. "I do, I *do* wike it."

"What do you say, Major? Dinner out as a family?"

I could see the happiness and hope in his eyes, and I wanted so much for it to be real—for him to get the happy ever after he wanted and deserved.

But he'd never been gay in public before, and the world wasn't going to take kindly to two men raising kids together in our small town.

I nodded. "Should I tell Stan and Lois?"

"No, I called and told them we were taking the kids out to give them a night to themselves. I thought maybe we'd go see the new Benji movie afterward. The girls have been asking."

Billy piped up asking if we could go see a deep-sea treasure-hunting movie instead, but he knew there was no way the girls could go to that one.

"Uncle Major and I could go. You and the girls could see the kids' movie," he said.

"Uncle Major wants to see Benji," I corrected. "But I'll share a Coke and popcorn with you. How about that?"

He grinned, almost the same as Doc. "Yeah, okay. And I can sit next to you? I mean, I'll have to for us to share."

I messed up his hair. "Of course. But I want Jackie on my other side so I'll have someone's hand to hold in case it gets scary."

Jackie giggled and held her arms out for me. I took her from Doc and propped her on my hip. She was getting so big.

Doc told Billy to run go tell his sisters to get their shoes on and get ready. Once he was gone, he grinned up at me. "Dang, Major. I was hoping to sit next to you at the theater," he said with a wink. "What if I get scared?"

Before I could tease him back, Lois came out of the house. I could tell by the way she was dressed she had plans to go into town for the evening.

"Room for one more?" she asked with a false cheer.

Doc's eyes flicked to me before glancing back at her. "Uh, sure. Of course. But I thought you and Dad were—"

"Jackie, run on inside, sweetie. See what's taking the girls so long," she said.

I set her down, and she took off inside the house calling for Gina and Brenda to hurry.

Lois looked more awkward than I'd ever seen her.

"What is it, Mom?" Doc asked.

"Billy said you and Weston were both going."

"Yes."

"Well, I just think… I mean… it will look strange, that's all."

Oh hell.

I glanced at Doc. "I can stay here."

Doc's forehead creased. "What? No. Don't be ridiculous. You're coming with us."

"Honey, maybe he's right. You know how people in town talk, and if you and the major go to dinner and a movie together with the kids you'll look like… well… a family, you know?"

Uh-oh. I knew Doc's angry face well. It didn't come out often, but when it did, it was no joke.

"We *are* a family," he said through clenched teeth.

"You know what I mean, Liam," she said with a frustrated sigh.

"Mom—"

The way he said it set off alarm bells. This was *not* the time to come out to his mother. The situation needed to be diffused ASAP.

"Doc," I said with a cough. "You remember Letty, whose son Chuck plays baseball with Billy?"

He stared at me in confusion before the lightbulb went on. "Yeah. The one who's always trying to set you up with her sisters?"

Bingo.

"Maybe we should see if they want a burger and a movie too," I said with a wink.

So that's what we did. And damned if that wasn't what started all the trouble. Sometimes when you choose a path without thinking, when a spur-of-the-moment decision sends you catapulting toward the inevitable whether you realize it or not, you can trace it back to one stupid moment, one idiotic decision.

Inviting those twin sisters out with us that night was it.

CHAPTER 31

LIAM "DOC" WILDE

At the time, I thought it was a brilliant plan. Hide my date with Major under a double date with two women. Easy, right? And it was. That first night.

But then we got the harebrained idea to do it again. There was a new roadhouse out on the county highway toward Valley Cross, and they had pool tables and dartboards. We'd already been just the two of us a few times, but the last time we'd been in, Major had overheard someone refer to us as the Bobbsey Twins and he'd gotten worried about my reputation. I'd told him to shove my reputation, but he'd somehow convinced me it would be a good idea to ask the girls out again.

So that's how we ended up at the Nutcase Roadhouse with Bonnie and Deb. They were both super sweet. I knew Deb from work at the clinic. She was one of Dr. Holben's nurses, but I'd still shied away from being too personal with her. Her sister Bonnie had gotten a job at the regional hospital in the labor and delivery ward, so I focused on asking her how she liked it there.

Deb was perfectly happy to flirt her fool head off with Major. Clearly she felt that she'd won the lottery as soon as he'd taken the seat next to her in the red vinyl booth by the pool tables, which was funny because I felt the same way the minute his cowboy boot slid alongside my loafer and pressed in. I looked at him over the top of my beer glass. His denim blues met mine.

Why in the world hadn't we just stayed home to watch television and make out on his sofa?

As Deb and Bonnie chatted animatedly throughout the night, Major's and my eyes couldn't help but meet from time to time and pass unspoken messages across the wooden table. I was struck by how different it was to spend time in the company of someone you knew almost as well as yourself than to spend time getting to know new people. But since we'd invited the ladies out with us, I tried very hard to give them plenty of attention.

Major wasn't nearly as good at it. What they didn't know was that he was simply a quiet man. He was a better listener than talker. He was a steady rock who didn't get riled up over little things, so he wasn't the best person to gossip with if he didn't know the players involved. Because of his sexuality, he tended to keep himself apart from people which meant he *didn't* know any of the players involved most of the time.

At one point a man I recognized as a mechanic who worked at the same marina where Letty's husband worked came over and asked Deb to dance. She looked downright offended since she was clearly there on a date with Major. As far as she knew.

"No, thank you, Randy. I'm fixing to dance with the lieutenant colonel here in a minute."

That was news to Wes but he simply nodded agreeably.

Randy's eyes narrowed at Wes before turning to me. "You saying you'd rather be out with these baby killers than—"

"Watch it," Major said in a low voice. Since he'd served so much longer than I had, he'd experienced military prejudice more than I had. It still shocked me. "You don't know what you're talking about."

"Did you serve in Vietnam or not?" he asked. His tone was loud enough to draw the attention of his friends from around the nearest pool table. They wandered over and stood behind him, eyeing us. "Did you kill innocent people for no good reason or not?"

The faces of the men we'd killed were nothing compared to the faces of all the American soldiers we'd saved. All the young men who'd gotten to return home to their families because of Major's phenomenal command of a medevac operation. I started shaking with anger and a little bit of fear. If those men wanted a fight, I would stand no chance.

Major stood up slowly, towering over the man despite Randy's muscular frame.

"Please leave us in peace," he said slowly and calmly. "If your issue is with me, you're welcome to find me another time when I'm not out with these nice ladies."

"Peace isn't something you'd know much about, is it, *LT*?" The man spat at Major's feet, and that was enough for me. I stood up and hauled my fist back, but Major grabbed my elbow before I could take the swing. His other arm came around my waist and hauled me back.

"None of that," he said low enough for only me to hear. "We'll just get out of here and go somewhere else."

There wasn't really anywhere else. We were a one-horse town that rolled up its sidewalks at eight on the dot.

I pulled out of his grip, still angrier than hell. "No. We're not leaving. We served our country while these pissants stayed home and did shit-all. They have no idea what it was like over there!" My voice wobbled and cracked, and I could tell by the look on Major's face that he thought I was going to lose it.

He was right.

"C'mon, ladies," Major said to Deb and Bonnie. "We'll drop you at home."

The girls started scooting out of the booth when Deb batted her eyelashes at my... major. "Let's go back to your place and continue the party."

Maybe he wanted to poke a stick at Earl or maybe he was willing to agree to anything just to get us out of there, but Major nodded. "All right, let's go."

Thankfully, Randy and his thug friends let us leave without further incident. We made our way out to the car and drove back to the ranch in relative quiet. It wasn't until we parked outside of Major's house that I realized what a mistake this was.

How in the world were we going to take these two into the house without raising false expectations of more than a few drinks?

Well, it turns out one option was to concentrate too much on the drinks. Within an hour of sitting around the kitchen table talking and listening to music—and drinking screwdrivers—I was a few hairs past a freckle.

Bonnie was giggling and leaning into me. Somehow her chair had gotten progressively closer to mine over time. At one point Deb had pulled one of Major's big hands into her two small ones to "read his palm" which I assumed was Deb-speak for getting his sexy mitts on her.

I ignored it and doubled down on talking to Bonnie until Major's growl caught my ear.

"It's time I drove you ladies home."

I blinked at him and found him staring at me. I knew that look. That was the look that told me to get naked and wait in his bed.

"I think maybe I need to lie down. Ladies, will you be very mad at me if I don't accompany you home?" I tried pulling the puppy dog face.

Bonnie looked disappointed but rallied anyway. "Will you walk me out?"

Oh hell.

"Um, sure." I followed them out to the truck and thanked them profusely for a nice night. When it was clear Bonnie was waiting for a kiss, I leaned in and kissed her cheek. Not daring to look at Major, I waved and turned for the house. As soon as I got to the bedroom, I stripped down and jumped under the covers to wait. I was asleep within seconds.

Sometime later I woke up to the feel of scratchy whiskers on my back, soft lips on my skin, and a slick finger circling my hole.

"Oh *god*." I gasped in relief knowing he was back, he was here, and he wanted me like this. The evening's events had been a strange kind of hours-long foreplay, and even though I'd passed out on him, I was desperate for a physical connection. "Want your fingers," I muffled into the pillow. "Feels good."

He pressed one inside, and I arched back to take more. I bent one leg up to give him more room and tilted my hips back at him like a wanton horndog.

"Mine," he grunted as he slid a second slippery finger inside of me. "*Mine mine mine.*"

The growly possessiveness made my dick ache. "Yours," I moaned, humping back into him in an effort to find a rhythm. "Please, Wes."

His lips nibbled at my ear lobe. "I love you," he breathed. "I love you so much, Liam."

"Show me," I choked out. "Make love to me. I'm ready."

When his lubricated dick began pressing in, I sucked in a breath and panicked at first.

"Shhh," he whispered in his calm way. "I've got you. We're going slowly, just relax, sweetheart. Breathe for me."

I knew that in my brain, but my body needed reminding. I took a deep breath and forced myself to calm down. His thick length pushed a little farther inside.

"So damned tight, Liam," he muttered behind me. "You're killing me. Breathe, baby, that's it."

Suddenly it seemed easier. His length continued to slide into me, and I ended up pushing back for more. When Wes pulled out and pushed back in, we both groaned in pleasure.

"More," I begged. "Again."

The rumble of his laugh made me so damned happy. It was one of my favorite sounds.

"You feel so good." He groaned hotly into the back of my hair. The hand he'd used to spread one of my ass cheeks open moved around to grasp my dick, which almost set me right off.

"Christ, Major, fuck. Yeah, jack me, shit." I made a choking sound, almost inhaling my own drool like an idiot. More rumbling laughter behind me warmed me from the inside. A happy Major was the best thing in the world.

He did a little move with his thumb on my cock that made me see stars. My eyes rolled back, and I almost broke his nose with my skull, but I didn't care because at the same time, the head of his cock brushed against that spot inside that sent me into the stratosphere.

"Coming," I gasped. "Coming, Jesus. Oh god, *Wes*."

Sticky fluid shot out onto the sheets as I clamped down on him and came. My brain was like late-night television static for a few beats until I sucked in another breath. Major's sticky hand was clamped over my heart now, and his thrusts pounded into me twice more before he shoved in hard one last time and stayed there. The muffled sound of his bit-back whimpers surprised me.

When he finally pulled out, I turned over to face him. "Why did you hold back with me?"

He looked confused for a beat until he realized what I meant. His hand came up to cup my cheek, and his smile was sweet. "I didn't want to deafen you. My mouth was right by your ear, and I knew I was going to roar if I wasn't careful."

I grinned and kissed him. "I love you too," I said softly after a while. "I don't ever want you to doubt it for even a minute."

His thumb brushed my cheek. "I don't."

I laid my head on his chest and snuggled closer. "We shouldn't have taken the sisters out."

"No, we shouldn't have. I'm sorry. It was my stupid idea."

"I agreed to it. Anyway, let's just forget it. No harm, no foul."

Major didn't say anything, but I felt his body tense. I lifted my head up and met his eyes with a lifted brow.

He sighed. "Deb came onto me after I dropped Bonnie off."

I moved to sit up, leaning back against the headboard and pulling the sheet up with me. "I thought they lived together."

"They do. But Bonnie had me drop her off at Letty's place for some reason."

"Christ, Major. *Some reason*? Yeah, it was so she could get you at her place alone." My arms crossed in front of my chest. "*Christ*," I repeated for good measure.

Major grinned, dimple and all.

"Don't be cute," I muttered. "What'd you do?"

185

He shrugged. "I slept with her. Figured it was easier than—"

I tackled him and held his wrists above his head. "Asshole," I accused. "Don't even joke about that."

Major's face got serious. "She made a play for me, Liam. I had to tell her no."

"Well, I mean, sometimes that happens. Why is it such a big deal?"

"She got a look on her face, and I have a bad feeling about it. She didn't want to take no for an answer."

"She'll get over it. And anyway, I don't want to talk about her." I kissed him because I couldn't not. "We had sex."

"We did," Major said with a satisfied grin. He moved his hands down to squeeze my butt. "You're a ringer."

"Stop. Wait, don't stop. Tell me I'm the best ass you've ever had," I teased, batting my eyelashes. "Tell me my body was made for you. Tell me—"

"I love you."

My breath caught. "Even better," I said softly. "Never fails to surprise me for some reason."

He laughed and moved his hands up my back, burying one in my hair. "It shouldn't. It's been like this for a while now."

I thought about Betsy, and for the first time, I saw my marriage from his point of view. I imagined our roles reversed where he was married with kids while I had a hopeless crush on him. My chest hurt and my throat thickened. "God, Major, how did you stand it? If you had feelings for me while I was with Betsy… I couldn't have stayed here like you did. I wouldn't have been strong enough."

His strong fingers massaged my scalp. His eyes looked at me like I was the second coming of Christ. It was heady, being on the receiving end of his affection.

"You would have stayed because you wouldn't have had a choice, Doc. Having one tiny, narrow shaft of sunlight is so much better than living in full darkness. With you around, I always had some sun. Did I wish for more? Every day. But I was lucky, you know? I loved Betsy enough to want her drenched in the light too. It wasn't that I wished she didn't have it. I just wanted it too."

My love for Weston Marian bloomed full and wild like the acres and acres of wildflowers we were always trying to tame on some of our grazing land. He was truly the kindest, most generous person I'd ever known. Not only was I grateful to have him in my life, but I was doubly thankful that my children had him as a role model.

We drifted back to sleep in each other's arms and woke up with the sun. I made my way back to the farmhouse to spend my day off with the kids, and Major got ready to work. He and the hands were doing some repair work on one of the equipment barns at the farm. I didn't hear from him or see him for the rest of the weekend, which was strange. Normally he showed up at the farmhouse for most meal-times, and he especially rarely missed Sunday dinner.

My mom had sent Billy out to the equipment barn to take the guys some big thermoses of lemonade and a tin of cookies late Sunday afternoon. When he returned, I overheard him mention Major's black eye to my mom.

My heart jumped. "What did you say? How did he get a black eye?"

Billy turned to me after handing the dirty thermoses to Mom. "He told me it was a stupid accident. I asked Jonny about it, and he said Major banged his face into the kitchen sink pipe when the phone rang and startled him. I guess he was working under there." He shrugged. "It looks worse than it is. He told me not to tell you, Dad. He knew you'd be upset."

"Of course I'm upset. I'm a doctor. He's my... friend."

"He's fine. The man's a soldier like you, Dad. I'm sure he's had much worse," Billy said before wandering off.

I stood up. "I'm going to run over there and check on him."

My mom turned from the sink where she'd been washing the ther-moses and dried her hands on a kitchen towel. "Liam, honey. You need to stop treating Major like he's one of your kids."

That stopped me in my tracks. If she only knew. "I don't treat him like one of the kids, Mom."

"You act like he can't protect himself. Like he needs looking after. The two of you have gotten so close since Betsy's death, I feel like maybe it's time you should give him some space."

"Of course we got close. He's my best friend, and lord only knows where I would have been without him this past year."

"I'm just saying maybe you two don't need to be in each other's pockets so much. There are rumors about him in town, and I'm afraid you might get caught up in them."

My blood ran cold. "What rumors?"

Mom looked flustered. "You know the things they say about men who are still single over forty, Liam. *Those* kind of rumors."

If I was already tired of hearing about people's prejudices, I couldn't even imagine how Major felt. To think he'd had to live his entire life in the shadows because of it just made me angry. Furious.

"And what if it's true, Mom? Would that be so bad?"

"Liam!" My mother gasped. "Don't even joke about such a thing."

"I'm not joking. Why is it anyone's business? Why can't a man's love life be his own concern?"

She studied me. "It's our concern when he's like an uncle to your children. When he's in charge of all the hands for the farm and ranch, some of whom are impressionable young men away from home for the first time. Son, even if it didn't matter to *us*, it would matter to the entire town. We would be a laughingstock. The kids would be ostracized. If he really is—" She lowered her voice in case maybe Jesus was listening. "—a homosexual, then we need to consider encouraging him to move along. It would be best for everyone."

The reality of my life, my decisions, my actions hit me like a kick to the chest. My father had always taught me that decisions had repercussions, and this was one of those times I couldn't deny the truth of it.

What had I been thinking? That we could just... be together? Like a true couple, a real family? Was I crazy? What had I been thinking? I *hadn't* been thinking.

My mom was right. The kids would be bullied. All the farm hands and ranch hands would quit. Well, some of them anyway. And my father's life's work would be all for nothing. My parents would be whispered about behind their backs and left out of events at the church.

I'd known all of that. Of course I had. But I hadn't stopped to be deliberate about my actions. I hadn't thought to sit Major down and go through what we could and couldn't do if we wanted to be together like this. I needed to talk to him.

But before that, I needed to think through what was best for my children, my parents. Me.

My mom's cool hand covered mine. "I know you love him like a brother, Liam. I know this is hard for you."

I looked up at her, trying desperately not to cry like a child. "You have no idea, Mom." I wanted her to understand. I wanted her not to be a bigot like everyone else. "When you... when you're facing the enemy and you have to make a split-second decision about who lives and dies... well, it puts a lot of things into perspective. Even when you have to decide when to take a man's leg off, you don't stop and think about his race, his sexuality, where he's from, or whether or not he has a family back home. You think about his quality of life, his health, his happiness. Period. In Vietnam I learned about what was really important, Mom. And if that man—" My voice cracked. "If that man is happiest in the arms of another man, I will shout my thanks to the heavens that he is happy and whole and here with us, and that he's found the love he deserves."

I mumbled an excuse me and made my way upstairs to the privacy of my own room before I broke down completely. I fell asleep and didn't get woken up for supper which was probably for the best. Eventually I rallied enough to put the girls to bed. We were reading *The Lion, The Witch and The Wardrobe* together, so I knew they wouldn't have let me skip it anyway.

I tried calling Major, but there was no answer. Despite knowing he would have welcomed me there, I forced myself not to go over to his house to check on him and spend some time with him before bed. But since I had an early shift at the clinic in the morning, I went to bed instead.

The next day was nuts at the clinic the way it always is on Mondays, so I didn't have time to tune in to the gossip. But when I moved from one patient room to another, I heard a nurse telling

LUCY LENNOX

another about the man they'd found beaten half to death out on one of the lesser-traveled country roads. It was nowhere near the ranch, thank god, so I didn't do much more than send up a little prayer for the man and his doctors over at the regional hospital. Until I realized one of the nurses was Deb and she said something about the bastard deserving what he got.

"What are you talking about? Who is it?" I asked.

She didn't even need to say his name. I could tell by the guilty look on her face it was Major.

I dropped everything and ran.

CHAPTER 32

WESTON "MAJOR" MARIAN

I hadn't told Doc the whole story of what had happened with Deb. As soon as I'd brushed off her advances, she'd accused me of being gay. Not in those words, of course. She'd spat nasty slurs and threatened to out me to everyone in town. After retiring from the army, I'd sworn to myself I'd never blatantly lie about my sexuality again, so I didn't lie to her. I simply apologized for upsetting her and went on my way.

It came as no surprise that she went right out the following day and flapped her jaws all over town, or at least to her family and friends. When I stopped at the filling station Saturday evening before going to the market for some beer, the man behind the counter looked at me funny. Unlike at the main full-service station in town, this one was farther off the beaten path and had pretty bad turnover behind the cashier counter.

"Evening," I said as I pulled out my wallet. "Frankie's stays open till eight, right?"

"Mpfh," he grunted. "You're the one they's been talking about, ain't you?"

"Can't say I know what you mean. Thanks," I said, pocketing the change.

As I turned to leave, he muttered something about laying down with dogs and getting up with fleas. I made my way out of the little building and walked toward my truck, feeling the hairs on the back of my neck prickle.

When I got to the shop to get the beer, Letty's husband, Phil, was waiting out front. I walked up to greet him and he took a swing at me, right there in front of Frankie's. I staggered back, clutching my face.

"What was that for?" I asked, even though I could have guessed.

"For leading my sister-in-law on, you pussy."

"Phil, you and I both know I didn't lead her on. We went out twice. You're mad because I didn't sleep with her by the second date? Jesus."

Before he could take another swing at me or say anything more, I stepped into the store where Frankie, a huge guy with an even bigger brother who'd served in Nam, greeted me pleasantly.

"Your jaw still work, LT?" he asked. "What the hell was that for?"

"Apparently, someone around here doesn't kiss and tell. And by that, let me emphasize the *doesn't kiss* part," I muttered, reaching into one of the coolers for a six-pack.

"Yeah, I heard you got stuck with the feisty one. Probably for the best. I can see Doc Wilde and Bonnie making a sweet pair." He punched the price of my beer into his register. "He deserves it after losing poor Betsy."

I made a noncommittal noise and paid for my beer. Thankfully Phil was gone when I came out of the shop, and my drive home was uneventful.

But the next night, I didn't even have to leave the ranch property. A group of men caught me at the end of my long drive checking the mail I'd forgotten to get the day before. This time, there was no holding back. Phil, Randy, and a couple of the other guys who worked in the machine shop at the marina all took turns whaling on me and screaming gay slurs at me until I couldn't stay up any longer. And once I was on the ground, it wasn't long before it was lights-out.

My last thoughts were of Liam and the kids and how very lucky I was I'd known what true love and family were before I died.

~

I WANTED to stay under where it was fuzzy and painless, but someone I loved was screaming in agony. How could I rest here while he was so upset? After struggling to open one of my eyes, I saw Doc being held back by a strong orderly. Tears and snot covered his face, and he was screaming for all he was worth.

"Weston! Wes, wake up, goddammit! Wes!"

I blinked open the other eye and tried to tell him I was awake, but there was something in my throat. My eyes barely opened at all, but I could see him.

Baby, I'm here. I'm okay.

"Weston," he cried. "Please, please don't leave me. *Please.*"

He finally pulled out of the orderly's hold and came tripping toward me. I tried to hold out my hand, but only a finger twitched.

"Sir. Dr. Wilde, we need to work on him," a voice said from my other side. I couldn't turn my head to see who was speaking. "You know as well as anyone how critical these first hours are. We need to get him into surgery."

Doc's hands shook as they held the sides of my head too softly for me to feel. He met my eyes.

The deep blue China Sea.

"I love you," he said firmly, unafraid of anyone hearing him. He looked fierce despite the tears. "And you're going to come out of this if I have to drag you kicking and screaming. Do you hear me, Major?"

I blinked to tell him I heard him. The pain was overwhelming, and the thought of surgery meant I could at least escape the pain for a little while.

He leaned in and pressed a kiss to my forehead and then a soft one to the edge of my lips before saying the words again more softly this time. "I love you so much. When you get better, we'll go away. We'll take the kids to California or New York. Or maybe Miami. But I'm not living without you, do you understand? I'm not losing you too."

And it was that last word that saw me through the pain and agony of the following days. I would not let William Wilde lose another person in his life who loved him as much as he deserved.

When I was finally well enough to start coming off the heavy sedatives, I realized Doc looked almost worse than I did. Every time I opened my eyes, he was there, either on the chair or on a little cot in the corner of the room.

"Baby?" I croaked when I could finally move my throat enough to speak. Doc woke with a start and jumped up, rushing to my side and grabbing the hand that didn't have an IV in it. I squeezed it a little to let him know I was there even though I wasn't sure I could say another word until I got something to drink.

"Wes, hi. Oh my god, you're awake." His bloodshot eyes filled, and I wondered how many tears he'd shed while I'd been happily high on pain meds.

"Water," he said, snapping his fingers. "Hang tight."

As soon as I got a few sips down, he sat beside my hip on the bed and ran his fingers through my hair.

"Hi, beautiful," he said with an affectionate but worried smile. "You're still here."

One of my legs was hanging up in some kind of contraption, and I had aches and pains in too many places to count, but I was alive. "Still here," I said in a rough voice. "Love you."

His chin wobbled and he tried to breathe away the tears.

"It's okay, Doc. I'm fine. But it's okay to cry too."

He leaned in and pressed his face in the crook of my neck before letting go. His arm lay across my chest, but he was clearly trying not to put any weight on it. I wrapped my arms around him as much as I could and held him while he cried.

Doc took a fortifying breath and pulled back, wiping angrily at his face. "As soon as you're well enough to move, we're leaving. I'm not staying here in this godforsaken—"

"Shh," I said, reaching out to try and smooth away his tears too. He was so damned beautiful it took my breath away. Maybe it was the pain meds still talking, but I just wanted to stare at him like an idiot and drink him in. "We're not leaving."

"Oh yes we are," he said, narrowing his eyes. "I'm not letting these good old boys get their hands on you again with their ignorance and their hate."

"We're going to raise your kids on their family's land and show them how to combat hate, Liam. We're going to at least try it first. We're going to give our friends and neighbors the benefit of the doubt and teach them that we're a family just like they are, only a little different."

If his chin trembled one more time, I was going to be the one bawling.

"Our kids," he said.

"What?"

"*Our* kids. Yours and mine. Our kids."

Well, now he'd gone and done it. Tears flowed down my face until I couldn't see him clearly anymore.

"This is a lot to wake up to," I mumbled, reaching out for a tissue.

Doc snorted a laugh and leaned over to kiss me on the lips, and that's when his parents walked in.

"William!" His mother gasped, and his father froze in his tracks. I pulled away from Doc quickly, but he reached to pull me back closer again.

"You already know I love him," he said with a firm chin now. "And I'm not hiding it anymore even if I could. Everyone in town's already figured it out seeing as how I threw myself over his body like a war widow when he almost died."

Doc grasped my hand and held on tightly. "We're together. Forever. This is it for me, Mom and Dad, and I hope... I really, really hope you can be happy for me. Because Weston Marian makes me so happy. And no one has ever loved me as much as he does. And I've never wanted someone's happiness the way I want his. I'd do anything to make him happy and to ease his pain."

Lois had begun crying. When Doc realized it, he squeezed my hand and stood up to wrap his arm around her. "Mom, I know you loved Betsy dearly. So did I. But she's gone. And she approved of Wes. The children adore him. He's a good man, and he takes care of our family and our legacy."

While he spoke to his mother, Stan edged closer to me and reached out for the hand Doc had released.

195

"How are you feeling, son?"

That word was everything. I was so choked up, I couldn't answer, so I nodded instead.

"We were worried about you," Stan said. His voice sounded almost as emotional as it had when we'd lost Betsy. "I'm so glad you're okay. Don't worry about anything at home. Jonny found a couple of temporary hands to fill in while you recover, and Billy's been keeping an eye out on your place. He made me promise not to tell you he's riding Thunder in your absence, but I told him you wouldn't mind."

"No, sir. He needs the exercise or he'll get ornery."

Stan nodded and released my hand with a final squeeze. "That's exactly what I told him. Hurry up and get better, Major. We miss you. And, uh... well, I think I might want to talk about you taking over the reins soon at the ranch. If you're up for it."

Doc's hand was clapped over his mouth as his eyes met mine.

"Yes, sir," I said, clearing my throat. "Yes, sir. I'd be honored. And I won't let you down."

"Course not." Stan walked back over toward Doc and clasped his shoulders. "We are your parents first and foremost. When God sent you into our lives after all the years we'd tried for a family and failed, well, we knew we'd cherish you no matter what. We were simply grateful to have a baby, a son. And when you came back whole from Nam, in part because of that man there in that hospital bed, we were even more grateful. So you aren't going to lose us no matter what. Now, I'm not saying it's going to be easy living in this small town with a lifestyle people don't know much about. But you two are some of the bravest men I know. If anyone can do it, you can. We love you, son."

Doc stepped into his father's arms and embraced him. I closed my eyes and thanked any god who was willing to listen for putting me on that helicopter with William Wilde all those years before.

CHAPTER 33

LIAM "DOC" WILDE

It wasn't easy, living in Hobie, Texas, in 1977 as a gay man. Well, as a bisexual man in my case. But it wasn't as hard as we'd expected either. We realized very quickly there were quite a few people in town whose deep respect for Weston didn't waver much when they discovered he liked men.

He'd already spent several years putting down solid roots in town. He'd volunteered at the vocational rehab center and had spent years doing free upkeep and repairs at the Boys & Girls Club. Wes was already well-known as one of the men in town you called when you need an extra hand moving something heavy or shoveling snow. He was quiet and polite. The man had never made waves in town before the night at the Roadhouse.

And as for me, my family had been around longer than anyone, and my children were descended from the two most historic, prominent families around. Not to mention, there were quite a few Hobians who were bound and determined to see the two of us as nothing more than brothers, joined at the hip and raising "those poor motherless children" the best way we knew how.

We never corrected them. In fact, for many years we continued to live our lives relatively quietly and tried not to make waves. We rarely touched in public, and we did our best to keep our private life private. After a while everyone settled into a kind of détente in which we didn't flaunt our sexuality and everyone else politely pretended it didn't exist.

It didn't hurt that one of my father's closest friends was the sheriff, and he arrested four of the five men involved in the assault the same day Weston said their names.

Things would have been very different if we hadn't had the support of the sheriff during those years, but we did. And he was one of the first people to congratulate us when word got out two years later that Weston Marian had legally changed his last name to Wilde. Back then, we didn't really think of it in terms of marriage. It was more like wanting, *needing*, him to officially become part of our family.

We found a good lawyer down in Dallas who drew up paperwork to protect Wes in case something happened to me. He would become the trustee of the ranch and farm after my parents' passing, and he'd take guardianship of the kids. We even had paperwork giving him rights to make medical decisions for the children, but not once in the remaining years of their childhoods did anyone accept them. Even my colleagues and coworkers had insisted on getting my approval before Wes could so much as consent to an X-ray the day Billy sprained his ankle sliding into home base during a high school baseball game.

Hobie itself also changed during that time. Pastor Dickerson retired and Pastor White took his place in charge of the largest congregation in town. While he never came out of the closet, he also made sure his focus was on modeling and teaching love and acceptance to his congregants. It made all the difference.

The biggest negative repercussion to come out of Major's assault besides the damage to his body had been me losing my job at the clinic. As soon as the powers that be had heard the rumors about my relationship with another man, they'd used my walking off the job that day as cause for termination.

When Major had found out about it, he'd lost his ever-loving mind.

"I'm going up there to give them a piece of my mind," he'd fumed.

"That's cute. Who's going to push your wheelchair?" I'd drawled lazily from the hospital chair next to his bed where I was working on a crossword puzzle.

"Dammit, Doc. This is serious."

"Mm-hm. What's an eight-letter word for stoic and gruff?"

"Liam," he'd snapped.

"Babe," I'd replied, writing in *taciturn*.

"What are you going to do? Apply here at the hospital and wind up with a longer commute?"

I'd looked up at him, appreciating the strong jaw under all the bruising. There was more salt in his pepper hair than there'd been even a year ago.

I sighed. "You're one of those men who gets more handsome with age. It's not fair."

His face had lit up with an idea. "I've got it! You should open your own practice in town. We could look for office space and set up—"

That's when I'd pulled out the folded piece of paper from my back pocket and handed it to him. He'd looked at the photo of the historic Victorian house we'd admired many times while walking around town. It wasn't far off the square and had the perfect setup for a small private medical practice. It even had space upstairs that had already been made into a separate apartment in case we ever needed or wanted to spend the night in town or needed a rental to bring in extra income.

Major had studied the For Sale flyer before looking up at me. "They're going to love you, Doc. It's going to be the best decision you ever made. I'm proud of you."

And they had loved me. My practice had grown so quickly, I'd had to bring in another two doctors over the next five years. I'd justified hiring the gay applicant over the straight one because he was an army vet just like me which meant we had a lot in common. And when the next hiring decision had come down to choosing between a well-qualified man and a younger but equally qualified woman, I'd chosen the woman because I'd remembered Betsy wishing she'd had access to female doctors.

With the new docs on board, I'd had more time at home with the kids and Wes. My dad had spent a full year transitioning management of the ranch over to Wes before showing up one day with a gigantic recreational vehicle and declaring himself officially retired and inviting my mother on the road trip from hell. At least, that's what my mom had called it. My dad had called it "seeing the world one campground at a time."

They'd already built a small "retirement nest" on the ranch property and moved in to give Wes and me free rein over the large farmhouse. We'd argued with them about it, but in the end, we'd had to admit it couldn't have been easy for them to think about their son sharing a bedroom upstairs with another man. And even after they'd moved into their own place, my mother had still retained ownership of the farmhouse kitchen, letting herself in and out whenever she wanted and making all the meals as usual.

It took me a while to realize that Weston had been right to insist on staying in Hobie. As hard as it had been dealing with the stares and whispers, I began to recognize how our children were thriving in a way they wouldn't necessarily have experienced in a big city.

For one, Billy had gone down to Dallas one summer during high school to participate in a high-level baseball camp at the university there. While he was there, he managed to take some kind of seminar course in accounting. He returned to the ranch and threw himself into optimizing our finances. By the time he applied to colleges, he was essentially the CFO for a large family agriculture business. That led to his work in international finance, which was how he eventually met his wife, Shelby. Shelby had fallen in love with Hobie and the ranch and had insisted on raising their ten children there. We'd helped build them their own home on the property so Wes and I could help with the kids. Our first grandchild, Hudson, was born less than ten years after Wes and I got together. At that time, we still had Jackie at home with us. Since she was only fourteen, she made a killing babysitting for Shelby and Bill.

Then there was Brenda, who might have been happier in a big city, but whose fierce determination to love "Uncle Major" despite how strict he was had turned into the feisty commitment to defending him from anyone who dared disparage him. She was the first one of the four of them to start calling him Pop, and she'd even come screeching like a banshee into his hospital room after his assault, insisting that no one was allowed to touch him except Daddy because he was a doctor. But when she decided to attend SMU, she got super prissy and preppy. And when she met and married Hollis, they decided to live the country club life in Dallas which seemed to suit the two of them just fine. We loved how, despite marrying a socialite and becoming a stay-at-home mom, Brenda never lost her fire and sass. And when any trouble hit the ranch, she was the first to jump in her fancy Wagoneer and come running.

Gina, on the other hand, always stayed close. When my parents took off on their RV trip, Gina begged Wes to let her take over Granny's kitchen garden. By the time she graduated from high school, she'd fallen in love with growing things. We had to strong-arm her into going to college, but she insisted on the closest agricultural studies program she could find. As soon as she got out, she took over running the Hobart farm until convincing us in 1990 to let her go organic. Wes sat me down and proposed gifting her the farm.

"She's ready, Doc," he said.

"I just worry about her finding a partner. She throws herself into work so much, she doesn't have a life."

His eyes went soft, and he reached for my hand across the kitchen table. "She's in love with Carmen Segura."

I stared at him, picturing the young homeless woman I'd hired six months before to clean the office. She'd been kicked out of her house for being gay as soon as she'd turned eighteen. One of my nurses had heard about her predicament and asked me to help her. We'd put her up in the apartment over the practice. "*My* Carmen?"

Wes lifted a dark eyebrow at me. He was so fucking handsome, I couldn't stop staring at him even after twenty years of seeing his face. "*Your* Carmen? You have some news for me, sweetheart?"

"Shut up, you know what I mean. Is it reciprocated?"

He nodded. "At least I think so. I stopped by Gina's place two days ago to drop off some mail that had come here by mistake and Carmen's bicycle was propped against the house. It was seven in the morning."

My jaw was hanging open. Wes's finger lifted up, and then he leaned over to kiss me on the lips. "Brenda gets her dramatics from you. You know that, right?" I swatted him away.

"Did we know Gina was gay?" I cried. "How did we not know one of our children was gay? Jesus fucking Christ, Wes. She's *gay*? Wait. Maybe she just spent the night as a friend."

I thought of all the nights I'd spent in that foreman's house "as a friend." Wes must have been thinking the exact same thing because his eyes twinkled at me before he bounced his eyebrows seductively.

"God, you're so smug," I said. "And for your information, Betsy was plenty dramatic."

"She was. But you gotta admit, you Wildes sure are easy to turn gay."

I couldn't help but bark out a laugh. "Stop. It's not funny. Should we talk to her?"

"About lesbian sex? Give her the birds and birds talk?"

Weston Wilde made me laugh every single day. I loved him so damned much. "Yeah, maybe. Don't you think? I mean, we need to at least…"

"Force her to come out to her parents?"

"Argh!" I dropped my face in my hands. "You're such a know-it-all."

Wes's thick fingers brushed through my hair. "You're adorably naive, sweetheart. Gina had a girlfriend in college. I also caught her kissing Taffy Yarborough behind the bleachers during a high school football game."

Okay, maybe he was right about the dramatics because I gasped. Loudly. "Are you kidding me? Why wouldn't you have told me? I feel like I'm looking at a stranger right now."

Wes reached for me, tugging me out of my seat and onto his lap. I straddled him and leaned my head on his muscular shoulder. His arms circled me and held me tight. I loved having my very own cowboy.

"Liam, honey, you would have wanted to confront her about it and make it a thing. You would have gotten in her face with aggressive acceptance and labeling, when she really needs to manage her sexuality on her own time and in her own way."

I hated him knowing me so well.

"I never should have gotten together with you," I muttered. "Nothing but a pain in the ass."

His hand came down to run a strong finger down the seam of my pants, reminding me of the pounding I'd taken up against the shower wall that morning. "You want me to distract you with some more ass pain?"

"No." *Yes.*

His laughter rumbled against my face, and his hands began kneading my butt possessively.

"We were talking about Gina," I reminded him. "And her *girlfriend.*"

"Actually, we were talking about the farm."

"Yeah, fine. Whatever. I don't care about the farm. I care about our baby."

"She's twenty-two."

I sighed. "At least we still have Jackie at home for one more year. Then we'll have an empty nest."

"Unless your mom and dad come back to live with us in the main house," Wes suggested in a teasing voice. "Anyway, I think it's highly likely Jackie will stick around after high school considering she's refusing to apply to college."

But she didn't. The day after her high school graduation the following year, she hopped a bus to LA with the money she'd been saving up from all that babysitting and decided she was going to become the next big Hollywood star. She got pregnant within the year and had our sweet Felix, rebuffing all our efforts to help until finally allowing us to bring him home to the ranch when he was nine and raise him as our own.

During all those years of kids and work, ups and downs, I begged

Wes to look up his long-lost family in Bakersfield and attempt a reunion of sorts.

It was the biggest source of contention in our relationship during all that time. I'd ask him to look them up, he'd grunt for me to mind my own business, I'd remind him he *was* my business, and he'd distract me with a blowjob.

And so it went for almost twenty more years. Until a Marian showed up in Hobie out of the blue.

CHAPTER 34

WESTON "MAJOR" MARIAN

I was terrified of doing anything that would jeopardize my incredible life and the loving family I'd been welcomed into. Even after the internet became a thing and we discovered Clayton and Mrs. Burns had survived the attempted home invasion all those years before, I was too scared to go crawling back to Bakersfield and open up a nasty can of worms with my father.

My sister, Tilly, was the only person in my family I still cared about, and there was no way I could ask her forgiveness for disappearing all those years ago.

So anytime Doc brought it up, I did my best to change the subject. Once Doc started calling them Tilly blowjobs, it was all over. Clearly, his purpose was to deflate my cock with heinous and horrific association. My poor little prim sister would surely keel over dead if she only knew.

One day when our oldest grandchild started falling in love, we stumbled upon a woman named Rebecca Marian. Doc immediately blurted out that his husband's birth name was Marian, and we quickly discovered she was married to Walter's son, Thomas Marian. Through Rebecca, we learned that everyone was gone except Tilly.

My sister was not only still alive, but apparently thriving in San Francisco.

"We have to go see her!" Doc said excitedly. I looked at him in panic.

Rebecca must have sensed my unease. She reached out a hand to clasp mine where we sat at Nico's little kitchen table. "I don't have to tell anyone in my family who you are, Weston. You can decide this on your own time. If there's one thing I've learned in all my years as a mom, especially a foster and adoptive mom, it's that family issues are deeply personal. It's up to you how you want to proceed. I'm fairly confident Tilly would hug you, chew you up, spit you out, and then hug you again. She's pretty damned sassy."

I laughed through my tears. "Sounds like you definitely have the right Matilda Marian."

"She's everyone's favorite, Weston. She's funny and fun. Rich as hell and determined. Stubborn, and inquisitive. The best part about her is that she refuses to get old. If a frat house invited her over for strip poker, she'd not only go but she'd bring all her lesbian friends."

"She's *gay?*" Doc and I asked at the same time.

Rebecca laughed so hard at our synchronized routine, she almost doubled over. "Oh my god, you two. No. She's not. She's never been married, but she's dating a nice man right now. Her two besties are gay though, and one of them is even crazier than she is. I really hope you'll decide to come meet them all someday soon."

We agreed we would.

And then we didn't.

The Tilly blowjobs started again and lasted two full years. Until a stranger named Miller Hobbs showed up at our door. The young man claimed to have done an ancestry DNA test that gave him results pointing to me which made no sense since I'd never done anything like that before.

After the young man had left, I turned to my beautiful husband, who radiated guilt and had particular knowledge of how to collect DNA without telling a person.

"Don't look at me like that," he said. *Guiltily.*

"I never did a DNA kit."

"Well, yeah, maybe you did." He'd looked over my shoulder back toward the kitchen. "Is your chili burning, because I think—"

"*Doctor* Wilde. Explain how someone got my DNA without my knowledge."

"Um, you know what I'd like to do right now?" Even at seventy-five years old, Doc's voice still got higher-pitched when he was nervous. He tried to give me a sexy look. Little did he know, he always looked sexy to me. "I'd like to suck that big fat cock of yours. Let's go to the bedroom."

"You sound like a porn star. It's not as sexy when I know your knee is acting up," I muttered, sliding my arm around his waist and kissing his cheek. "But I'm still going to take you up on it. Later. We'll put some pillows down."

Instead of going to the bedroom, we went to the big farmhouse kitchen that had been renovated several years before into our absolute favorite space. Waiting for us there was a collection of many of our grown grandchildren, Brenda, Gina and her wife, Carmen.

I explained to everybody about Miller coming to the door. "He did one of those ancestry DNA kits and discovered he's a close match to me and an even closer match to a Matilda Marian in San Francisco. My sister. Since I've never had biological children, I explained it either had to be through my brother, Walter, or my sister, Matilda. It looks more like a match to Tilly."

Doc cut in. "There are no records of Tilly ever marrying or changing her name. Miller's mother was born to an anonymous unwed mother in a home in California. Tilly would have been eighteen at the time."

"Has Miller met her yet?" our grandson Saint asked.

I sat up straight. "She refuses to meet him or acknowledge him. He came here in hopes I could help get through to her." I paused for a moment, thinking about whether or not I was truly willing to help this kid. "His mother is dying. She wants to meet her biological mother if possible before she goes. Miller wants to do this for her."

Silence descended.

"Well, shit," Saint's twin, MJ, said. "What are you going to do?"

"Go to California to see my sister," I said with a sigh, wondering if I truly had the balls to confront her after all this time. "And try and figure out how the hell to say 'sorry I disappeared, hey can you do this kid a favor' when I get there."

But then, of course, I chickened out again. Well, it was more like I put it off and put it off a little more until the kids took it into their own hands. I still wasn't sure if Doc had anything to do with it or not, but suddenly I found myself part of a giant entourage of fellow Wildes flying to Napa for a vow renewal ceremony. I assumed part of the reason they'd selected Napa for the event was its proximity to where my sister lived.

Regardless of the reason behind the gesture, I was thrilled for a chance to renew my vows to Doc.

Several years before, he and I had raced to the county clerk's office first thing in the morning on Monday, June 29, 2015, after the Obergefell decision in the Supreme Court. We'd grinned like loons while the clerk had processed our marriage license in front of half the town and Judge Timmons had performed the brief ceremony. When we returned home the farmhouse had been covered in rainbow banners, balloons, streamers, flags, and Wildes. Music blared from speakers on the front porch, and I'd recognized the song as "Same Love" since Felix had played it on repeat sometimes in his glass work-shop. It had been an amazing day none of us would ever forget.

But now we were on a plane to California to renew the vows in an actual wedding ceremony, complete with fancy reception at a winery.

I looked at the snoozing man in the seat next to me. Doc's blond hair had thinned, and laugh lines creased the skin next to his eyes under his glasses. He'd missed a spot with his shaver that morning, and I leaned over to kiss it softly. He still smelled like Old Spice after forty-something years.

"I love you," I murmured into his ear before kissing him again on the temple. After sitting back in my seat, I reached a hand out to rest on his thigh and felt his own warm hand land on mine.

"Only because I give good head," he murmured back.

"Gross! Oh my *god*. Stop." Brenda's voice cried out from the row behind us. "So gross. You're eighty-five years old, for the love of *god*."

Brenda with the dramatics. She was so easy to rile.

"Doc's not," I answered with a grin. "He's a spry seventy-five. The man has a lot of life left in him, not to mention creativity and drive."

"Jesus, Pop. Gag me. Max, give me your headphones. This has to stop."

"Here you go, Mom. You think maybe Doc can give me some pointers? My last Grindr hookup—"

"La la la!" Brenda said loudly.

Doc held a fist over his head for Max to pound. "When we get to the hotel, find me a banana and I'm all yours." After bumping fists with Max, Doc leaned over to doze off again on my shoulder.

After a while I realized Brenda was telling Max the story of the time she barged in on us while we were having sex. Thank god we'd been under the covers or it would have resulted in therapy for all.

I interrupted her story. "We tried to teach you guys not to ever barge in unannounced," I said over my shoulder. "So you're the only one to blame."

"Hush, Pop. I'm telling the story. Even the dogs were mortified. All of them had their paws over their eyes and were whimpering."

Doc stirred on my shoulder. "They weren't the only ones whimpering. Badda bing."

Max and every other Wilde sitting around us groaned. Brenda ignored us and continued. "Anyway, there was a giant vat of lube on the floor by my feet and some strappy underthing I'd never seen before nearby."

West's husband Nico coughed. "*Jockstrap.*"

"And rubber... *bananas*, for lack of a better word, scattered about," Brenda continued.

Hudson, who was sitting in front of me, started howling. His husband, Charlie, asked politely if he could get a new rubber banana in San Francisco because he'd heard they had the very best ones in specialty stores there.

"You sure were observant for only being in there long enough to shriek to the heavens," Doc mumbled against my shirt.

"I was traumatized."

Gina piped up from her spot across the aisle. "You were nosy. Imagine sharing a room with her. Or a womb for that matter."

I looked over and saw Carmen's hand on Gina's boob, clutching it like a security blanket. Carmen herself was dead asleep, her thick brown braid resting inside Gina's shirt collar, while Gina laid into Brenda about years' worth of misdeeds.

Our family wasn't what you'd call quiet or private.

Before any more unseemly details came to light, I needed to nose the hound off the trail.

"Tell it to me straight. Have you all invited my sister to this wedding?"

Suddenly, ours was the quietest family who'd ever snapped their jaws shut and feigned ignorance.

I looked down to find my husband's familiar guilty face. I narrowed my eyes at him. "Et tu, Bruté?"

"Amor vincit omnia," he replied.

"What does that mean in English?"

"You mean besides don't speak Latin to a doctor? It means love conquers all. Or as my old buddy John Lennon used to say, 'All you need is love.'"

I rolled my eyes. "You haven't met my sister. Sometimes you also need a flak jacket."

CHAPTER 35

LIAM "DOC" WILDE

When we entered the large wooden lodge building at the Alexander Vineyard, the first person I saw was a little old lady with white hair. I immediately assumed she was Tilly until I saw her grab a taller woman's face between two hands and pull her down until they were eye to eye.

"Need me some sugar," the old lady murmured. "Pronto."

The taller woman leaned in for a kiss that took a sharp turn toward granny porn.

"What the hell?" Gina murmured beside me. "I mean, go lesbian power, but still."

Carmen swatted at her. "It's refreshing to see two older women not afraid to be affectionate in public. You could learn a thing or two."

Gina turned and grabbed Carmen's ass. "I'll show you PDA. Peachy damned ass is what this is."

"Can we focus please?" I asked, trying to ignore the shaking clamminess of my husband's palm in my hand. Wes was being even quieter than normal, and it was disconcerting. "Despite what Stevie Devore called our trip to San Francisco, this isn't Wildes Gone Wild."

"How many old ladies could there possibly be?" Charlie asked.

211

Hudson held Charlie's hand beside him. "Wait a second. I know those women."

"How?" Charlie asked.

"I don't know… I just recognize them from somewhere."

"Would anyone be bothered if I bailed early and got some sleep?" Hudson's younger brother King asked.

His sister Hallie wasn't having it. "Yes. Me. You promised to tell me about the museum you visited in Prague. Not all of us are international travelers, you know."

"Bitter much? Believe me, it's not all it's cracked up to be." King sighed and muttered an agreement to rally for Hallie's sake.

Rebecca Marian popped her head out of a hallway past the reception counter. "Oh my goodness, they're here!" She came rushing out to greet us, followed by a good-looking man in his late thirties or early forties with strawberry-blond hair and a friendly smile. "Hi, everyone, this is my son Blue. He and his husband, Tristan, own the vineyard. Welcome."

Everyone introduced themselves which drew the attention of the two older ladies. Granny and Irene were Tristan's grandmothers and also best friends with Tilly.

"Is, um, is she here?" I asked. Wes had gone pale. I'd been worried about his heart condition, so I'd been keeping a close eye on his pulse and blood pressure periodically throughout the trip, but he was fine physically. That didn't mean he was fine emotionally. I'd already tried nudging him toward the sofas arranged in front of a huge stone fireplace, but he'd stayed glued to my side instead.

Rebecca nodded and shared a soft smile with me. "I asked her to stay in her suite so you could meet with her privately. We had to bribe our big crew to stop loitering in hopes of watching the spectacle. You'll meet everyone tonight at dinner."

Wes shifted beside me and made a strange noise. I turned to see him truly struggling. "Baby?"

"I don't know if… Doc…" His eyes were frantic, and a bead of sweat appeared at his hairline over his temple. "I think I need some water."

Blue thrust a key card envelope into our hands. "Why don't you go take a break in your room first? You must be exhausted from the trip."

I smiled and said my thanks before allowing Rebecca to lead us away to our room. When we got behind closed doors, Wes pulled me in for a tight hug.

"I don't want to lose you," he said into my neck. The sound was muffled, and I wondered if I'd misheard.

"Weston, at this point you could shoot someone in the face and you wouldn't lose me. In fact, I've actually seen you shoot someone in the face, and it was after that I fell in love with you. What that says about me, I'm a little unsure. But I'm sure as shit not leaving you now. For one, I'd never find a replacement foot warmer for my bed."

"Stop. Be serious. I mean it."

I pulled back and looked at him, caressing the sides of his handsome face with my fingers. "Why are you so affected by this? I've tried to understand it, but... I mean, Wes, life's too short. What do you have to lose?"

He moved us over to the sitting area by the sliding glass doors that led to a patio off the back of the lodge. Before joining him on the love seat, I slid the doors open to let some of the cooler air into the stuffy room. The pale winter sun streamed over a long expanse of lawn, and I could see rows of dormant grapevines in the distance.

When I joined him on the love seat, he tried to explain. "It started off that I was afraid to show myself to my family because they thought I was a deviant. Then I thought maybe I was a criminal. Then it became this... almost like a habit to stay away. It was easier to put it aside and forget about my old life. But now?" He sighed. "Now I feel like an idiot. I feel like I have to explain why I wasted sixty-seven years. *Sixty-seven years* when I could have had Matilda in my life."

"It's never too late. The past is done."

Wes's voice croaked in agony, and his eyes filled. "Her best friends are gay. Her grand... nephews, or whatever, are gay. How could I have thought she wouldn't want me in her life because I was gay? How can I face her now and try to make her understand?"

I'd known all along it had been fear and shame of her judgment, of letting her down, that had kept him from his beloved sister all this time, but it was still impossible to witness my love in pain. I threw my arms around his neck and held tight while he cried out his nerves and regrets.

A woman's voice came from the open sliding doors. "You don't have to make me understand, Weston. You just have to let me get to know you now."

We looked up and saw her there. Tilly stood upright and regal, her expensive clothing and hairstyle telling of her comfortable life. An attractive white-haired man stood quietly by her side with an arm around her waist.

My husband was a complete wreck. "I'm so sorry, Tilly," he choked out, standing and reaching out a hand for her. "How can you ever forgive me for leaving you?"

She reached out a slender-fingered hand like a queen, but the quiver in her chin revealed her own nerves. "I forgave you a very, very long time ago, brother. All I ever wanted for you is what I've wanted for my own nieces and nephews and all of their children. Peace. Love. A happy life."

They clutched hands for a beat before falling into each other's arms and holding tight.

"And it sounds like you had all those things," Tilly said softly into Wes's ear. "I'm so happy for you, Weston."

They pulled back and chuckled at the emotional mess we all were. I spotted a box of tissues on the side table and held it out to them. "I'm Liam Wilde, Weston's husband. It's so nice to finally meet you."

Instead of offering her hand again, Tilly stepped into my arms for a hug. "Thank you for loving him," she said in my ear.

"Easiest thing I've ever done," I croaked. "Now stop making me cry and introduce me to your handsome man in case I want an upgrade someday."

Tilly pulled back and chuckled. "This is my better half. Harold Cannon."

The man smiled and shook my hand. "So nice to meet you, Liam."

"Please call me Doc. Everyone does. Wait. You're Senator Cannon."

He nodded. "Used to be anyway. Call me Harry, please."

Tilly couldn't stop staring at Wes. "God, you're an old man. Look at those ears."

Wes barked out a laugh. "Brat."

"She's right though. I call them his Ferengi ears," I confided. "Please come on in and have a seat. I'm going to hunt down some drinks and snacks for us while you two catch up."

Harry stepped up next to me. "I'll join you."

While we walked to the hotel lounge, we made small talk until I mentioned we lived in Hobie, Texas. "You're kidding?" he asked. "My son and daughter-in-law have a vacation home on the lake there. What a beautiful place."

"You'll have to come visit sometime. We'd love to show you around. It's a great little town. My family has lived there for generations."

Harry studied me. "How in the world did Tilly's brother wind up in tiny Hobie, Texas?"

I grinned at him. "Long story."

CHAPTER 36

WESTON "MAJOR" MARIAN

We spent the rest of the afternoon talking each other's ears off. Tilly was the same sassy girl I'd known as a child, but now she also had an entire life's worth of experience and wisdom behind it. And maybe a healthy dash of irreverence. She was a riot and had Doc laughing so hard at times, I thought maybe I was going to have to make a joke about needing adult diapers before long.

At one point we moved our foursome out to the lobby where both Wildes and Marians congregated around us, quietly at first. They asked us questions about growing up together and asked more about our lives between Bakersfield and now. I discovered that she'd somehow ended up in the same kind of wild and wonderful extended family we had. I'd never seen so many gay men under one roof in all my life.

After I'd finally convinced Tilly to join me for a visit to Miller and his sick mother the following week, my granddaughter Sassy came up and looped an arm through mine with a soft whine. "What the hell, Grandpa. All the good ones really *are* gay. This is worse than going to Stallions with my brothers on dollar martini night."

I kissed the top of her curly hair. "Meh, you're better off anyway. They're all related. Sort of."

Once heavy hors d'oeuvres appeared out of nowhere and began circulating, the party ramped up in volume and excitement. Tristan Marian made sure everyone who wanted some had a glass of wine in hand and distributed bottles of water to everyone else. Someone turned on music while someone else stoked the fire and turned on twinkle lights around the large space as the sun went down outside.

Doc and I eventually snuggled into the corner of one of the giant sofas and talked to absolutely everyone at some point. We got to know Thomas and Rebecca's children, and I had a chance to ask Thomas about his father, my brother, Walt. It sounded like he'd been a milder version of my strict father because Thomas credited Rebecca with turning his own life around and opening his mind.

Rebecca cut in. "Don't get me wrong, Walt was a nice man. But if he hadn't passed away already, he would have died when he realized our boys were gay. And that's before we got involved in the shelter and adopted more kids. He was just... well, we always told the kids he was from another generation."

"How the hell did Tilly make it out with such a different outlook?" Doc asked.

Thomas's eyes crinkled with laughter. "She roomed in college with a total hippie. Her name was Maureen, but she went by Moonbeam, swear to god. Let's just say, she introduced Tilly to the wild side. They spent spring break marching on Washington and summer vacation allowing Maureen's rich family to fund their escapades to Europe and the Cape."

Doc leaned across me to ask a question in a low voice. "Where'd she get all her money?"

Thomas leaned in, squishing Rebecca against me. "To this day, nobody knows."

I caught my sister's eye across the coffee table. She winked at me and then seemed to notice my grandson Hudson sitting on a nearby chair. She tilted her head and then narrowed her eyes at him.

"Holy crap, it's you!" she cried. "The dumbass who accidentally proposed to someone."

Hudson's eyes grew comically wider as the lightbulb went off. "The flight to Ireland! That's where I know you guys from!"

He turned to his husband to explain. "Right before I first met you. This is the lady on the airplane who told me to, er, I mean…" His face flushed deep red.

Charlie turned to Tilly with a giant grin and his enticing lilt. "Thank ye kindly for suggesting the sausage over the tacos, ma'am. He turned out to have a wee taste for it."

The entire room tittered with excitement and laughter before demanding the whole story. Tilly seemed enchanted by Charlie. After asking him a million questions about his meeting Hudson, she finally winked at him and said, "I don't really give a shit. I just wanted to hear you talk."

At one point, a stranger entered the lobby and looked around until locking eyes on King. King froze and stared at the man as if seeing a ghost. When the stranger approached, King stood.

"This is a private party," he said, colder than I'd ever seen. Clearly he knew the man.

"I'm sorry. It can't wait."

"Are you here to arrest me, because if so—" Now, instead of icy, King looked angry.

"No, no. Not that. I…" He seemed to realize a room full of people were hanging on every word he said. He swallowed and looked back at King. "I need your help. I have a plane waiting on a private airstrip nearby. We need to be in…" He looked around again. "We need to leave right now."

"I don't work for you," King said incredulously. The rest of us looked on like mesmerized spectators at a tennis match.

The strange man narrowed his eyes at my grandson. "You do now. Let's go."

King's nostrils flared like he wanted to lay into this guy right here. Instead, he let out a controlled breath. "Let me gather my things."

My grandson Saint finally stood up. "What the hell is going on? Who are you? King, who is this guy?"

King suddenly looked sad and resigned. He shook his head at

West. "It's fine. Really." Then he turned to me and Doc. "I'm very sorry to miss the wedding."

I didn't know what to say, but if there was one thing Doc and I were on the same page about, it was respecting our children's and grandchildren's independence. "We know you love us no matter where you are tomorrow. We just want you to be happy."

He let out a laugh that was more like a scoff. "Yeah. Happy." He looked at the stranger, who seemed taken aback by King's look of resignation.

The stranger turned to us. "I'm really sorry to do this. He's needed on a... very important project."

He was an attractive man, older than King for sure, but he radiated military or law enforcement. King asked him to wait with us while he ran to pack his things, but when he didn't come back after a little while, the man asked to be shown to his room.

King was gone. And so was all of his stuff.

"Motherfucker," the man spat. "Someone give me his phone number, please."

Suddenly every Wilde in the room was looking at each other with clueless expressions, and my grandchildren proved themselves to be master liars. "Whose number?" MJ asked.

"King's number. Who else?"

"King who?" Otto asked.

"We don't know any kings."

"Uh, hello?" Felix chimed up from his spot on a giant floor cushion. "What about this guy?" He pointed to his husband, Lior, who just so happened to be... well, yeah.

The stranger was pissed. "He's getting away. Believe me when I tell you he wants this job."

Saint flexed his huge pecs and shoulders at the guy. "I'm thinking he doesn't. I'm thinking if he did, he'd have stuck around and asked a few questions."

What the hell was King up to? And why had he thought this man was going to arrest him?

MJ leaned over and whispered in Doc's ear loud enough for me to hear. "Don't worry. I know what's going on. It's fine."

I glanced at her, our smart attorney. I could tell by the look in her eyes she was telling the truth. After reaching for Doc's hand, I looked up at the man. "It would seem to me that if you wanted to catch him, you wouldn't be standing here looking at a bunch of people who obviously aren't going to help you."

The man exhaled a curse and took off, calling back over his shoulder for us to tell King to contact him.

"Wanna maybe give us your number?" Saint called out.

"He has it."

To break the tension in the room, Granny and Irene suddenly passed around shots of something unnaturally purple. Doc refused to let me try one. "If I wanted you dead, I'd kill you myself," he muttered, handing it off to one of the kids. "I have plans for your old fogey ass."

I realized how tired I was, and we had a big day—*wedding* day—ahead of us the following day. I looked at my beautiful husband and turned his chin toward me.

"Come to bed with me, sweetheart."

His face melted into the gushy lovestruck one that always warmed my heart.

"Ew, gross," someone said. "They're totally going to do it."

We were. We really, really were.

Doc stood up and reached out his hand to help pull me up. He spoke over his shoulder at whoever had spoken. "You're just jealous. Admit it. Your grandfathers have more game than you."

I realized it was one of our youngest grandsons, Cal. He blushed. "True story, bro."

We waved good night and made our way to the hotel room. Once the door closed behind us, Doc pushed me up against the door and kissed me softly.

"You were amazing out there," he said between kisses. "I'm so fucking proud of you, old man."

I ran my fingers through his hair and tilted his head so I could deepen the kiss. "Couldn't have done it without my wingman. You're like social lube. I should squirt you out more often."

Doc's fingers began unbuttoning my shirt as his mouth moved under my chin and down my neck. "Sounds like someone has lube on the brain."

"Mm-hm. Want you. Want to be buried deep inside you and stay there forever." I tried unbuttoning his shirt, but he pulled mine off before I could get any of them open.

Once my chest was bare, he ran his hands up it and over my shoulders. "So damned handsome. So strong, so sexy," he said softly. "All this white fur just kills me. Is there such a thing as a polar bear on those gay phone apps? We need to ask the kids."

I grumbled out a laugh and reached for his shirt again. Once I got it off, I pulled him close again so I could feel his warm chest and the reassuring thump of his heart against mine. "You're the best thing that ever happened to me."

"Shut up. I've already cried too much today." He kissed me before removing both of our glasses and moving farther into the room to drop them on the bedside table. I followed behind and wrapped my arms around his front to undo his pants.

"No crying. Only cries of ecstasy tonight." I teased his earlobe with my lips.

"Hot damn. My favorite kind of cries. How we gonna do this? You have a hot guy coming over to help?" He turned and reached for my fly too until we were frantically getting into each other's pants like horny teens.

"I'm going to suck your dick and then fuck you."

The front of his pants twitched under my hands. "Uh-huh. Sounds…" He swallowed. "Sounds like a solid plan."

I squeezed his cock through the front of his pants before shoving them down so he could step out of them. Once he was completely naked, I told him to get his sweet ass on the bed and wait for me.

He climbed up and lay on his side with his elbow propped under him. "Where are you going?"

"To get the plastic banana." I opened our suitcase and pulled out my Dopp kit with the lube in it. After removing my pants and boxers, I made my way to the bed and climbed on top of him, kissing him again just because I still loved the feel of his lips on mine after all this time. His body was warm and familiar. I knew every single hot spot and weakness. I moved my lips down his chest to tease his nipples and suck marks into his belly. When I got to his cock, it was hard and ready. I licked up and down until pulling it up and taking it into my mouth.

Doc's hands landed on my head. "Fuck, *Major*, god. Please, please. Just like that."

While I sucked him, I fumbled the lube open and warmed some up between my fingers before reaching for his hole. We hadn't done this for a while, so I took my time prepping him while using my mouth to keep him nice and hard. Just seeing him arch up in pleasure had me hard as a rock too, and by the time he was ready, I was well past ready.

I moved back up and kissed him on the mouth again. Doc's hands came up to clasp the sides of my face.

"God you're good at that. Hurry."

I grabbed several pillows and propped them under his hips before moving back over him and pressing in. Our eyes met.

For the millionth time since 1968, I sank into the South China Sea.

"I will love you for the rest of my life, William Wilde," I promised, hoping like hell we still had a long time left together.

His eyes leaked precious tears. "Damn you for making me cry." His hands reached for my face again. "I have loved you over half my life, and I will continue loving you till my last breath. You are everything to me, Weston Wilde. *Everything.*"

We kept our eyes locked together as I continued to make love to him, rocking gently at first until finally pressing into him faster and faster, trying desperately to get as close to him as possible.

I reached for his shaft and pulled with a slick hand until he gasped. "*Wes!* Oh god—yes!"

As his body tightened around me and the cool evening air blew in through the partially open sliding doors, I closed my eyes and cried out his name.

CHAPTER 37

LIAM "DOC" WILDE

Waking up in Wes's arms was always a gift, but knowing I was going to be able to renew my vows to him in front of our friends and family made the day even better. I stretched up and kissed his prickly cheek. "Morning, husband."

He nuzzled the side of my face. "Nah, I'm a bachelor this morning. Marrying a hot dude this afternoon. Until then I can sleep with whoever I want."

"Hearing a geezer like you say the word *dude* is off-putting."

Wes took my hand and put it on his morning wood. His deep morning grumble got my heart going better than a cup of coffee. "I don't want to do anything off-putting. All *on*-putting."

I stroked him slowly, teasing him while I propped my head on my hand. "What are we doing this morning?"

He thrust up into my hand. "Each other, hopefully."

I reached down to cup his balls. "After that."

Wes groaned and squeezed his eyes closed. "Keep touching me. I can't think."

After leaning in to kiss underneath his jaw, I moved over to lie on top of him. He was still solid and barrel-chested, sexy as hell. I kissed down past his collarbone to his chest.

"After sex and showers, I mean," I murmured.

Wes's hand cupped the back of my head gently as I began to lick and nibble below his belly button. "Whatever you want, Doc. I will do absolutely anything if you'll put your mouth on my dick."

Which is how he ended up wearing his full dress uniform at our wedding.

My sexy cowboy walked down the aisle a highly decorated retired lieutenant colonel. The medals and ribbons I'd snuck in my suitcase shone brightly in the California winter sunlight. When I'd originally asked him to wear it for the ceremony, he'd balked, claiming he felt strange in it after all this time. But I knew the truth. He was scared about being openly gay in uniform for the first time.

Major and I had been together for decades by now, and I knew him almost better than I knew myself. The fear of being outed in the army was so deeply ingrained in him, it was one of the reasons I'd decided to push him to wear the dress uniform for our wedding. He needed to fully feel how different things were today than they were in 1968 or in 1954 when he'd first enlisted.

So watching him stride across the lawn toward me with that thing on? Holy mother of god was it powerful. He was tall and proud, brave and determined. He carried himself with the confident, competent grace he'd always had, and that alone was enough to nearly bring me to my knees.

I loved him so damned much, I was dizzy with it.

When we arrived at the end of the grassy aisle hand in hand, Felix stood under an arch covered in peach and cream flowers and greenery. He wore a stunning dark suit with a bright purple sash and some kind of royal insignia above his breast pocket signifying his position as king consort of Liorland. Despite standing tall and proud, his eyes were wet already which, of course, set me off.

"Our boy," Wes murmured under his breath, his hand tightening in mine. "Look at him, Liam."

"Stop. Don't make me cry harder, asshole."

"You're not supposed to call me that right now," he *tskd*. I turned to face him. His faded denim blues were full of all the love and tenderness they'd always carried when pointed at me. Those eyes and his soft smile made the kind of promises that rendered vows completely unnecessary. They always had.

"I love you," I said in a voice broken by the memory of decades of commitment already passed, years spent aching and desperate for his comfort, moments of the two of us exchanging a simple look that said absolutely everything without speaking a word.

Wes reached out and thumbed a tear off my cheek. "You are the greatest gift of my life."

Tilly piped up from her spot at his elbow. "Can it. That shit's supposed to come later." If she surreptitiously swiped at her own eye with a dainty linen handkerchief, then it was probably just for appearances. Even if the linen was already noticeably damp.

Bill chuckled by my side. "They're polar opposites."

"Right?" I muttered. "It's weird."

Bill's hand came up to squeeze my shoulder. "Marrying Pop was the greatest gift you gave the four of us, Dad." His voice was thick with emotion. "I don't know if we ever thanked you, but we couldn't be happier to be here today for this."

Brenda murmured her agreement from his side, and I caught Gina's wink and nod behind Tilly. Movement out of the corner of my eye caught my attention. We turned to see Jackie sneak up to Gina's side with an apologetic expression on her face. *I love you*, she mouthed at us.

Oh god.

The waterworks came like a fountain then. I couldn't help it. I stepped forward and buried my face in Wes's neck. His arms automatically came up to wrap me in their strength as always.

"Shh." I could hear the indulgent smile in his voice. "Shh, baby, it's okay. Take your time. No one is going anywhere." His hands rubbed my back through my suit coat, and his lips brushed the top of my head.

"Can't I just say *I do* when the time comes?" I asked into his shirt.

"No way," Felix said with a wink. I tried not to think about the conversation he would have to have with his mother later. "I was promised original vows, and I'm holding you to it."

I shot him a faux glare before sniffing and standing back up straight. Before I could reach for my own, Wes offered me his handkerchief.

Once I'd gathered my composure, I tucked the linen in my pocket and reached for his hands. "Okay. I'm ready."

Felix turned to everyone gathered in the rows of wooden folding chairs on the back lawn of the lodge. The sun was still out, warming up the cool winter afternoon enough to make it tolerable for the ceremony.

"Friends and family, we are gathered together today to celebrate forty-five years of the kind of love we all aspire to. We're here to support and honor these two men, who dared to love each other in a time of great change in our country and despite war, loss, kids, ranching, and late nights on call at the hospital. For forty-five years, Doc and Grandpa, Liam and Weston, remained steadfast to us and to each other. They formed the foundation for our family, the anchor, the true north we could always come home to and rely on. Most of us are here because of their love and commitment to each other, and I especially am a direct result of it." His voice wobbled and his eyes took a moment to find his husband's in the front row. What he saw in Lior's face must have strengthened him because he continued. "So it is both an incredible joy and a true privilege to witness their vow renewal today."

I seriously wasn't going to make it through this ceremony. But I kept my eyes glued on Weston's and let that be my own anchor. Because Felix was wrong. All of those things—the foundation and true north—were because of Wes, not me.

"Doc, would you like to begin?" he asked softly.

I kept my eyes on Wes, whose hands squeezed mine in encouragement.

"Felix was right. Together we gave our family a loving home they could always return to, but it was mostly because of you, Weston. You're the rock-steady one, the one who watches out for all of us and makes sure we always have what we need to thrive."

I swallowed. "In 1968 I met a man who impressed me with his strength and poise, his battle-worn patience, and his innate ability to handle anything that was thrown at him. I fell into hero worship back then. I saw how brave and steady you were and let those qualities provide shelter to me long before I even realized that's what was happening."

My lower lip began to quiver. "When we got back to Texas and I felt overwhelmed, I didn't even think. I ran straight to the strongest, smartest man I knew. Because there was no doubt in my mind you'd keep me on the right path. And you did. You stepped in and took care of everything.

"Major, you've been keeping me on the right path for over fifty years. And in all that time, you've always put me first, always made sure I was happy, and always stood by me patiently. I have never once doubted your love for me or your commitment to me. Because of you, Weston Marian Wilde, I have felt fiercely loved and cherished for over half my life."

Tears poured down my face. "I promise that I will continue to do my very best to honor your love for me by giving it back to you as fiercely and devotedly as I possibly can. Because you deserve love more than anyone I've ever known. And you are worthy of it. Weston, you are the very best of men, and I am honored to call you husband, best friend, and beloved soul mate."

Wes's face was tear-streaked too, but his beautiful eyes remained serene and his smile was as tender as always.

Felix's voice was thick when he turned to Wes. "Top that, Grandpa," he teased.

Wes's smile broke wider. "My pleasure."

Before he began, he brushed tears off my face. When he was done, he held my face in his big hands.

"Liam." He took a breath and let it out. His grin returned as wide and dimpled as I'd ever seen it. "Don't misinterpret these tears on my face. Standing up here today exchanging wedding vows with you is like being accepted into the gates of heaven. I cannot think of a gift greater than your love, and my heart overflows with it today and every day."

His thumbs brushed gently along my cheeks as he spoke, and I almost wanted to close my eyes and lean into him. He was home to me, the personification of comfort and ease, and with him I was able to let go. Always.

"Doc, when I first met you, I was a soldier. Period. The only thing I had was the army, so I dedicated my life to it. But when you offered me the gift of your friendship, suddenly I had something more to live for, to fight for, to return home for. And when I did return, *you* were my home.

"I never in a million years expected to have children, a partner, *family*, a home to be proud of. Even when you were still married to Betsy, you gave me those things. *She* gave me those things. Your parents welcomed me like a second son, your wife like a close friend, and your children—*our* children now—like another father. From the very beginning of my life in Hobie, I had everything I ever dreamed of. My life was full. And then I got you too."

He reached for my hands again and brought them up for a quick kiss to my knuckles, a move he'd done a million times over the years without thinking.

"Sweetheart, the day I first met you I swore in my heart to keep you safe. The day I first kissed you I swore in my soul to love you forever. The day we first married I swore to stay with you forever. And today I swear to you that you will never live a day of your life without feeling my love for you. It is a living thing that has grown wild and strong between us like Betsy's roses on the farmhouse porch rails. After all these years of loving you, I don't think I'd know how to take a single breath without it. You are my home, Liam. The one I never thought I'd be lucky enough to have."

I stepped into his chest again and held him tight, crying into his uniform coat and letting all the emotion come out. Our four children gathered around us to form a group hug, and I could distinguish the sounds of each of their happy sniffles.

When we stepped back into position, Felix cleared his throat. "You people are killing me. Liam, do you promise to love, honor, cherish, and protect Weston forever?"

"I do," I said loud and clear. I wanted to shout it from the rooftops.

"Weston, do you—"

"I do. I *dooooo*," he said with twinkling eyes. I couldn't hold back a snicker.

Felix rolled his eyes. "Okay, Doc, do you have the ring?"

I turned to Bill, who handed me Wes's wedding band. As I slipped it onto his finger, I repeated the words Felix prompted. "This is a symbol of my love and oath. With this ring, I renew my vow to you."

When it was Wes's turn, he reached for my ring from Tilly and placed it on my finger, repeating the words.

Felix looked at each of us in turn, grinning like a loon. "It is one of the greatest honors of my life to declare you husbands. Now kiss each other's brains out so we can eat cake."

Wes's hands returned to my face, and his eyes bored into mine. In them I saw everything. Every man we'd tried to save in the jungles of Nam and the night I'd crawled into his bed to take my comfort from him. Every time he'd made Betsy smile through her pain and the knitting he still attempted in her memory. Every scrape on the kids' knees he'd kissed and every time he'd been the disciplinarian when my heart wasn't strong enough. Every dirty look we'd received holding hands in town and every time someone had surprised us with support or a kind word instead. I saw late nights crawling into bed after losing a patient when Wes would wake up just to remind me I was human and loved. I saw his face across the kitchen table the day he decided to retire from ranching. The way his hand felt in mine while I watched the preacher lay my mom and dad to rest. The way his hands moved across my body with the knowledge of how to play it like a fiddle after all these years.

In his eyes I saw a lifetime. One that stretched long into the past, but stretched forward into the future too.

I leaned in to kiss him. This wasn't the end of our time together, after all.

It was a new beginning.

EPILOGUE

AKA CAN LUCY WRITE A SCENE WITH EVERY MARIAN AND WILDE IN IT?

(best appreciated if you've read the previous Made Marian and Forever Wilde novels)

It wasn't until late Saturday night well after the wedding ceremony that things got a little... exuberant. Or as Granny called it, "Off the chain-link fence." To which Simone rolled her eyes and muttered to her about maybe leaving off the fence part.

They'd all migrated from the barrel room where the reception had been to the lodge lobby where there were tons of sofas and chairs to lounge in while the giant blaze in the fireplace added to the atmosphere. This location had the added benefit of being within spitting distance of the bar where all the beloved liquor lived.

Anyway, suffice to say Simone was the only sober person for miles around. She'd gotten pregnant again when Joel Junior, or JJ as he was called, was only ten months old, and poor Joel Healy had been forced to nurse blue balls for a solid three days because of it. But then pregnancy horniness had kicked in and Joel's beloved seducer had returned, albeit under duress. She may have wanted an orgasm or three, but that didn't mean she had to like it. Er, whatever.

So Simone looked down her nose at the rest of the group and drank her LaCroix like it was a nice glass of champagne. It wasn't. It was more like the taste of being haunted by Carmen Miranda's ghost.

Stevie swayed nearby. "What's it called when…? When…"

Chief Paige wrapped an arm around his man and pressed a kiss to Stevie's royal blue hair. "When what, baby?"

"When two old married men get married again. Hey, that rhymes. I'm a poet and didn't know it."

"Except you did. Because you say that all the freaking time," Sassy muttered under her breath.

"It's rhyme time," Stevie slurred.

Sassy rolled her eyes. "How about mime time? That would be better for you, lightweight."

"Is this a joke?" Augie asked. "'Cause I like jokes."

Saint pulled Augie onto his lap. "Is what a joke, cutie?"

"Gay marriage," Augie said.

"*What?*" cried half the room, heads swiveling and drinks sloshing.

"Calm your tits," Granny called out from her position… on the floor. She lay with her head on a pillow and her legs spread wide in front of the fire. When Tristan had politely asked her to close her knees earlier, she'd told him ladies of a certain age had circulation problems and needed a little external help preheating the love flaps. Honestly, that last word out of her mouth had been what had caused the current extreme level of drunkenness in the room. Everyone had thrown themselves into a glass of liquor to forget.

Granny continued, still spread-eagle in front of the flames. "He wasn't calling gay marriage a joke, people. Which is a good thing because then I would have had to grab Reenie for a demonstration about…" She'd been picking at a loose sequin on her dress and it finally popped off, bringing its neighbors with it and leaving a zigzagged pattern of bald fabric behind. "Well, I'll be damned. This is how it happens. I've finally lost my sparkle."

"Never," her wife said affectionately, delivering a new drink to her before lowering herself onto the colorful floor pillows scattered in front of the stone hearth. "Here. Sweet nuts."

"What did you just call her?" Teddy Marian asked with a giant grin. "Because that shit's gonna stick."

Jamie leaned his head onto Teddy's shoulder and groaned. "I shouldn't have had the third piece of cake. Why didn't you stop me?"

Teddy rubbed Jamie's belly. "I just assumed you and Simone were competing for whose belly was the most robust. You'll never beat her, babydoll. Look at that thing." He pointed to Simone's belly covered in one of Joel's hoodies. She'd torn off the too-tight dress as soon as they'd returned to the lodge.

"Asshole," Simone muttered. Ginger reached over and caressed the bump.

"Awww," she said to her favorite (only) sister-in-law with a schmoopy tone. "I see you this pregnant and think, 'Thank god that's not me.'"

She turned to her husband, Pete, for a high five.

"Preach, wife. Never again," Pete said with a laugh.

Simone shot her brother the bird and snuggled back against her big beefy man. Joel chuckled for a split second before cooing at Simone about how beautiful she looked. He lied.

Hallie Wilde leaned forward to grab a handful of candied almonds from a dish on the coffee table. "I thought these were sweet nuts."

Tilly waltzed into the sitting area from the direction of her suite looking decidedly unkempt. The senator ambled after her with a flushed face and swollen lips. His shirt was buttoned wrong, and there was lipstick smeared on it down by his belt.

"Honey, this room is chock-full of sweet nuts," Tilly said, wiping the side of her mouth with the tip of her pinky finger. "Look around you."

Everyone looked around. There were over twenty gay men and their partners.

Stevie's eyes glazed over. "Soo many sweet nuts..."

Chief Paige stood up and threw Stevie over his shoulder. "All right. That's enough. I can't compete with all you buff young ones. I'm taking my baby to bed."

"Can we do naughty things when we get there, Chief?" Stevie

asked from upside down. His hands snuck into the back of Chief's pants.

Chief's big hand swatted Stevie's pert ass. "Always."

Bill Wilde, the oldest of Doc and Grandpa's children, looked around in a daze similar to Stevie's but for much different reasons. "I still can't believe it's possible for this many men in one—okay two—families to be gay."

"Samesies," his wife, Shelby, said. "Clearly it was your sperm. Just saying."

"Men? Gee thanks, Dad," MJ muttered. "Lesbian erasure much?"

"Shh," Neckie said. "If you start arguing, you'll stop massaging my feet, and this feels really good."

Beck Wilde looked around the room in similar awe. "I thought your family was homophobic and that's why you had to marry a woman," he said to his partner, Quinn. "Like... I don't get it. You're from the gayest family who ever worshipped Gaga."

Jude sat up from where he'd been leaning against Derek's shoulder. "Beck, holy crap. I just realized we're related now."

"Are you though?" Winnie Wilde asked while trying to wipe off the Reese's Peanut Butter Cups crumbles that had fallen onto her chest from Granny Sweet Nuts when Irene had walked by her earlier. More to herself than anyone else, she asked, "Is it rude to eat candy off your own shirt in public?"

"Not if you share," Hallie asked, reaching over to grab a big chunk off her sister's boob. "If only my boobs were big enough to collect snacks from passersby."

Derek chimed in. "Beck's grandpa-in-law—"

Augie giggled. "We don't need no stinkin' Stevie to bust a rhyme."

Derek ignored the little drunkard. "Beck's grandpa-in-law is Jude's great-uncle."

"My head hurts," Dante Marian muttered. "Angel, I'm waiting for you to do me like that hottie silver fox did to Stevie."

AJ's eyes lit up. "Done." He stood up and swooped his man into his arms fast enough to make Dante squeak. "Later, dudes," AJ said with a nod before disappearing down one of the hallways.

West eyed Nico. "What say we—"

Nico cut him off with a raised palm. "No way. We're in this until the last Marian-Wilde horks over the balcony railing. This is going to be the night that bards talk about in generations to come."

Charlie reached over for a high five. "Couldn'ta said it better m'self."

Hudson grinned like an idiot at his husband. "You're so beautiful when you talk Irish. Isn't he beautiful? He's so…"

"Yeah, we know, Hud. The man's a treat," Brenda's daughter, Katie, said with a sigh of longing. "Whatever happened to the plan where you two were going to take me and Web over to Ireland so we could find our own redheaded lovers?"

Web opened his eye from his spot on the sofa. "No gingers. Not after the last one."

"Hey," Blue cried. "I resemble that remark." He set down the bowls of something or other on the table by the nuts.

Tristan yanked him down onto his lap in the wide leather chair. "Gingers give the best hea—"

"Stop it right there," Maverick called across the space. "Don't want to hear about my brother's oral talents."

"I do," Beau muttered from Mav's shoulder. "Give a man some wank material please."

Mav gave his husband a look. "You need wank material?"

Beau was transfixed by the gorgeous man he'd known practically his whole life. The man who'd only the day before surprised him with a private picnic and hot-air balloon ride over the vineyard.

"Never," he sighed with a goofy smile. "I just look under the covers at your hot bod and—"

"Things are getting out of hand," Griff said to Sam. "I love it."

Sam ran his fingers into Griff's crazy curls. "It's strange though. Usually you're the instigator."

"Right?" Nico called out.

"Or Aunt Tilly," said shy little Ammon Marian, the newest member of the family and the only sober one there besides his sister Simone. "Or Granny."

"True dat," Irene said holding out her glass for a cheers with someone. Otto leaned in from his spot on a nearby pillow and clinked his whiskey glass against her Sweet Nuts shooter.

"Need a refill, gorgeous?" he asked her with a little slur. Granny scrambled up to defend her wife.

"Git your skanky paws off my woman, you big ole beefcake!" Okay, maybe the scrambling was a bit... slow-motion. But she eventually got up on her knees in Otto's face and held her little knobby fists up like she was going to fight 1920s style. "Put up your dukes."

Otto looked back at his husband Seth in drunken confusion. "I... I don't know if I have dukes... Baby, do we have dukes?"

Seth's eyes twinkled. "No. But maybe they sell them at the plastic banana store in San Francisco. I think we should check it out before we fly back to Hobie."

Granny deflated. "Well, hell. We shoulda brought the Love Junk. Coulda made a killing."

Noah rolled his head off Luke's shoulder long enough to glare at Granny. "If you're going to lecture me again about getting out of the dildo business, zip it."

Luke pulled Noah's head back down on his shoulder. "Shh. I don't have the energy to pull you off her again tonight. Plus we're out of Neosporin."

Granny shot him the bird.

Teddy lifted his hand as if in a classroom. "Hold up. Jamie and I have enough of a personal collection of Love Junk, we could probably—"

"Nope," Jamie said quickly. "Think again, big guy."

"But that new little corkscrew-shaped thingie—"

Jamie slapped a hand over Teddy's mouth and whispered something in his ear. Teddy's eyes widened comically, and the front of his pants tented.

"That's all you needed to say, sweetheart. Bedtime. *Now.*"

Jamie turned to the group with a triumphant grin. "Later!"

His brother Thad watched him go. "Maybe I should have been

gay," he mused. "I would have had a better chance at getting lucky tonight."

"Same," Jackie Wilde lamented. "Men suck."

Agreeable, appreciative titters mixed with agreeable, annoyed ones.

"Not sure Sara would appreciate it if you were," Thomas said to Thad. Thomas's hands toyed with Rebecca's hair as she lay curled up next to him on one of the sofas. "And the baby in her belly will be worth all the nausea eventually. Be glad she went to bed early. She needs the sleep."

Thad closed his eyes and sighed. "She told me before she went to the room that if I show up later without a pint of ice cream, I'd have to sleep on the floor."

Rebecca stirred on Thomas's lap. "You take my grandbaby some ice cream, son. Even if you have to steal it from Simone's personal stash."

"Hey!" Simone cried. "If I can't have my own Sweet Nuts, then I need my BJ."

"That's not what anyone calls Ben & Jerry's, baby," Joel said. "I've told you that a million times."

Cal, the youngest of the Wilde brothers, stretched his arms up. He was sitting on the stone hearth in front of the fire and was half-drowsy from the warmth. "I could go for some BJ."

"I volunteer as tribute." A breathy voice escaped Ammon, but no one heard it.

Cal continued. "Anyone want to show me where the ice cream stash is? I'm happy to run grab it."

Ammon got up the nerve to stand up. That kid was too cute to pass up. "I, um, know where the—"

Tilly flapped her hand. "Oh for the love of god, Ammon, just take the man to the storage closet like Ben did with Reese that one time."

"You *knew* about that?" Ben gasped.

Reese's chest puffed up. "Babe, everyone knew about it. We weren't exactly quiet."

"Omigod," Ben said, hiding his face in Reese's shirt.

There was a commotion by the hallway to the sleeping rooms and out walked a semifamiliar woman with a glamorous red mane of artful beach waves all down her back. "What the hell?" Grandpa asked in surprise.

"I recognize that wig," Doc said with a grin. "That's... that's Betsy's wig from a million years ago."

Grandpa pulled Doc close and kissed him on the cheek. "No, sweetheart. That was the one she bought for *me*."

Granny bounced her eyes lasciviously. "Irene, tonight's threesome night at the O.K. Corral."

Chief Paige appeared behind the stunning redhead in platform heels and offered her his arm.

"Well shit," Granny said. "It's just Stevie in drag."

Chief Paige looked at the group. "How much you figure an Uber is to that plastic banana store?"

Blue snorted. "In the city? Uh, about a million dollars. Which we're happy to pay if you let your lovely lady there perform for us."

Doc squinted his eyes at Stevie. "Is it wrong to think he's sexy on my wedding day to another man?"

Grandpa squeezed his hand. "Babe, Stevie in drag is like a bisexual's wet dream. You can't help it. But he is young enough to be our—"

"Don't say it, or I'll need to turn myself in to law enforcement," Doc admitted.

"Law enforcement's drunk. Like suuuuper drunk," Seth slurred. "But my man's sexy as fuck, and he's young enough to be your—"

Otto barked out a laugh. "Stop. I think it's high time someone show these folks what a fireman's carry really looks like." He tossed Seth over his shoulders like a sack of seriously sexy spuds.

Quinn turned to Beck with a pointed look. "This. All this right here is why I felt pressure to marry a woman. There was already so much fucking gay and weirdness in this family, *someone* had to take one for the team."

Beck tilted his head. "Huh. Didn't take though, did it?"

Gina studied their oldest adopted son with eyes that probably saw double of everything at the moment. "Quinn, admit it. You saw the two of us and wished you could have a piece of that action."

"Ew," Quinn said. "Time to cut the moms off."

Carmen nodded. "Probably an Oedipal thing. Oedipal... Oedipal... sounds like... Oh, hey, anyone want to make me a buttery nipple?"

Their middle son, Max, groaned. "For the love of god, is there any gay man willing to toss me over his shoulder and take me to his bed?"

King Lior's valet, Arthur, who had been standing quietly off to the side still immaculate in his wedding suit, bent at the waist in a formal bow.

"Sir, allow me."

Felix's jaw dropped and he leaned over to whisper to Lio without taking his eyes off the fastidious valet. "Is he strong enough to—"

Lio interrupted his husband but also refused to stop watching the spectacle. Sure enough Arthur approached the younger man and threw him over his shoulder. Lio held out a hand in a *see?* gesture. "He once bodily carried me out of a cabinet meeting after someone called you gorgeous."

Felix finally turned to him, a pink blush sneaking up his neck to his face. "What do you mean?"

Lio looked at him and smiled that sweet, tender smile reserved only for his king consort. "It was the fourth time it had happened that day, Fee. I couldn't take it anymore. I was..." He sighed and looked down. "Jealous, all right? I was jealous. Everyone in the world looks at you and fantasizes about you. But you're mine."

Felix swooned in his arms, and the room filled with aww's and smoochy sounds as the two of them shared a sweet kiss.

Which set off a massive kissfest the likes of which neither family had ever seen before, or would ever speak of again.

What happened at the vineyard, stayed at the vineyard.

And lots of things happened at the vineyard.

Want to see what happens when Arthur carries Max off to bed? Sign up for Lucy's newsletter for a link to a free short!
www.LucyLennox.com

LETTER FROM LUCY

Dear Reader,

Thank you so much for reading *Wilde Love*, book six in the Forever Wilde series. There are so many things I want to tell you about writing this book. How I both dreaded and loved the research. How I ended the story but then had to write "one more scene" four different times. How I struggled not to include more important historical events like Stonewall, the AIDS crisis, and even the moon landing. Finally, I want you to know that I am more in love with these two men than ever before, and I didn't know that was possible.

I wanted to write all those intervening years between Vietnam and now, to tell you what it was like raising the kids together and how they felt when Jackie had Felix so far away, to describe in greater detail the day the Wildes learned gay marriage was legalized and the day Doc and Grandpa became grandfathers for the first time. But I had to make some tough choices. The result is a story of how they met and fell in love, how that love lasted decades, and how family once lost can be found again. I hope you enjoyed this visit with the Wildes and Marians as much as I did.

If you're unfamiliar with the Forever Wilde series, check out the first book *Facing West* which is about Nico, a tattoo artist from San

Francisco, returning to his small-town Texas roots to take custody of his sister's baby. There he meets the local uptight physician, West Wilde, who thinks this urban punk is in no way prepared to take on the care of a newborn. And he's right.

There are already six novels in the series with more to come, so please stay tuned. Up next will be King's story which involves an uptight law enforcement agent and a Wilde who's been living a secret life overseas all this time.

If you're unfamiliar with the Made Marian series, check out the first book *Borrowing Blue* which is about a straight, divorced vineyard owner agreeing to do a guest a solid. Tristan kisses Blue in the bar one night to make Blue's ex jealous. But when Tristan and Blue discover the wedding weekend they're there for is between Blue's sister and Tristan's brother, what began as one hot kiss turns into lots of big trouble.

Be sure to follow me on Amazon to be notified of new releases, and look for me on Facebook for sneak peeks of upcoming stories.

Feel free to sign up for my newsletter, stop by www.LucyLennox.com or visit me on social media to stay in touch. We have a super fun reader group on Facebook that can be found here:

https://www.facebook.com/groups/lucyslair/

To see fun inspiration photos for all of my novels, visit my Pinterest boards.

Happy reading!

Lucy

ABOUT LUCY LENNOX

Lucy Lennox is the creator of the bestselling Made Marian series, the Forever Wilde series, and co-creator of the Twist of Fate Series with Sloane Kennedy and the After Oscar series with Molly Maddox. Born and raised in the southeast, she is finally putting good use to that English Lit degree.

Lucy enjoys naps, pizza, and procrastinating. She is married to someone who is better at math than romance but who makes her laugh every single day and is the best dancer in the history of ever.

She stays up way too late each night reading M/M romance because that stuff is impossible to put down.

For more information and to stay updated about future releases, please sign up for Lucy's author newsletter on her website.

Connect with Lucy on social media:
www.LucyLennox.com
Lucy@LucyLennox.com

ALSO BY LUCY LENNOX

Made Marian Series:

Borrowing Blue

Taming Teddy

Jumping Jude

Grounding Griffin

Moving Maverick

Delivering Dante

A Very Marian Christmas

Made Marian Shorts

Made Mine - Crossover with Sloane Kennedy's Protectors series

Hay: A Made Marian Short

Forever Wilde Series:

Facing West

Felix and the Prince

Wilde Fire

Hudson's Luck

Flirt: A Forever Wilde Short

His Saint

Twist of Fate Series (with Sloane Kennedy):

Lost and Found

Safe and Sound

Body and Soul

After Oscar Series (with Molly Maddox):

IRL: In Real Life

LOL: Laugh Out Loud

Free Short Stories available at www.LucyLennox.com.

Also be sure to check out audio versions here.

Made in the USA
Middletown, DE
12 March 2020